BEWARE
THE
ABANDONED

Ian Duncan
MacDonald

Library and Archives Canada Cataloguing in Publication
MacDonald, Ian D., author
BEWARE THE ABANDONED / Ian Duncan MacDonald
Issued in print and electronic formats

ISBN 9780991931798 (paperback).
1.   Wealth 2. Crime I. Title. II Beware The Abandoned

Published by
Informus Inc, Publishing Division, 2 Vista Humber Drive, Toronto, Ontario,
Canada, M9P 3R7
www.informus.ca
tel. 929-800-2397

Cover Design by Ian D. MacDonald.

THE STORY BEHIND THE STORY

BEWARE THE ABANDONED started off as a screenplay about a beach volleyball tournament in Delaware. I thought it was a good story and came back to it, years later, to turn it into this novel. It ended up going far beyond the movie script.

It can take thousands of words to describe what ten seconds in a movie can convey. I found something magical happens when you start to turn a screenplay into a novel. As you describe the action, instead of photographing it, you must first create an explanation for the action. This is when the story starts to write itself. Your mind searches all your life's memories; everything you have seen, heard, read and experienced. Your objective is to create an interesting, entertaining, believable story. I read somewhere that novelists are liars. They turn lies into believable realities.

Settings:
I knew little about New Mexico until I began to research them.
Paris, Las Vegas, Laughlin, Washington, Delaware and Philadelphia I have visited..
A friend with a yacht shares his yacht club experiences with me.
I have not played golf for years but I found researching the business side of golfing interesting.
Commercial collection agency management is something that I do have an intimate understanding of.
I know business because I worked as a senior executive in several large international organizations.
I have a tall son who was captain of his university volleyball team. He exposed me to that world.

Editing:

 I would like to acknowledge the help of my friends in completing this novel:
J.G. Peter King my longtime friend whose first edit of the book and warned me that over editing could ruin my style.
Dr. John Turner patiently read through the book and brought to my attention many words, that I had erroneously believed readers would understand. He suggested I find substitutes, which I did.

Ivana Tupone brought to my attention that there were no female Sanctuarians and caused me to address that issue.

Evelyne Kazo who was recuperating from a broken wrist, brought many spelling and grammar errors to my attention.

Brent Arlitt got me to do a better job of justifying one of the murders and making the ending more satisfactory.

My wife **Carmen**, who has encouraged and supported my writing and all my other endeavors. Her preliminary review of the novel were encouraging.

The Novel:

I hope this novel entertains you. I enjoyed the hundreds of hours it took to write, rewrite, edit and format. I especially liked exploring the morality issues. Is John Cross a saint or a sinner? Is he a psychopathic killer or someone dedicated to a nobler cause? Could an organization like The Sanctuary ever exist? Does wealth guarantee happiness? Should abandoned street children just be left to perish? Would street children be your best candidates for turning them into exploitable wealthy entrepreneurs? Can a murderer be creative and charming? Do the ends ever justify the means to get there? Can murder ever be rationalized? I would be interested in following any debates about Murderous Little Bastards.

This is the third of two novels I have completed. The first was Massive Retaliation, and it is available as an eBook and hardcopy. I have now gone back to editing and rewriting a second novel, Manifest Destiny, which I jumped over to complete Beware The Abandoned which left some of those who have read it wanting the story of John Cross to continue. I left the ending open so this could be possible.

Ian D. MacDonald
imacd@informus.ca
November 12, 2018

Table of Contents

PART 1

BEFORE THE FALL

CHAPTER 1

SCREAM

The yacht rocked as the first early morning breeze rippled across Delaware Bay. The sun already felt warm on the back of his neck. It was going to be a warm, cloudless day.

John Cross tied the fifty-pound weight to his wife's legs. As he did, she sighed deeply. John concluded that the tranquilizer must affect people in different ways. Her lover had never stirred before he had been heaved overboard. Time was of the essence. He had better hurry before she gained consciousness.

Tying the final knot, he dragged her body across the teak deck. As he stepped back, to push her, feet first, into the sea, her eyes opened, her body stiffened. She tried to scream but couldn't. The tranquilizing drug still paralyzed her vocal cords.

Her body followed the fifty-pound weight into the depths. John stood back and watched her disappear. He turned, made his way to the bridge, started the diesel engine and set a course to where he was going to abandon the yacht.

At this juncture of the recurring dream, John would always wake. He looked at the clock on the night table. It was two-thirty in the morning. He wondered if he was now going to lie awake for hours running through his mind, over and over, what happened on the boat?

It had been necessary. She was threatening the money he had set aside to save hundreds of children living on the mean streets. Her decision to meet with a divorce lawyer had forced him to act

CHAPTER 2

PARIS

T en years before Naomi's murder, John Cross had been flown to Paris. He had been sent there by The Sanctuary to recruit abandoned, disposable children. He had once been one of those discarded children. Two hours after landing at Charles De Gaulle Airport, he was standing, at attention, in The Sanctuary's Paris Mission, listening to Lester Simpson.

In a Cockney accent, Lester recited his standard greeting, "Welcome to Paris. I am sure the last ten years were a challenging a journey for you. You are now, two years away from having repaid the first part of your debt to The Sanctuary. Two years, from today, you will receive your grant which you will invest in an entrepreneurial venture of your choosing. This venture will reward both you and The Sanctuary. These two years will pass very rapidly."

Lester was responsible for The Sanctuary's Paris operations. He paused to make sure he had their attention. Smiling broadly, he displayed a mouthful of teeth going in unconventional directions. Tall and fit, he looked the part of a leader, tasked with setting an example for young men who had just completed ten years of rigorous physical and mental conditioning. He was deliberately dressed, to both impress and inspire his new charges. In direct contrast to the young men's dull apparel, his clothing had been chosen to reassure them that there indeed was a pot of gold waiting for them at the end of the two years. His suit was Armani; the shirt was Bartoli; the tie was Hermes, and the shoes were Gucci loafers.

Lester knew, like all Sanctuarians, that when death stalks a child, and that child escapes death's clutches, that child is both changed and liberated. While such children may have cheated death, they learned, from those who had not cheated death, that they were not immortal. These children also learned that you survive by being ruthless and doing whatever you must do to survive. On the hard streets, they learned that conventional laws and attitudes were for other people. A fear of consequences would never constrain them. Even murder was not sacrosanct.

The Sanctuary had saved John Cross from a short, brutal life They had then nurtured, protected, educated and guided him for ten years. During this time, they had applied a thin veneer of civility to him. Was The Sanctuary foolish in thinking that they could banish the raw jungle rules he had survived under for the first twelve years of his life? No, The Sanctuary counted on those jungle instincts to drive John to achieving incredible financial success. A success in whose rewards in they would share. The Sanctuary's greatest success had been in concealing the beast behind a cloak of middle-class respectability.

John had no illusions about human behavior. He had been conditioned to believe that only the powerful thrive and that showing any weakness would lead to his demise. While fighting for survival on the mean streets, he had learned to respond quickly and violently to any slight, or disrespect shown towards him. If you threatened his peace and harmony, he was prepared take away your life. He was the ultimate survivor.

There were two young men standing in front of Lester. Both had never known conventional boyhoods. John Cross was twenty-three years old. He had just graduated with the equivalent of a master's degree in Business Administration. The Sanctuary did not concern itself with how their graduates were perceived by other institutions. They were creating entrepreneurs who answer only to themselves.

The Sanctuary was dedicated to teaching knowledge and skills that made their graduates wealthy businessmen. Educational credentials acquired to impress potential employers were not relevant. The true value of their student's education was realized in the profits from the enterprises the students created that they would share in.

Standing beside John Cross was Raymond Powell. He was a year older than John. He had the equivalent of a Master of Business Administration with an emphasis in computer science. John's emphasis had been in marketing.

They were graduates of The Sanctuary's very private, very intense, educational experience that took place at their campus in Taos, New Mexico. Both were of medium build, six feet tall, with bright blue, intelligent eyes and sandy blond hair. Their short, military, haircuts and clean-shaven faces gave them that fresh, newly minted image, that U.S. Marine Corps officers have. Both were dressed, as they had been for the last ten years, in black socks, white shirts, black polyester tie, black wool slacks and unfashionable, but comfortable, black leather shoes with thick, soft, rubber soles. To chic Parisians, they would look like aliens from another planet.

Peering closely at the two of them, before continuing in an accent that betrayed his own deprived upbringing, Lester paused and asked, "Are the two of you related? You look like brothers."

John Cross was the first to reply, "No sir. We have been asked that since our first days at the college. People often got us confused."

"Interesting." Simpson paused again, looking at them even more closely, then he continued, "As I am sure you were told, the two of you have been paired. This is done so you can protect each other's backs. It means that for two years you are never going to be out of each other's sight. This does not mean you will be taking showers with each other or going to the bathroom together. It does mean you will be sharing the same bedroom, eating together and working the streets as a team."

Standing rigidly, John and Raymond nodded their heads. They understood. Their mentor at the college had prepared them for this commitment, just as Lester had once been prepared for his two-year commitment. Sanctuarians looked back on their two-year commitment, as a rite of passage. They expected that the shared two-year pairing experience would bond them for the rest of their lives.

No matter how much effort was put into preparing them for their missions, the mentors knew missions were a traumatic experience. After the ten years in the safe, warm, structured womb of the campus, The Sanctuary would no longer be there to protect them. Now, they were going to be again immersed into the cold, harsh, dangerous streets. The same ones they escaped when they were selected to become Sanctuarians.

Lester motioned for John and Raymond to sit. He continued with his well-rehearsed speech, "I am sure you have been told that pairing evolved because of the attacks on our young men. That is why, you must always be together. It will then always be the word of the two of you, against any accuser. Be assured, Parisians will view you with suspicion and hostility. You will appear strange and foreign to them. Years ago, the Sanctuary deliberately chose your black trousers, tie and white shirts so that you would be noticed but be easily dismissed as a threat."

To give added emphasis to his words, Lester stood and leaned towards them, "What Parisians don't understand, they often treat badly. A few will see you as a threat and try to remove you from their streets. Before pairing, we were open to false accusations of rape, selling drugs, robbery and even murder. We are only able to achieve our missions without interference if the authorities see us as a passive, weak, charitable, religious organization. You are to keep each other away from any temptations that threaten this image."

Sitting again, Lester continued, "You are returning to the same dangerous streets that you, and I came from. It is now your turn to find those exceptional, diamondsin-the-rough that can be turned into the highly trained, polished, confident young men just like yourselves. Your placement is in the Saint Germain-des-Prés area of the 6th Arrondissement. It is a poor area. The Sanctuary fishes where the fish are. It does not seek the pampered, weak, indulged children of the rich. You are there to recruit the toughest and smartest of the street kids. Those who are homeless, deprived of love and comfort. Living on the edge and unlikely to see adulthood if they do not escape these streets. They are the discarded ones, who only by their intelligence and internal strength, have managed to survive in what has been, for them, a cruel, hostile, ugly, dangerous world."

Raymond and John felt the tension of their long-buried survival instincts returning. They raptly listened as Lester said, "These children are just like you were before The Sanctuary instilled in you the confidence and the knowledge of capitalism. These children can smell phoniness. They trust no one, but you are not phonies. You are the real thing. You've been where they are now. Only you can convince them to put the rest of their lives in the hands of The Sanctuary, just as you were convinced by those who recruited you."

For dramatic effect, Lester paused before he continued, "Although they don't realize it, these children desperately seek a structure in their lives that will protect them. They need comfort, direction and wealth. While it may be suppressed, you and I know they have a longing to escape from the bleak and wretched path they see before them. You must convince them to put their future in the hands of The Sanctuary, so that ten years from now, they too can save children from a short and wretched life."

While John Cross sat, staring straight ahead, his mind raced back to the garbage strewn, bleak, streets of Los Angeles, bounded by Main St, 4th, 7th, and the LA River. He had never known a father. His mother had been a raging alcoholic, long abandoned by the man who fathered him.

By the time, he was four years old he had taken on an adult role of trying to feed and protect his mother. She had died when he was ten. No one noticed that he had been orphaned. His new reality was living in abandoned buildings with a pack of children who were older than himself. They survived by begging, shop lifting, robbing drunks and eating the discarded food tossed into dumpsters by restaurants and grocery stores. While one child was vulnerable to a street predator, the pack, by their very numbers, deterred any attacks. Even the authorities avoided them and regarded them as dangerous.

One-day, Frank had approached their group. With his white shirt, black tie, short hair and clean-cut image, he was as alien a presence as these children had ever encountered. Most of the pack quickly sought safety in flight. They assumed that any adult approaching them was either from social services or a pervert. John had not been afraid. He did not run away. His intelligence made him curious to find out why this alien was interested in them.

Frank told John a story of how he too had lived rough, on the streets, just like John, until The Sanctuary rescued him. Over ten years they trained and educated him. They promised him a life of wealth and security. This reward was in return for Frank agreeing to spend two years recruiting lost children and to donating 15% of his lifetime income and assets to The Sanctuary.

Even at thirteen, John had experienced enough fear and abuse to recognize an opportunity to escape his circumstances. He accepted Frank's offer with the hope that the Sanctuary would become both his mother and his father. For the first time in his life he saw a purpose and a direction. Unless he could escape the streets, he could already see that his life was destined to be short and brutish.

Raymond Powell was also reflecting on growing up hard on East Van Buren Street in Phoenix, Arizona. His mother had never been sure who his father had been. She was a prostitute who would disappear from his life for weeks at a time. When he was not much more than a toddler, she would leave him alone to fend for himself. One day, when he was twelve, she left and never returned. Years later, he concluded that she must have been murdered by one of her clients and now lay in a shallow desert grave.

After her disappearance, Social Services had collected him and warehoused him in a group home. The next day, he fled the group home and returned to East Van Buren Street. Here, he survived by shoplifting and acting as a delivery boy for drug dealers. Being a child, if he were apprehended by the police, he knew the worse they could do was to put him in a group home. Each day, he managed to earn just enough to survive to the next day.

Although Raymond was grateful that the Sanctuary had plucked him from those hard streets, he knew even as a child, that nothing in this life was free. It was now time to repay his debt. It was only fair. The Sanctuary were responsible for everything that he had gained and hoped to gain. He would serve his two-year mission and genuinely hoped that he could help a few outstanding children to escape from the misery of the streets.

Interrupting their reflections, Lester continued, "We have rented a clean, safe room for you in the Montmartre section of Paris. This maison de chambres is owned by an elderly lady. She will prepare only breakfast for you. You should not expect much more than a croissant, coffee and jam. You will get your other meals from the restaurants in the neighborhood. She speaks no English, but I understand that French is no problem for the two of you. Your file says that after ten years of French immersion studies, you speak it fluently. I also noticed that you have both achieved high ratings in martial arts. That is good because you will be on your own and I cannot stress enough that you must always be prepared to defend yourselves. Paris is not the Disneyland of the tourist brochures. Tomorrow you will be out on the streets looking for potential recruits. Be careful."

Looking very serious, he continued, "Fifteen thousand people are sleeping rough on the streets of Paris. Many are children. The have come to Paris looking for jobs but have found only misery. Some are gypsies. Many are from the Balkans. A few are from Afghanistan. Most are from North Africa. While the French social service does provide shelter for refugee children under sixteen, most of these homeless children are unable to prove how old they. This conveniently allows, the French authorities, to abandon them to the street where they fend for themselves as thieves and pickpockets. The girls often become child prostitutes. Too many of them get pregnant. Usually, these children are being exploited by adults who train them to steal. These adults then fence whatever they steal. I understand if these kids don't bring in a few hundred Euros every day, they get beaten."

"Poor kids," Raymond murmured.

Lester looked at him and said, "True, but be careful around them. To rob you, they work as a team. Several will swarm you and while you are distracted, one will steal your wallet. For their protection, they carry knives and they will use them, if you resist their attack. Be wary when you are on the street if anyone is standing too close to you because this behavior is unusual for Parisians. The French do not care for close physical contact. I would recommend, that from now on, you keep your wallets in your front pocket. It makes pick-pocketing more difficult. Be especially careful on the Metro. It is their favorite hunting ground. Just before the doors on the subway car close, thieves will snatch your cell phone and wallet and escape through the closing door."

"Why can this thievery not be stopped?", Raymond asked?

"Children under thirteen can't be prosecuted. The police cannot even be bothered chasing them."

"Are there areas in Paris we should avoid?"

"Yes, areas called *Zones Urbaine Sensibles*, or ZUS for short. These are the no-go zones. Even the police will not go there. It is just too dangerous. However, unlike America, few Parisians have guns. Even many of the policemen don't. While you are unlikely to be shot, the robbers do carry knives and will use them if you put up a fight."

Raymond and John now understood they really were returning to the same dangerous environment that they had left ten years ago. Lester let his warning sink in for a few seconds, before he said, "I have a present for you."

He went over to a closet and took out what appeared to be two ordinary, black umbrellas. They were new with the typical hook handle that old fashioned umbrellas have. John could see a small tag on one of them. It advertised, "Unbreakable Umbrella".

Lester handed them each one as he explained what they were, "These are special umbrellas manufactured for the protection force that guards the president of the Philippines. They are incredibly strong and were designed to be used as weapons. These handles and shafts are so strong that you could easily suspend your entire weight. If you hit an attacker hard enough with the handle, you will break their arms or legs. Hit them in the head and you will kill them. The shafts are a super strong alloy that will not bend or break. You hold it by the umbrella end and use the hook end as a sledge hammer or to twist a knife out of an attacker's hands. They can be opened to shield you from an attacker. Oh yeah, they are good at keeping you dry. Since they are umbrellas, you will have no problem taking them through security checks. I want you to carry them with you every time you leave your room, even if the sun is shining. It is better that you look eccentric, for carrying an umbrella on a sunny day, then to be attacked and wish you had them with you."

John noticed that they felt heavier than a regular umbrella. Treating his as if it were a golf club, he took a few practice golf swings with his. He found they were nicely balanced and easy to handle.

The introduction of the umbrellas further removed any illusions that this mission was going to be a holiday. Lester was not being an iconoclast; he was trying to protect them.

He ended their meeting with his final instructions, "On Saturdays, all the Sanctuarians in Paris, congregate here at noon. We have lunch and a group discussion on the candidates being considered for recruitment. Saturday is also when you hand in your expense report and your activity report for the previous week. It is also when I hand you your cash advance for the next week. Any questions?"

John and Raymond looked at each other and then shook their heads in unison to show they had no questions. Lester reached into his drawer and took out two envelopes. He smiled and said, "Here is your first week's advance. It will cover your meals and incidentals. Madam Leblanc, your landlady, will receive payment for your room from me. We don't expect you will be spending much time in your room. It is a warm, dry, safe place for you to sleep. The driver is waiting to drive you there now. Bonne chance, mes amis."

Lester stepped forward shook their hands and then walked over to the office door. He held it open for them. It was one of those incredibly high doors you get in the old Paris mansions. The Sanctuary, although keeping a low profile, made sure that the public only saw an image of wealth and privilege. It had been chosen as their French base of operations with great care. It was a large three-story building, surrounded by high stone walls, in a stylish area of embassies and high-end retailers.

They made their way to the large black Mercedes limousine that was waiting for them. Their bags were already in it. The chauffeur had put them in the trunk when he picked them up early in the morning at Charles de Gaulle Airport. As they approached the vehicle, they casually swung their new umbrellas.

Seeing them, a security guard stepped out of a small guardhouse, across the courtyard from the mansion. He opened the tall, wrought iron gates to the street to allow the Mercedes to exit.

They were unusually subdued as the Mercedes gracefully wound its way through the narrow, congested streets. Their journey had begun early the day before. On the plane, they had been too excited to sleep. Now, they were looking forward to a quick nap before exploring their new neighborhood.

The Mercedes pulled over to the curb on a long, wide street. It was walled by stone buildings, four stories high, flush to the sidewalk and to each other. Retail stores occupied the ground floors. Residences occupied the three upper floors. They had stopped in front of 41 Boulevard Rochechouart. It had an entrance between a vegetable store and a laundry.

Raymond pulled up a Google map of Paris on his cell phone and keyed in the street address. The map showed that they were a few blocks away from a landmark, the Sacré-Cœur Basilica. That explained the tourist buses, like huge whales clogging the busy street. In the crowd of tourists, swirling by, Raymond picked out the beggars, thieves and prostitutes. The street people were busily assessing the revenue potential among the tourists.

A small sign above the door for number 41 announced that this was Pension Rochechouart. They learned that this entrance, opened to a small vestibule, with stairs leading to the upper levels.

They unloaded their luggage from the Mercedes' trunk and rested it on the sidewalk. John tried the door. It was locked. He pushed a door bell and waited. Within a few minutes, a thin, elderly, white haired woman in a stylish but faded, silk dress, opened the door and greeted them. She ushered them in, clucking away in French like a mother hen. With suitcases in hand, they climbed the steep stairs behind her.

Stopping on the first upper level, she showed them the breakfast room. It had half a dozen small wooden tables with hard looking, old fashioned, high backed chairs. It was not a place to linger. The rest of that floor was Madam Leblanc's private apartment.

Lifting their bags again they followed her to the second level and then onward to the third level. She explained that the resident on each floor shared that floor's common bathroom.

Madame Leblanc opened the door to what was going to be their home for the next two years. It was Spartan, but adequate, with two twin beds, a desk, a dresser, an armoire, a chair and a small sofa. A large, old fashioned, window with a web of small glass panes allowed sunshine to flood into the room. High, above the roofs of the buildings across the wide street, they could see the glory of the brilliantly white Sacre-Coeur Basilica.

The Basilica sits on the highest hill in Paris. Only the Eiffel Tower gives tourists a better view of the city. Muttering away to herself, Madame Leblanc gave each of them a key to the pension's front door and another to their room. She left them to unpack.

They had few possessions and did not fill the drawers in the dresser. Both removed sketch pads, paints and a few canvases from their suitcases. The college had exposed every student to the arts. Some chose musical instruments. Raymond and John had both chosen drawing and painting. Over the years, they had become talented artists. Creating art gave them pleasure.

To help prepare them for their ascension into the middle class, the college had also made them choose a sport and a foreign language to study. They coincidentally had both chosen golf and French. Both choices were as alien to them as camel racing and Swahili, but they had learned to love the game and the language.

Exhausted, they closed the drapes and lay on their beds for a short nap. Much to their surprise they did not awake until the next morning.

CHAPTER 3

BASILICA

After quickly eating their meagre breakfast of coffee and croissants, Raymond and John were eager to explore the neighborhood. They made their way down the stairs to the street and headed East on Boulevard de Rochechouart. It is a wide street with a green boulevard that separates the traffic lanes. Both were carrying their umbrellas and small sketch pads.

They found a Metro entrance at the end of their block. Here, they crossed the street and turned North onto Rue de Steinkerque. This short street led to the elaborately manicured public gardens that bordered the walkways leading up the hill to the majestic Sacre-Coeur Basilica. Architecture snobs derogatorily describe the cathedral, covered in white stone, as looking like a salt shaker. To the tourists, it just looked large, old and impressive.

The neat garden pathways and stairways were crowded with tourists, babbling away excitely in a rainbow of foreign languages. Finding a shaded bench, just inside the entrance to the gardens, John and Raymond sat down to study the players and the interplay. They soon began to draw in their sketch pads which were a prop, to disguise their true objective. Their umbrellas rested against their legs, ready to defend them, if necessary.

They sat for hours and watched the parade of tourists flow by. Initially, the permanent players in the park, eyed them suspiciously. However, within half an hour, Raymond and John were drawing no more interest than the park's trees or the flowers. The players on this stage had concluded, from John and Raymond's unusual apparel and demeanor, that they were neither potential victims to be fleeced nor policemen to be avoided.

It was not unusual to find artists in this park. For a hundred years, armies of artists had lived within walking distance of the Sacre-Coeur Basilica. They could usually find buyers for their paintings of the cathedral. The constant flow of tourists was always looking for souvenirs to take home to impress their neighbors.

John and Raymond's attention was caught by a young boy, perhaps ten years old, approach a tourist. The boy held a string in his hand which he suddenly tied around the tourist's finger. The surprised man chastised the boy and started to remove the string. The boy's accomplice deftly removed the distracted man's wallet from his back pocket and quickly disappeared into the crowd. The first boy quickly abandoned his string and ran away.

Later, an older girl with a clipboard, made her way among the milling tourists. She was looking for the most vulnerable. Stopping by an elderly woman with a shoulder bag, she asked if the tourist would sign a petition to provide a shelter for homeless children. The sympathetic tourist removed her shoulder bag, and handed it to her elderly companion. As she began to sign the petition, an older boy appeared. He wrenched the bag from her elderly companion's weak hands and ran. The girl with the petition disappeared in the confusion. The tourists' screeches for help went unheeded until finally two unenthusiastic gendarmes strolled over to address the transgression.

Just inside the entrance to the gardens, an older woman, dressed in filthy rags, lay on the hard sidewalk shaking, seeming to be in great distress. She appeared to be suffering from some horrible neurological disease. A shiny tin can, strategically placed close to her, attracted spare change from sympathetic tourists. It worked well. John calculated that at least twenty percent of the tourists were moved by the pitiful performance.

Later in the afternoon, a large, expensive Mercedes pull up close to the park entrance. They watched, as that horribly disabled woman, leaped sprightly to her feet and quickly made her way to the Mercedes. Her money can, was clutched firmly in her grasp. It was full to the brim.

John turned to Raymond and laughed at this miraculous transformation. They agreed that such a performance deserved to be richly rewarded.

For the first week, they observed. Identifying, the most skilled of the child thieves, was not difficult.

The next week, they started to follow one boy that they both agreed had displayed the most skill and creativity. They did not get too close to their target, just close enough that the target was aware that he was under observation. It took another week before their target angrily confronted them and asked them why they were following him.

They told him that they had business proposition they wanted to discuss with him. He looked at them with suspicion. They asked their target if he were hungry and if he would accompany them to a restaurant. The only strangers who had ever previously propositioned him were pedophiles. He ran away.

The next day, they waited for him at his usual haunt. He saw them but ignored them. When they again followed him, his intelligence led him into the trap of curiosity. He said he would listen to them but it must be in the park. Over the afternoon, they explained who they were and what they had to offer.

He did not commit himself. The next day he returned with questions. He told them his name was Gabriel LaChance and that he worked for Andre, an adult who expected him to generate 200 Euros a day. In exchange, he received protection, a place to sleep and food. He was Andre's top earner and Andre had warned him, if he ever ran away that he would find him and kill him. The boy wanted to know how they would protect him from Andre. He pointed out Andre to them.

Andre was tall, with long scraggly hair and a greasy beard. He was slouched against a pillar, a hundred feet away, observing his money makers at work. Andre's snake like eyes kept shifting to Gabriel. He did not like any interference with his money machines. He made eye contact with Gabriel and then made a hand gesture for Gabriel to get back to work. He scowled at John and Raymond, making it very clear that they were interfering with his property.

John explained to Gabriel that as soon as he joined The Sanctuary, he would be immediately moved to a safe house. Within a few days, he would then be flown to the United States. Here, thousands of miles away from Andre, he would be safe. Gabriel said he needed more time to think about it.

For several weeks, at their Saturday meetings, with the other Parisian Sanctuarians, they discussed Gabriel. The group agreed that he was a good prospect.

Under Lester's direction, a tentative plan was made to transport Gabriel to New Mexico. The passport of an American child, living in Paris, would be used to get him into the United States. The American boy's parents would be paid well to transport Gabriel to New Mexico. Once he was in New Mexico, he would assume the identity of another child and Gabriel LaChance would disappear forever.

A few days later, after receiving a particularly vicious beating from Andre, Gabriel sought out John and Raymond. He told them he was ready to join The Sanctuary. Raymond immediately took out his cell phone and contacted Lester Simpson. Within minutes, The Sanctuary's limousine appeared to remove Gabriel from danger.

John and Raymond noticed Andre, over the next few days, frantically searching for Gabriel. Someone told Andre that they had last seen Gabriel talking to the two strange looking artists. Andre did not know, what they had done to Gabriel, but he now believed they were responsible for his disappearance.

Late one afternoon, Andre sidled up to them and whispered that they would be sorry for having interfered in his business. John and Raymond grasped their umbrellas ready to defend themselves. They stared him down. Outnumbered this time, Andre angrily turned and strode off. They were now on their guard.

CHAPTER 4

MALCOLM

Each day as the sunset and the park emptied, they would always make their way back to their room to stow their drawing pad. Then, they would begin their evening ritual of wandering through the narrow, twisted lanes of old Montmartre looking for somewhere good to eat. Their generous food allowance and an almost infinite number of interesting restaurants made this choice difficult. Finally, hunger would force them to make a choice.

One day, just as they were leaving their building to begin their evening search, an artist they had often seen in the park, passed by carrying a blank canvas under his arm. He nodded at them, smiled and stopped. In what sounded like unaccented English to their ears, he asked, "Did you have a good day in the park?"

"Yes, we did. Are you an American?"

"No, I'm a Canadian."

"Do you live close by?"

"Actually, I live in the building next to yours."

"Really. We are just off to dinner. Would you like to join us?"

"Great idea. Wait here a minute while I run upstairs and put this canvas in my studio. Oh yes, I should introduce myself. My name is Malcolm Edwards."

They introduced themselves and waited. In a few minutes, Malcolm returned and led them to what he said was his favorite restaurant. It was only a few blocks away. Over a delicious meal of stewed rabbit in a red wine sauce, they established a friendship.

Malcolm appeared to them to be very old. He was in his early sixties but the white, bushy beard and shoulder length hair made him look older. As they ate, he told them that he had owned a company in Canada which had been sold to a large American conglomerate.

The sale had given him total financial independence. At that time, he was only in his early fifties. Life was sweet. Unfortunately, within a year of the sale, his wife and only child were killed in a car accident. After the funeral, he left Toronto and everything that reminded him of them.

He had dreamed of a career as an artist. However, the responsibilities of providing for a wife and child had relegated this dream to a minor role in his life. He had always found time to paint but the growing demands of his successful business had relegated his painting to a hobby status.

Paris had been the mecca for artists for centuries. Malcolm wanted to explore why Paris had become this magnet for artists. He came to Paris and after living six months in a Montmartre apartment, he knew that this was where he wanted to spend the rest of his life. Having the financial resources, he bought the building on Boulevard de Rochechouart.

Malcolm rented out the ground floor of his building to a grocer. The rooms on the other floors were rented out to artists as studios, except for the top floor. This is where he had his apartment. He also kept a large studio, at the top of the first landing. It had a large window that overlooked the busy street. The door to his studio was always open when he was in residence, so he could keep an eye on the comings and goings in his building.

Over the years, his studio had become the unofficial meeting place for the neighborhood artists. They drank his free coffee and warmed the comfortable chairs that circled his easel. As Malcolm stood, painting at his easel, he would periodically pause to participate in their passionate arguments. Colors, artists, techniques, composition, framing, shadows, clients, thieving gallery owners, lying politicians and relationships were the participant's usual topics.

With no real need for more money, Malcolm put little effort into selling his paintings. The walls of his studio and the halls of the entire building were crowded with his paintings. He painted for the pure joy he got from creating images.

Selling paintings is hard work and requires a dedicated, consistent effort. Malcolm wanted to spend the rest of his life doing exactly what he wanted to do and that did not include chasing after gallery owners and collectors. Some of his inventory did momentarily shrink. A rare buyer would stumble upon one of his paintings or Malcolm would give one to a friend as a present.

When they finished their dinner, Malcolm invited them back to his studio for coffee. They followed him back to his building and up the stairs. Within five minutes, after he unlocked his studio door and turned on the lights, they heard the clump of footsteps on the stairs. Other artists, who had been waiting for the light go on in his studio window, now gathered.

Now most evenings, Raymond and John joined the group in Malcolm's studio. As the evening wore on, often only the two of them and Malcolm would be left.

Being only students of business, John and Raymond were interested in taking advantage of Malcolm's decades of real business experience. They described to him the business opportunities that they were considering when their two-year commitment ended. Malcolm was intrigued by the whole concept of The Sanctuary and the grant that they would receive to establish a business.

One day, he suggested that they should consider building a commercial collection agency. He explained that this was where he had acquired his wealth. It was an enterprise that they had never been exposed to. When Malcolm explained in detail how the business worked, they were intrigued.

For more than a year, Malcolm taught them how to make money operating a commercial collection agency. He shared with them the contents of his laptop. It was full of letters, proposals, operating manuals and articles that brought the business alive. They transferred much of this documentation to their own laptop.

What intrigued Raymond, when he reviewed the documentation, was how much of the operation could be computerized for even greater efficiency. Motivated by Malcolm's concepts, Raymond built sophisticated systems in their laptop. He showed Malcolm the computer systems that he had created. Malcolm enthusiastically encouraged their initiative while tactfully pointing out problem areas that he thought needed further work.

Raymond would never see his systems being used. Man plans. God laughs.

During the day, Raymond and John's hours were filled with observing possible recruits for The Sanctuary. Their evenings were dedicated to building and refining the systems they would use to build their commercial collection agency.

As their first acquisition, Gabriel motivated them to search for more candidates. Every few months, they were responsible for a few of the smartest and the brightest of child thieves disappearing from Paris streets. Andre and the other controllers were enraged at this theft of their best resources.

The two years flew by. As their departure date approached, they became more and more excited about leaving Paris and establishing their commercial collection agency.

Their final day in Paris was spent preparing for their new life. Fashionable new clothes were bought. On returning to their room with their purchases, they took great pleasure in consigning their black shoes, white shirts and black pants to the trash. They were amused when returning to the street, dressed in their new attire, that their neighbors, who had seen them daily for the two years, did not recognize them.

They packed and prepared to go out for one last celebratory dinner. They had hoped that Malcolm would join them, but he had a rare meeting with an art dealer, interested in his work, and could not make it. Since they would be leaving for airport early in the morning, they said their final goodbyes to him and promised that they would keep in touch.

It was almost midnight when they left the restaurant and strolled home through the dark, empty streets of Montmartre. As always, they carried their umbrellas.

They talked as they made their way home for the last time. Excitedly, they speculated about how much money The Sanctuary would grant them and where the best location to establish their collection agency should be. John walked on the outside closest to the road. Raymond was on the inside, next to the buildings that lined the poorly lit street. The hard soles and heels of their new shoes echoed in the quiet street as they approached the entrance to an alley. Both had celebrated with a little too much of the restaurant's cheap red wine. They were feeling relaxed, pleased with their lot in life and dulled by the wine. They were looking forward to their beds and to flying home in the morning.

As they passed the entrance to the alley, John caught a sudden flash out of the corner of his eye. Raymond crumbled to the ground. He had been stabbed in the heart. The attacker now lunged for John. Spinning quickly, John managed to club Raymond's attacker in the temple with his umbrella's handle.

John didn't know if that was what killed the attacker or when the attacker's head had hit the concrete curb. There had been a wet and hollow sound when his head had hit the curb. A sound John had last heard when he had dropped a watermelon onto a concrete floor.

A second attacker, with his knife drawn, now leaped out of the alley. John, moved backwards into the street, fending him off with the umbrella. Using the umbrella's handle, he was finally able to twist the knife out of the second attackers' hand. It clattered to the ground. John swiftly picked it up.

Disarmed and seeing his accomplice's smashed, bloody body on the ground, the second attacker turned and ran. John raced after him with the knife firmly grasped in his hand. Being younger and in better shape, he quickly caught up to the attacker. Reaching out, he grabbed the attacker's long scraggly hair with one hand and yanked his head back, exposing his throat. With one quick, sweeping motion, John cut that throat from ear-to-ear, almost severing the attacker's head. It was only when he stared down at the blood gushing from the attacker's severed arteries that he realized it was Andre.

He wiped the blade and handle of the knife on Andre's shirt and dropped the knife beside the still body. Remembering the instructions that they had received on their arrival in Paris. He looked for evidence that could connect this murder scene to

The Sanctuary. Walking back to Raymond's body, he retrieved Raymond's cellular phone and his wallet. He checked Raymond's pockets for anything else that might connect the body to The Sanctuary. Finding nothing, he walked away, intent on quickly putting as much distance as possible between himself and the three bodies.

Blocks away, he stopped in a door way, pulled out his own cellphone and phoned Lester Simpson's emergency number. The phone rang just once, a sleepy Lester answered it. John explained what had happened. Simpson, who was now wide awake, asked, "Did you get Raymond's wallet?"

"Yes, and his cellular phone as well."

"Good. It is doubtful that the police will ever be able to identify him or connect him to The Sanctuary. How far are you from home?"

"About five minutes."

"Okay, get back there. Pack everything. Leave nothing behind. I'll have a car over there within half an hour. In France, unlike the United States, you are guilty until proven innocent. This could get messy. We've got to remove you while we still can."

"What about Raymond's body?"

Lester paused before answering. He sought comforting words but realized such words did not exist, "I know you were close to him and this sounds terrible but right now my sole concern is flying you out of here in the morning and removing any link between The Sanctuary and those three bodies. With no next of kin, only we will miss Raymond. The French authorities will bury the body after they complete their investigation. Now go. The car will soon be there."

As he raced back to the room, he could not shake the feeling that he was having a nightmare and would soon wake up. It did not seem real. One minute, the two of them had been laughing and making plans for the rest of their lives and the next moment Raymond was gone. They would never again share hopes and fears. Raymond would never be there to protect his back and he, Raymond's back. Why was he spared, instead of Raymond? Was it luck? Fate?

While he felt no remorse for having killed the two men, he did feel that somehow that he should feel remorse. After all, he was responsible for taking two lives. It frightened him that taking the two lives had affected him no more than if he had swatted two irritating mosquitos. Was he a psycho killer? Was it the martial arts training that had automatically taken over his body and responded instinctively to the attack? Was it the kill, or be killed, lessons he had learned on the rough streets of Los Angeles?

There really was no one, other than him, to mourn. Raymond's life seemed to have made no more of an impression than footprints on a beach washed away by the tide. John wondered, for the first time in his life, if anyone would mourn him when he was gone and whether it mattered. He had accepted the concept of life being temporary but facing the reality of how quickly it could be ended, was traumatic. The Sanctuary had lost on their investment in Raymond

When he got back to the room, he hurriedly packed his bag with the laptop and everything linked to Raymond. This included Raymond's passport and his plane tickets.

When he went down to the street, he was surprised to find the Mercedes was already waiting for him. He felt he had lived a lifetime in the last hour. The driver took him back to the Mission, to wait a few hours, before they headed to the airport.

⌧⌧CHAPTER 5

TAOS

Getting to Taos, New Mexico from Paris is neither quick nor easy. Conscious of cost efficiencies, The Sanctuary had chosen the least expensive route. The early morning flight from Paris to Madrid took two hours. After a two-hour layover, John Cross caught a much longer flight in the afternoon to Dallas, Texas. Another two-hour layover in Dallas, delayed his arrival in Albuquerque until the evening.

He felt lucky when he exited the airport to find the Taos shuttle van waiting. It took over two hours to make the one hundred and thirty-five mile drive up State Road 68. Upon reaching the outskirts of Taos; the shuttle pulled over to the side of the highway ⌷and let him off in front of the Days Inn. It was the van's first stop in the small town.

Coming into Taos is like coming into most small American towns. Along each side of the four-lane highway are the icons of American retail: A Ford dealership, followed by a Chevrolet dealership, followed by Sears, followed by Walmart, followed by a Quality Inn, followed by a Sonic hamburger restaurant.

Land is cheap in New Mexico. Businesses can grow horizontally, instead of being forced to grow vertically. You see, very few two-story buildings. Businesses have big parking lots, often with vacant, undeveloped land between them and the next business.

Low, scruffy trees and bushes add a hint of greenery to the grey-yellow desert landscape. Encircled by distant, dark mountains the Taos valley seems flatter and broader than it is.

John took out his cell phone and called the main college number. The receptionist told him they had been waiting for his call and said they would send someone to pick him up. He stood, with his bag at his feet, watching the parade of pickup trucks go streaming by. There were no pedestrians.

A fiery red ball of a sun was setting. It put on a glorious show. After spending two years in the narrow canyons of Paris, John had almost forgotten how the big New Mexico skies could make one feel so small and inconsequential. Tainted pink by the dying light, puffy clouds sped across the darkening blue dome.

This had been his home and refuge for ten years. After living in a vibrant city like Paris, it now felt foreign, empty and dead. He no longer wanted to be here. It brought back too many memories of Raymond Powell. He wanted to get on with the challenges of living and use all the skills he had acquired.

A pimply faced kid, driving one of The Sanctuary's white pickup trucks, pulled up beside him. John threw his suitcase into the cargo bed and climbed into the cab. It only took a few minutes to get to the college. Most places in Taos took only a few to get to.

Twenty-five years earlier, The Sanctuary had purchased five hundred acres of desert land on the outskirts of Taos. One of the first things the contractors did, when they built the campus, was to drill for water. They had got lucky. They had drilled into a large aquifer. The trapped ground water, that had been compressed by an ancient geological formation, gushed with great force to the surface. Ever since, it had been irrigating the lawns, flower beds, trees and the eighteen-hole golf course.

The college was at the end of a long dirt driveway, a half mile in from the highway. A high chain link fence surrounded the Sanctuary's property. It controlled who got into the campus, not who got out. The guard at the only gate, was there to make sure only the invited, got in.

While cocooned in this compound for ten years, it had never felt like a prison. To John, it was an oasis in the middle of a desert, a safe refuge in the middle of a hostile world.

After childhoods, full of horrors, the campus was somewhere its inhabitants wanted to be. Not somewhere, they wanted to escape from. The Sanctuary took care of their every need.

Anyone who had wanted to leave could have left but without a family to go to where were they going to go? To remind themselves of just how well off they were, all they had to do was walk to the edge of the campus and stare through the chain link fence at the endless grey, brown, dry, desert that surrounded their lush green campus.

They had all experienced the harshness of life. They understand what they had gained. You do not have to be an adult to know when you are well off. As far as

John Cross knew, no one had ever left The Sanctuary before they left to go on their two-year mission.

The Sanctuary gave them a purpose, a goal, an opportunity to do something honorable with their lives. They accepted that they were being prepared for the responsibility of saving children from the same dire circumstances that they had escaped. They also recognized that they could not save every abandoned child.

The children who grow up in conventional environments look upon their future as a mystery. They receive a general education. Those on The Sanctuary campus understood their learning had a purpose. They knew that the profits of their future enterprises and their personal incomes depended on how well they absorbed what they were being taught about running a business.

They also understood that the time spent on the compound's sports fields not only strengthened their bodies but prepared them to work as team members in a competitive environment. To prepare them to move with confidence, in the privileged social circles they were expected to join, they were also coached in manners, in using tableware, good grooming and preparing healthy food.

As they drove up the long driveway to the campus, John could see the leader's sparkling white pyramid rising above the leafy green trees surrounding it. It was the only three-story building for miles in every direction. On its ground floor was a reception area and a six thousand square foot library. A three thousand square foot administration center occupied the second floor and on the third level was the leader's one thousand square foot office. On the roof of the third floor was a four-sided white pyramid that soared another thirty feet higher into the sky. From his office, the leader could not only see the entire campus, but he could see all the way to downtown Taos and across the desert to the distant mountains.

Since the building was white washed adobe, from a distance, it looked like a wedding cake laid down on the desert. One story residences, lecture halls, labs, class rooms, a recreational center, a student center surrounded the three-story administrative building. All were in the same white washed adobe style.

Now that he was a graduate, John learned his status rated him a private guest cottage that overlooked the college's golf course. He had spent many enjoyable hours on its links.

The kid waited while John deposited his bag into the small unlocked cottage and then drove him to the student center cafeteria. As he was about to drive away, the driver remembered to hand John an envelope. It contained a letter from Winston Hawkins, the current leader and son of the founder of The Sanctuary. It welcomed John home and invited him to a nine o'clock meeting in the morning.

The only other time he had ever been in Winston Hawkins presence, was two years earlier. At his graduation ceremony, Hawkins had handed him his diploma and shaken his hand. He had been awed to be in the great man's presence.

The cafeteria was full of noisy students dressed in The Sanctuary's uniform of white shirts, black pants and black shoes. Heads in the room swiveled to check out John's colorful Parisian attire. John grabbed a plastic tray and pushed it along the stainless-steel counter. For nostalgic reasons, from a warning compartment, he chose the special of the day, Shepherd's Pie. There was no cashier. Once you were on the campus, money ceased to exist as a commodity of exchange. You helped yourself to whatever you needed when you needed it. Every student, every teacher, every administrator, every clerk and every visitor were a guest of The Sanctuary.

Arriving from the hard streets, the first impulse of the deprived children, was to eat to excess and to hoard everything they touched. They carried food, clothing, pens and paper back to their rooms. For the first time in their life they had a private room and a private bathroom. Their small rooms soon became so stuffed with acquisitions that they became uncomfortable. At that point, the student would realize that there was no point in stuffing their bodies or their rooms. They would never want for anything ever again. They were now Sanctuarians. The rooms, then reverted to functional neatness.

Even though he had left only two years ago, John recognized no one in the dining room. This did not surprise him. The campus hosted a thousand male students. Twenty percent of the students would have changed since he was last here. He would have only been familiar with those from his own year, some from the year that followed his year and those in the two years, ahead of him.

Each year had one hundred students divided into ten classes of ten students. The small classes allowed the instructors to meet, one-on-one, with students for several hours each week to make sure each student understood the lessons they were being taught. For twelve hours a day, seven days a week, students were in classes or in organized activities that would expand their minds and strengthen their bodies. Two hundred instructors taught the one thousand students. They were the best that The Sanctuary could attract to a campus in isolated community like Taos.

As he was finishing his apple pie, John felt a presence standing beside him. He looked up to see a student smiling at him. John knew he should recognize this face, but it was out of context in The Sanctuary's cafeteria.

With a slight, French accent, the student said, "John, how good it is to see you. I never had time to thank you. You saved my life."

It all came rushing back. With obvious surprise in his voice, John said, "Gabriel is that you? I can't believe how much you have grown in the last two years. I would never have recognized you."

Gabriel sat down with him. In perfect English, with all the appropriate colloquialisms, he told John about his studies, all the exciting ideas he had been exposed to and all the interesting people he had met. As John looked at this healthy, vibrant, young man, he felt a great sense of satisfaction and pride. Gabriel was standing in front of him instead of lying dead and forgotten in the mean streets of Paris. He had saved Gabriel. If he were to die today, Gabriel was living proof that he had already achieved at least one positive thing in life.

John finished his pie. He and Gabriel walked back to the cottage. The sun had set. The dry chill of the desert evening had crept in. As they parted, Gabriel said, "I hope that someday I can repay you for all that you have done for me."

There were no locks on any of the doors on the campus. John pushed open the cottage door, took a quick shower and collapsed on the bed. Sleep came as fast as an express train.

At nine o'clock, the next morning, he entered Winston Hawkins' large, very impressive office. It was a room filled with antique furniture, original oil paintings and book lined walls. The large picture windows, on all four sides, framed desert scenes and drenched the room in sunshine. Hawkins, dressed in a dark blue, pin stripe suit with a vest, peered at him over half glasses. This left John feeling like he was an interesting specimen under a microscope. With a grand sweep of his hand, Winston showed that John should take a chair across the desk from him.

"My condolences, yesterday I learned of your confrontation in Paris. We had looked forward to great things from Raymond. Thank goodness, you escaped any harm. Welcome home."

"Thank you."

"I am sure, over the last two years of your mission, that you have considered how you would serve The Sanctuary after your mission was over. Even when you first arrived here, you showed a natural inclination for business. We have taken great care in developing that natural talent. I am looking forward to hearing about your entrepreneurial plan."

This was John's cue. Not sure what to expect, he had been rehearsing his proposal for weeks. He was now both relieved and nervous about being able to present it. His future depended on the next few minutes.

He cleared his throat and began, "Raymond and I spent a lot of time discussing what we would do. We were planning on working as partners. Our first choice was buying and operating a golf course. We both loved the game and thought it would not only engage us but be something we both could be passionate about. Unfortunately, our research ruled it out."

"Why?"

"Lots of reasons. The biggest problem was that the majority of golf courses do not make a profit. The supply of golf courses exceeds the demand. We also found that we would have to take on a debt of between three and seven million dollars. That's a big burden when you are just learning how to run a business. There were other concerns too."

"Such as?"

"Uncontrollable things, such as bad weather, droughts, lawsuits from lawyers getting hit by 200-mile-per-hour golf balls or being run over by drunken golf cart drivers. We concluded that what we wanted was to start a small service business, that required a minimum investment, but had unlimited potential. One, where we can easily control expenses, minimize our risks and expand as quickly as our profits and experience would allow us. We wanted a business that would let us experiment and make mistakes, without destroying it. Maybe, once we had accumulated surplus cash, we could look at buying a golf course. Maybe by then, we would have learned enough about running a business to be the profitable exception."

"There are few service businesses that I can think of that would meet your parameters."

"The only one that we came across that met our criteria was running a commercial collection agency."

With a hint of disdain in his voice Winston Hawkins said, "Debt collecting?"

"Yes, debt collecting, but not consumer collections. We want to specialize in commercial collections. That is collecting money from businesses for businesses. We saw an opportunity for it to grow into a billion-dollar international business. Most collection agencies just want to be in consumer collections. They want to chase after the hundreds of millions of dollars that large credit card companies put out for collection. It is hard for small, new business to get a foothold in consumer collections. It is a cut throat, a messy business, with all kinds of consumer protection agencies interfering in your operations., The big national banks play off one consumer agency against another. They beat them down on their commission rates."

"How does commercial collections differ?"

"Well, to build a commercial agency, instead of selling retailers, you are selling to manufacturers, wholesalers and business services. You sell the credit manager of each business, one at a time. It requires providing a professional service that is consistent, effective and competitively priced. What is attractive, is that you can lever your success with one company as a reference for approaching another business in the same industry. You can then use this reference approach to move from one target industry to another target industry. You spread your risk among many customers. If you lose one customer, it has little impact on the overall health of your business. In consumer collections, if you lose one giant customer, it can bankrupt your business."

"You seem to know a lot about it for someone who has been on a mission for the last two years?"

"We had a mentor."

"Who?"

"An elderly man, by the name of Malcolm Edwards. He once owned the largest commercial collection agency in Canada and sold it to a large U.S. conglomerate. Shortly after selling it, his wife and son died in a car accident."

"How did you meet him?"

"Having lost his family, he wanted to get away from anything that reminded him of his previous life. He moved to Paris, to pursue a dream, that he had since he was a child, to be an artist. After seeing us sketching in the park, he approached us. It turned out that his studio was in the building next to our rooming house. The studio was the neighborhood meeting place for artists. Raymond and I spent a lot of evenings there. Having a theoretical business education, like we had, is one thing but being able to pick the brains of a creative entrepreneur is another. He had built his very successful collection agency over thirty years. When we showed interest in learning every aspect of the industry, he became like a father preparing his two sons to take over the family business. He was a great teacher

John paused, as he let the memories of those evenings in Paris wash over him.

Winston Hawkins had heard enough. Any concerns that he might have had about investing in John's proposed venture had been erased. He nodded his head and asked, "John, how much money do you need to establish the business?"

John was taken back by this question. He had expected a long, grueling inquisition before the subject of money arose. He answered, "Very little, based on the business plan I worked out with Malcolm Edwards. I will start off with one collector as the inside person and three sales people, including myself. We will be out there beating the bushes for collection claims and servicing our customers. I'll set up operations in the cheapest rental property I can find. I believe that within a year I can expect to show a profit. As the business grows, and the volume justifies the expense, I will add more collectors and sales people. To set thing up, I calculated that I would need $400,000. It's all laid out in my business plan."

John pushed a folder with his business plan across the desk. Winston Hawkins picked it up and spent several minutes skimming through the pages. John sat there waiting for his future to start. Winston looked up and said, "Where do you plan to establish this business?"

"In Las Vegas."

"Why Las Vegas? Do you like to gamble?"

"Not really, but in business you do have to take calculated risks. As for gambling in casinos? That holds zero interest for me. As I understand it, the odds always favor the casino. I picked Las Vegas because, first, I feel most at home in the South West. Second, it will only cost $400 to incorporate there. The state levies no corporate income tax nor personal income tax. All I must pay is a $200 annual business license fee. Maybe someday I might need to go public to finance a national expansion. If that should happen, Nevada laws allow corporations to operate with the least government oversight of any state. It is also important that Las Vegas has a ten-billion-dollar economy and a population of two million. It's big enough to give us a solid base to build on. We won't have to contend with the large competitors in the more established financial centers, like New York and Chicago. Las Vegas is dynamic and open to a new business. Everyone has moved there from somewhere else."

"You seem to have done your homework. To get you started, we will deposit an initial $50,000 in your account today, $10,000 of that should get you a good used car. You'll need it to get to Las Vegas and to get the company set up. We'll keep an eye on your account and transfer more to it as needed. Each Friday, I want you to write me a one-page summary of your progress. Tell us where the money is going and what your plans are for the next week. Also, keep us up to date on any changes you make to your master plan. We expect that you **will** revise it as you encounter problems and opportunities that you had not **expected**."

"Thanks."

"No need for thanks. You've earned it. We've been preparing you for this for twelve years. It is not a loan. It is an investment by The Sanctuary. I need not remind you that we are counting on the income from your business to help children escape the horrors of the hard streets. We want to see thousands of them realize their full potential, just like you are now realizing yours."

Feeling overcome, almost on the edge of tears, John choked out his thanks, "If it were not for the Sanctuary, I would be dead. You can depend on me. I will become a successful businessman so that I can save hundreds of children who are facing the same bleak future I once faced."

He paused for a few seconds to recover before asking, "Is there anything for me to sign?"

"No, everything between you and The Sanctuary, we do on trust. You agreed long before your mission that the sanctuary would own 15% of the shares of any business you established and that 15% of the annual profits would go to The Sanctuary. All the money that you give to The Sanctuary can be deducted by your company as legitimate business expenses. It will take a while for you to get established. Your initial profits will be **invested** into the business. It is important that your company have a good solid base. However, within three years, we will expect to be sharing in your profits. Now go, make your fortune. You are not alone in this world. The Sanctuary will always be there to protect your back."

⊠⊠CHAPTER 6

VEGAS

After leaving Winston Hawkins' office, John waited by the gate until he could hitch a ride to the car dealer on Paseo Del Pueblo Sur. It was a small dealership with a limited inventory. The best deal he could make was a five-year-old, Chevrolet Malibu that appeared to be in good shape. He closed the deal and arranged to pick it up the next morning.

The only other cars he had ever driven were the college's old clunkers that they taught the students to drive in when they turned sixteen.

⬜The car salesman drove him back to the campus. With reality staring him in the face, he took his laptop and started a search for cheap office space in Las Vegas and somewhere he could afford to live while he was setting up the business.

At nine the next morning, he left Taos. He breezed through Santa Fe, Albuquerque and Flagstaff. It took over twelve hours to complete the eight-hundred-mile trip. He had stayed just above the speed limit.

The most affordable decent hotel room in Las Vegas, that he could find, was in a fake Mexican adobe style building. It was close to the Nellis Air Force Base and twenty minutes from the Las Vegas Strip. Every morning that he was there, he awoke as the military jets took off before six a.m.

⬜He had never stayed in a motel. In a few days he had got used to the hard bed, the white towels that were yellowed and worn and the stench of stale tobacco smoke. What was important to him, was that it had a telephone with free local calls, free internet, free parking and a flat screen television. The free continental breakfast, each morning, was a welcome and unexpected bonus.

It was too late to start his search for office space to rent. It had been a long drive, and he was tired. The hamburger and fries that he ate in the motel restaurant were adequate. As soon as he returned to his room, he crawled into bed and was asleep within minutes.

☐

The first morning, he accessed the website of a Las Vegas agency that specialized in incorporating companies. He filled out the documentation they required and transmitted it to them. They responded that the documentation would be submitted to the Nevada Secretary of State. By noon the following day, he should expect to receive the filed articles of incorporation from the State, along with tax registration forms, licensing and other bureaucratic documentation. As he had laid out in his business plan, he incorporated the business as, FICA INC, trading as the First Industry Collection Agency".

To open a commercial bank account and a separate trust account for the collection agency, he had to wait until he had completed the incorporation. Initially he could open a personal account in a nearby bank. He deposited the thousand dollars in cash he was carrying and transferred what remained of the first $50,000 from his bank account in Taos.

☐A trust account for the business is necessary because a collection agency must be able to deposit checks from the client's debtors. These checks are usually made out to the client and not to the collection agency. The law requires that the trust account money be isolated from the collection agency's operating account. Each month, money deposited in the trust account from the preceding month, is sent to the client minus the collection agency's commission. For trust accounts to hold millions of dollars owed to their client's is not unusual. Since banks pay interest on trust account money, the interest can be an important source income for the collection agency.

Incorporation was also necessary before John could apply for a collection agency licence and purchase a required $35,000 surety bond that the licence required. This bond would cost a thousand dollars.

☐While he waited, he began his search for a collection manager. Without a licenced collection manager, he could not open the collection agency nor could he open it without having a physical address.

John took the first reasonable space the real estate agent presented. It was a 960 square feet office for what he thought was a low rent of $600 a month. It was in a two storey, yellow office building, just east of McCarran International Airport. He made sure it had reliable air conditioning and free outdoor parking

Since the great recession of 2008, property prices in Las Vegas had been the lowest of all large American cities. There were several empty suites in the office building. He had chosen the smallest one, with the belief, that he could upgrade to a larger space, when needed.

Finding a collection manager, to build the business around, was critical to its success. He wanted an experienced collector looking for a growth opportunity. This person would be gambling on their future on newly formed business. As the first employee, they would have to find, train and manage a growing team of collectors to handle, what John hoped, would be an ever-growing flood of collection claims.

An experienced manager would expect to be well paid. To create credibility with this first employee, John needed to show them an office. He had to assure them that the First Industry Collection Agency was more than just a pipe dream.

The next morning, he purchased three desks, swivel chairs and a meeting room table from a used, business furniture company. Their delivery charges, cost almost as much as the furniture.

John organized the desks in a U formation, putting himself in the middle and the collection manager's desk on his right and his future sales manager on the left. This would allow him to listen in on what they were working on and to give him the opportunity to ask, or answer, questions that they, or he, might have. This would expose him to the unfamiliar intricacies of the collection business. Other purchases included personal computers, two large digital screens, an internet linkage to the Cloud, and a telephone system. The communications company promised they would all be operational the next day.

John hung the two large digital screens on opposite ends of the room. One would display commission income made by each collector and the other would display the value of collection claims brought in by each sales representative. Every collector, sales representative and manager would know every minute of every day how they were performing compared to their quotas.

When everything was in place, John transferred the collection agency software, that Raymond had created under Malcolm's direction, from his laptop to the new computer system. Management reports, form letters, accounting records, schedules, the prioritizing of collection calls and sales calls were now easily retrievable and operational. The system also retrieved and displayed information on debtors and prospective clients that it found in Google and other databases. The storage of debtor and sales prospect conversations and correspondence was also part of the system.

John tested all three computer terminals to verify the system was working as planned. As a final test, he emailed, from his desk top terminal, to his iPad, FICA's new client contract form. Using his finger, he signed the contract on the screen and emailed it back to himself. Within seconds, an email, with a copy of the signed contract arrived. Satisfied with this final test, he was now ready to hire his first employee.

John took a direct approach, He phoned all the collection agencies listed in Las Vegas and asked to speak to the agency's legal manager. Malcolm had told him the collector responsible for legal claims, would be the smartest, most experienced collector in that the agency. They would make good managers and be most open to an opportunity with potential in a new agency.

On his third try, he got through to a legal collection manager. He told her what he sought. She showed interest but was reluctant to talk on the phone. John wondered if she would appear for the appointment they had set for the next day. She did.

Her name was Patty Horan. John learned that she was there because she felt slighted. Male collectors with less experience than her, were being moved into management positions ahead of her. She had been collecting for five years and felt that her employer would never move her into management because of the integral role she played as their legal collector. Being a single mother, bringing up a young child, this barrier to her advancement was frustrating. She had financial needs and moving into a higher paying management position was important to her.

John found her to be articulate and bright. To show credibility, in what was a start up, he showed her the slick computer system. She asked several good questions and appeared impressed with his plans for FICA. John laid out the management opportunity.

Patty hesitated. For her it was a gamble. She now had a good job with an established collection agency, but her daughter's future and a safer home environment was her primary concern. More money and management experience would give her greater security.

Patty closed her eyes and pondered the opportunity. Interrupting her thinking, John asked her how big a salary it would take to get her on board. He was anxious to fill the position. The modest figure she came back with surprised him. He speculated that the low figure was due to Nevada having no state income tax. This had made their salaries lower than elsewhere in the country.

It was then agreed, that if her reference checks were satisfactory, that she would resign from her current job in the morning. Patty thought since she was leaving, to join a competitor, that they would fire her that morning.

Pleased to have one of his two key positions filled, he asked Patty if she could recommend a good collection salesman. Without thinking for more than a second, she said, "Billy O'Malley."

"Who is he?"

"He is an older guy with many contacts who worked for a large national agency for at least twenty years. They closed their Las Vegas operation a month ago and moved it to some third world country. I don't think he has landed anywhere yet. Everybody likes him. He's professional and has a good work ethic. I am sure he could bring in a ton of collections claims."

"How do you know him?"

"Though the National Association of Credit Management golf tournaments."

"You a golfer?"

"Yep. Let me see if I can find his phone number for you."

She took out her cellphone, searched, located it and read it to him. They parted. He said he would see her in two days at nine o'clock.

John phoned the number and left a message for Billy. Within an hour, Billy had returned the phone call. They agreed to meet the following day.

When they met the next morning, John liked Billy. He exuded a warmth and a sincerity that made it easy for him to establish a rapport with strangers. Billy's grey hair and the fact that Billy could afford to lose at least twenty pounds led John to believe that Billy was in his mid-fifties. Although he had never known his own grandfathers, John thought he looked like someone's kind, old grandfather.

They spent two hours determining what each of them would bring to FICA. Billy listened as John outlined how he intended to grow the company. He wanted to know why John intended to concentrate on chasing commercial collection claims from the food industry. John told him how Malcolm Edwards had advised him that the food industry would be the best source of a consistent, steady volume of collection claims.

Malcolm had explained that everyone must eat. While other industries went through bust and boom periods, the food industry was steady. It included food wholesalers, restaurants, grocery stores, food transportation, food storage, food processing and the disposal of food waste. Food moved along this supply chain on credit. Credit equalled potential collections. In the United States, hundreds of thousands of businesses in the food industry, generated billions of dollars in revenue. Food would give FICA a fertile ☐field to cultivate.

Billy also liked John's idea of distributing a daily blog to all FICA customers. It would name commercial food debtors placed for collection and those claims that FICA had collected. Their curious food clients would want to check their accounting records to see if they were dealing with the same debtor and whether that debtor owed them money. If it was past due, they too would consider placing the account for collection with FICA, for fear that it was soon to become a bad debt. Such a daily blog would become a valued source of information to steer them away from possible bad debts in their industry.

Billy had made most of his income from a percentage of the commissions received from collecting his clients' claims. He had a hard time accepting that John's straight salary plan, could work. He asked John what incentive was there for a salesman to work hard if he were not being motivated by greed. Malcolm had warned John that paying a salesman a salary was a radical idea that the old guard would have a hard time accepting it.

John got Billy to admit, that the salary he was offering, would give him a higher income than Billy had ever made. He pointed out that just because a salesman was getting a salary did not mean management expected lower results from him. If a salesman wanted to keep his job, he still had to meet objectives. With everyone on a salary, there would be less caustic competition between sales representatives. They would be more prone to work as a team.

John also pointed out that rather than being frozen in mediocre territories, protecting commission incomes from established customers, he could reassign reps as needed, to territories where FICA would see higher revenue gains because of their experience and talent.

Being paid a salary would also give Billy greater credibility when he gave recommendations to clients. He could now say that he was not a commission salesman trying to pressure them into giving FICA their collection claims. Whether they gave him collection claims or not, would not impact would not impact his salary.

John also outlined how he would adjust Billy's salary once a year, based on how much Billy had exceeded his annual target. A target that they would both have agreed was fair and achievable.

John showed Billy the two thousand customer prospects that his research had identified and scored by potential. They were to be prospected by descending potential until they were all sold. John said that it was his belief that most sales people were unsuccessful because they were undisciplined and not working a set plan

Billy asked what would happen if he could not sell anyone on using the FICA collection service. John reminded him that just like commission sales, holding your job depends on reaching reasonable targets. He pointed out that as soon as Billy had landed a hundred and fifty clients that Billy would then hire a sales representative to service these new clients. This would allow Billy to concentrate on selling the next one hundred and fifty new clients. As soon as they had five sales reps, Billy would become a full-time sales manager. John's management plan was to convince companies to use FICA and make sure they never left.

John agreed to give Billy two months to switch any customers, he had had with his former employer, over to FICA. Billy had convinced John that this would bring in immediate revenue to offset his salary expense. While most of these clients would not be in the food industry, Billy did not see this as a problem. He started the next day.

Everything went as John had planned. In a few years, FICA employed thirty collectors, three collection managers, three sales managers, fifteen service representatives, ten new business sales representatives and thirty clerical staff. In six months, FICA had made its first monthly profit.

It gave John great pleasure when he could repay The Chosen's first $50,000 advance. Every month, he now gave them fifteen percent of FICA's profits. He invested the rest of the profits into growing the business. He and Billy discussed opening offices in Los Angeles and Chicago.

With the business on a firm footing, John splurged on a house in one of Las Vega's upscale neighborhoods and on various toys. The Sea-Doo, motorcycle and Lamborghini sports car were impractical because he had little time to enjoy them. To set an example for his employees, John was always the first one in the office each morning and the last one to leave at night which left little time for leisure activities.

As John's, general sales manager, it was Billy's responsibility to direct the new business sales representatives to the best prospects. One morning John called him into his office. "Billy, I don't understand it. You have a team of fantastic sales representatives. They've sold everyone we targeted except for one that sticks out like a sore thumb. Why have we never been able to sell Player Industries on using our collection service? They must control a hundred companies. I understand that they own casinos, car dealerships, advertising agencies, television stations, office buildings, golf courses, equipment wholesalers and who knows what else. I don't think we have a client now that has anywhere near their potential."

"You're right. They are big. Big and dangerous."

"What do you mean, dangerous?"

When I first came to Las Vegas, I had a run in with Mike Asino, the guy who owns Player Industries. He was a scum bag then, and he is scum bag now. You don't want to touch him with a ten-foot pole. He is a predator. To be honest, I have tried to keep FICA off his radar screen. If he sees you are making money, he will find a way to steal FICA from you. What do they say? When you sup with the devil, you use a long spoon. His mob connections make him untouchable. This means if he goes after you, you will have no one to run to for help. He's got all the politicians in his back pocket."

"He can't be that bad?"

"Oh, believe me, he is."

"I hear what you're saying but we are running out of prospects in Las Vegas. Sometimes to grow, you must take chances. People change. While I can understand why you do not want to get involved with Asino, it is a potential revenue source that we can't just ignore. I tell you what I will do. I'll take Players on as my personal sales prospect and keep my eyes open for any danger signals. If we see any, then we can drop him like a hot potato and you'll be able to say, I told you so."

Billy stared at John for a long time before he nodded and left the room with a great feeling of apprehension.

⌧⌧CHAPTER 7

PLAYER

John drafted a letter to Mike Asino at Player Industries. He mailed it and waited. He didn't get a response. A week later he tried phoning Mike Asino and could not get through.

Asino, proved to be almost impossible to reach. However, each day John would phone and leave a message. This continued for weeks.

One evening, when he was home, watching a baseball game, the doorbell rang. He had not been expecting anyone. He opened the door. A tall, distinguished stranger in a suit was standing there.

"Mister Cross, my name is Joe Palarmo. I work for Mister Asino. He understands that you would like to meet with him."

Surprised, John responded, "Mike Asino of Player Industries?"

"Yes, can you come with me now?"

"Sure. Let me put on a suit."

"Don't bother. Mister Asino isn't wearing a suit."

A large, black, Lincoln town car was idling in the driveway. John got into the back, along with Joe Palarmo. They took the Southern Highlands Parkway. Palarmo said nothing during the entire trip.

The chauffeur pulled off the highway onto a street lined with ostentatious mansions built around a golf course. When they reached the Asino's mansion, they drove down a ramp into an underground garage. John counted parking spaces for a dozen cars.

The Lincoln pulled into a parking spot, next to an elevator. They took the elevator up to the second floor and exited onto a wide corridor, tiled in white marble. Joe crossed to a door and knocked before opening it.

John entered a large office. Joe Palarmo closed the door behind himself as he left. Mike Asino was sitting behind an ornate, antique, mahogany conference table that could seat ten people. John recognized him, from pictures he had seen on the internet Asino was often photographed presenting checks to charities. With a dismissive hand gesture, he showed that John should take a seat across from him. He did not stand or offer to shake John's hand.

John guessed that Asino was in his early fifties. He was wearing a tight, black, Lacoste golf shirt that showed off a tanned, well-muscled, hard looking torso. His salt and pepper hair was cut short. Dark brown, intelligent eyes stared at John as if he were a bug under a magnifying glass. John could feel that this was not someone you would want to have as an enemy. In a quiet voice, he enquired, "You wanted to meet?"

"Yes, I do. I can save Player Industries several million dollars."

"How would you do that?"

"The larger the organization, the harder it is to keep close tabs on all the account receivables. As I understand it, each of your companies manages their own receivables. If one company has a problem collecting money from a customer, that customer can continue buying from all your other companies, until they too become a receivable problem. I propose merging all your companies' receivables into one database. Then, a consistent credit policy, can be applied to every customer. Consistency is the secret to minimizing account receivable problems. For example, some of your companies are placing their accounts out for collection at ninety days past due and some at one hundred and twenty days, some even later. This makes you a source of interest free money.

John noticed that Asino was staring at him. He continued, "I propose, that on your behalf, FICA will send out ten-day final notices, to all your slow payers, as soon as they reach sixty days past due. At seventy days all unpaid accounts would be placed for collection with FICA. Your slow paying customers have trained your credit managers to wait for payment. You now have to train your customers to pay promptly. When you do, you will see a big drop in your bad debt losses, a reduction in your borrowing costs and a big increase your cash flow."

John had been preparing this proposal ever since he had first talked to Bill O'Malley about landing Player Industries. He wondered if the proposal was too critical and blunt, but he felt he had nothing to lose. Asino interrupted, "Wouldn't we lose sales if we tightened up on our credit terms?"

"No, you increase sales when you make your customers adhere to your terms of sale. Past due companies go to other suppliers to avoid confrontations with suppliers whom they are past due. If you keep them current, there will be no interruptions in their ordering."

"What would it cost?"

"For us, to set up and co-ordinated the account receivable service will cost you nothing. Our contingency rate, when the occasional account gets placed for collection, will cost you 16% of the first $1,000 collected; 8% of the next $9,000 and 4% of the balance. If you check with your companies, you will find that these rates are lower than what they are now paying. So, not only will we be reducing your bad debts to a small fraction of what they are now but the increase in sales will cost you nothing. I can have it in place within a month."

With this closing statement, John shut up and remained still. Asino made no immediate response. He continued to stare at John. The room was silent. John waited because he knew to continue talking could kill the sale. After what seemed like an hour but was only seconds, Asino responded, "Thanks for coming. I have found your proposal interesting. I need to discuss it with my financial people. They'll be back to you if they think it has merit."

Asino stood, came around the table, shook John's hand and escorted him to the door. Outside, Joe Palarmo was sitting on an ornate, wrought iron, chair waiting to escort John home.

Three days later, John received an invitation from a Senior Vice President at Players Industries, to meet with the financial heads of their various companies. At this meeting, he was to explain what they would need to do to set up the proposed new account receivable system.

Within three months, Players Industries was generating 10% of FICA's revenues. John said nothing to Billy. Billy said nothing to John. Billy just waited for the axe to fall.

A year after their first meeting, John again had an unexpected knock on his front door. Joe Palarmo was again there to escort him to a meeting with Mike Asino. This time, when Joe knocked on Asino's office door, it a smiling Mike Asino opened it. He stuck out his hand to shake John's hand. He led John over to a corner of the office where three leather love seats surrounded a low square coffee table. They took seats across from each other.

"Can I get you a drink, John?"

"No thanks."

"It's been a year since we first met. What you proposed worked well. You've contributed to the profits of Player Industries. I wanted to thank you."

"You're welcome."

"I see great profits for the collection industry. It is a business that I had never considered getting involved in. It has so much potential that Player Industries wants to buy FICA and market it across the country."

John interrupted him, "I'm flattered that you see the potential for FICA but it is not for sale."

Asino's warm, friendly persona, became as hard and cold as granite. He continued, "How we resolve this is up to you. The easy way is for me, tomorrow, to put a million dollars in an account that my banker will set up for you in the Cayman Islands. However, if you choose not to work with me, I will save my million dollars and you will receive nothing. Easy or hard, I will take over your business before the end of the month."

"Based on its profits, FICA is worth at least five million dollars."

"What is your life worth, John?"

This statement hung in the still room. Asino continued, "Go home and think about my offer. I'll give you forty-eight hours to consider it. You know how to get hold of me if you want your million dollars. This is a onetime offer."

Asino did not get up to shake John's hand. After a minute of sitting there, in silence, staring at Asino, John accepted his dismissal. He stood, crossed the room and saw himself out.

As he rode down in the elevator, his mind raced. Billy had warned him. Why hadn't he listened to him? Was Asino bluffing? Could Asino take the business away from him without destroying it? His street fighter instincts had kicked in. These instincts would not allow him to walk away from his business without a fight.

On the third day, FICA received a letter from a Senior Vice President at Players Industries telling them that their business relationship was severed. He told them immediately cease working on all Player Industry collection claims. John waited further repercussions.

On the fourth day, Patty appeared at John's office door. She looked distraught.

"What's up Patty?"

"John, have you made changes with the bank that you haven't told me about?"

"No. Why do you ask?"

"Our trust account is empty."

"What do you mean empty?"

"There is no money in it."

"Maybe you or the bank have got our accounts mixed up?"

"Haven't I controlled the trust account since we opened our doors?"

"Yes, you have. It must be a banking error. Have you talked to them?"

"Of course, I talked to them. They thought it was strange when they processed a series checks from us before the twenty-eighth of the month."

"Checks? What checks?"

"They emailed me copies of the checks. They were all made out to Player Industries and all of them had your signature on them."

John stared at her in disbelief. He had hoped that Asino was bluffing. Now he knew he wasn't.

As FICA collected money for their clients, it was all deposited into FICA's trust account. Under the law, there are only two reasons for a collection agency to withdraw money from a trust account. One was to receive the commissions for their collection work. The second reason was to remit to the client the amount collected, less the collection agency's commission. This distribution of funds always took place at FICA on the twenty-eighth of each month.

FICA's earned commissions only represented about 12% of the money on deposit in the trust account. The total dollars, now missing from the trust account, would be equivalent to all of FICA's income for the entire year.

John concluded that Player Industries had forged FICA's checks. This misdirection of funds had effectively put FICA out of business. There was no money to pay the other customers what had been collected for them. Without a transfer of funds from the trust account to their operating account, FICA could not pay employees, the rent or the phone company. FICA was insolvent. As soon as the word got out that FICA's trust money had disappeared, no company would ever entrust FICA with their collections again. As a business, it would all be over.

Since his signature was on the Player Industries' forged trust account checks, John felt he would be lucky if he did not end up in jail. It would be difficult to prove he had nothing to do with the money ending up with Player Industries. They were not about to help him.

John could predict the future. Billy, Patty and all the other employees would be without jobs. The Commissioner of Collection Agencies would close FICA. He would lose his house, his Cadillac Escalade and all the expensive toys that he had bought on credit. With his connections, Asino would make sure that by tomorrow the state auditors were aware of their insolvency.

John weighed his options. In his mind there was only one option.

He phoned Players Industries. He was immediately put through to Mike Asino. John figured Asino must have left instructions to put him through.

"John, what a surprise. To what, do I owe this phone call?"

"You've won."

"But I always win. Now, what can I do for you?"

"I'll take you up on your offer of the million dollars."

"Oh John, it is too late for that. The forty-eight hours has passed. The best I can now offer is that you will not go to jail, and your employees will not lose their jobs. This new offer is good for only two hours. I'll see you are sitting in a cell before the sun goes down tonight unless you get down here and sign over your shares. As soon as this is done the money will be returned to the trust account."

John next heard the click of the phone being hung up. Almost too agitated to drive, he did get to the Player Industries office. Here, he was led to the office of their corporate lawyer.

Their lawyer explained each clause in the agreement. He drew attention to a clause that stated that John was terminated for cause with no hope of suing for future compensation. Receiving John's shares, gave Players Industries total control of FICA.

The value of the fifteen percent of the shares that The Sanctuary owned and the five percent that Patty and Billy each owned, would be in jeopardy. John hoped Asino would understand how valuable the two employees were to the success of FICA, but he had his doubts that he would.

John Cross had massive personal debts and no way to pay them. He was insolvent and expected his creditors would soon seize their secured assets. The two years of planning and programming in France and the years spent establishing the business, would now only benefit Mike Asino.

Street fighters don't cry. They get angry. As he drove away from Players Industries he was already plotting his revenge. Mike Asino would soon learn that he had robbed the wrong person. On the mean streets of Los Angeles, John Cross had learned about retaliation and how to respond to disrespect.

For twelve years, The Sanctuary had groomed John Cross. Their share of the profits from FICA could have saved hundreds of children. John would not allow Michael Asino to divert him from fulfilling his responsibility to The Sanctuary.

⊠CHAPTER 8

REVENGE

In May, a casino parking lot in Laughlin, Nevada at 10:30 in the morning, is blistering hot. Less than a month, after losing FICA to Players Industries, John Cross sat on a mountain bike fingering a Glock 26, subcompact pistol, in an open, black leather pouch fastened around his waist. As he waited, he practiced quickly pulling the pistol in and out of the open pouch. It was a Monday morning after what he expected would have been another very busy, prosperous weekend for the Player Industry's Cheers Casino.

At this time of the morning, there were few cars to hide behind in the massive parking lot. Every few minutes, John would straighten and peer over the roof of the car that concealed him. He was looking for any unanticipated problems.

It was five hundred feet to the concrete apron in front of the main entrance to the casino. The shimmering heat waves performed a liquid dance on the black pavement.

The popular Cheers Casino was one of the first casinos that Player Industries had purchased. It was so successful that Mike Asino had bought several casinos in Las Vegas and Reno.

Laughlin, Nevada has a population of only seven thousand. While it is only an hour and a half south of big city of Las Vegas, the two cities are as different from each other, as night is from day. To reach Laughlin, you drive south from Las Vegas across ninety miles of empty, flat, dry, barren desert, until you are confronted with several giant casino hotels rising from that desert. The second shock is seeing a narrow wall of green, in the middle of a desert. The third shock, in a state thirsty for water, is the oddity of seeing a wide, fresh water river.

Laughlin competes with Las Vegas for tourists. It offers gamblers with families more than just gambling. Water sports on the Colorado River are a big attraction.

The larger city of Bullhead City Arizona is directly across the river from Laughlin. It has the shopping and restaurants that Laughlin doesn't have. A long bridge over the river links the two cities. Many of the employees working at the casinos in Laughlin, live in Bullhead.

John Cross had chosen the Cheers Casino as his target because it was the most vulnerable of Mike Asino's assets to attack. Escape would be much easier from the small town of Laughlin than from any of Player's Las Vegas casinos. Laughlin does not have the police protection and security infrastructure of Las Vegas.

Mike Asino, with his mob connections, was a bully. No one stood up to him. John Cross' middle class shell of respectability had fooled him. He had expected John to lick his wounds and accept that he had lost his collection agency. John was supposed to slink away like a dog with his tail between his legs.

Asino, was unaware of John's harsh up bringing on the rough streets of Los Angeles. He had dismissed John as just another Anglo, white bread, wimp. If he had known of John's background, he might have anticipated that he was going to pay for his disrespect and for stealing the collection agency. Mike Asino was about to learn that he had screwed the wrong person.

John's wraparound sunglasses and a bicycle helmet were an effective disguise. His racing T-shirt and tight spandex bicycle shorts outlined the lean, hard body of a serious athlete. The mountain bike had a black metal rack fastened to the handle bars. It was now inconspicuously folded but could be expanded to hold a large package.

At last, the large, grey, box of an armored truck, rolled up to the casino, as it did every Monday morning. It stopped at the casino's main entrance. A concrete apron jutted out into the driveway. John Cross watched the uniformed guard climb out of the truck and amble towards the glass doors pushing a small cart. The sun reflected off the guard's shiny, brown, leather gun holster. It wasn't there for decoration.

To John, it was no surprise to learn that Player Industries owned the armored truck company that picked up cash at their casinos and delivered it to the bank. Asino believed in the efficiencies of vertical integration.

John took the Glock out of its pouch and released its safety. He put it back in the pouch and waited. It wouldn't be long now.

The middle-aged guard finally exited the casino. He was pushing his small cart. It now held one, large, white, canvas money bag. He was walking more quickly than when he had gone in. It was hot. He wanted to get back into the air-conditioned armored truck, to cool off before the next boring pickup.

It was dead still. Heat waves rippled across the parking lot. Only the guard with his bag of money was on the apron. The casino's doorman was hiding from the heat, just inside the lobby doors.

From behind the parked car, Cross pushed off. He pedaled swiftly toward the guard as he had every Monday for the previous two weeks. John rolled onto the concrete apron via the curb opening graded for wheelchair access. He slowed down so that he would rendezvous with the guard as he reached the rear of the armored truck. Noticing that the guard was suddenly moving faster than usual, Cross pedaled harder to compensate for the guards change in speed. This encounter had to be timed right. The hot morning sun was burning his back.

The armored truck driver was able to see the guard, with the money bag, in his side view mirrors until he was directly behind the truck. He had also noticed Cross bicycling across the parking lot but safe inside his mobile fortress; the driver had no interest in a bicyclist that had appeared every Monday morning for the last two weeks. He returned to reading an amusing email from his wife on his cell phone. He never saw John Cross stop, behind the returning guard, jerk the bike's folded carrying basket to its maximum size, pull out his Glock and motion with his drawn weapon for the guard to put the large money bag into the carrier.

The guard stared at John's Glock, at first frozen with surprise, then he leaned over to pick up the money bag from the cart. Holding the bag in two hands, as a shield, he shoved it with great force into John, trying to knock John off the bike.

Knocked off balance, staggering, John unconsciously squeezed the trigger of the Glock, as he hopped on one foot and attempted to regain his balance. The bullet went through the money bag and smashed into the guard's chest. Falling to the ground, an ever growing, pool of fresh red blood soon encircled the guard.

Astride his bike, John Cross leaned over, ripped the money bag from guard's hands and rammed it into the bike's carrier. He stood on the pedals and pumped vigorously across the concrete apron.

The driver, frozen with fear by the gun shot, finally got his locked door open and almost fell out of the truck. He was old, overweight and out of shape, he had to hold onto the door with both hands before he could stand and reach for his sidearm. He fired off two shots at the escaping thief now over two hundred feet away.

The driver made a motion as if he would chase after John but after a few steps; he stopped his futile chase and turned back to aid his fallen comrade. Hotel employees cautiously approached from the lobby not understanding what had happened. It took fifteen minutes before the police and an ambulance arrived.

John Cross disappeared around the corner of the Casino as he turned down a laneway that ran along the south side the casino. The lane slanted down towards the

Colorado River. With his heart was pumping and gasping for breath, he pedaled faster than he had ever pedaled before.

When his adrenalin high dissipated, his pedaling slowed to the pace of someone out for a leisurely ride on a very hot day. Soaked in sweat, he reached the walkway that runs along the wooded bank of the Colorado River. He turned north, toward the bridge that crosses to Bullhead City, Arizona.

No one else was on the river walk. Joggers and strollers used it in the cool of the evening and in the very early morning hours. A few hundred feet south of the bridge, he turned up a path that lead to a parking lot. This was where earlier that morning, he had parked his black Cadillac Escalade.

He threw the bicycle and the money bag into the back of the Cadillac and drove carefully away, not wanting to draw any attention to himself. Even before the police and ambulance had arrived to assist the fallen guard, John had crossed over the bridge into Arizona.

He finally became aware he was still wearing his bicycle helmet and leather riding gloves. He tore them off and threw them onto the back seat.

Only on leaving Bullhead City behind did he consider the enormity of what he had done. He hoped that the guard was only wounded and would recover. The weapon had only been for show. It was an accident. He had never intended to hurt anyone. The guard should never have tried to knock him over. Since he could not turn back the clock, he accepted that he would have to live with the consequences of his actions for the rest of his life.

He took the highway East. A few miles from the small, desert town of Seligman, he turned off the highway onto a dirt road. He followed it until the wheel tracks disappeared in the sand. He was miles away from any signs of civilization. Only cacti and scruffy bushes dotted the surrounding desert. Getting out of the Cadillac, he walked around to the back, opened the hatch to the cargo area, took out a shovel and found a place to dig.

He took almost an hour to dig a large hole three feet deep in the sandy soil. When he finished, he reached into the pouch, belted around his waist, and took out his wallet, his passport, and the Glock. After removing the bills from his old wallet, he threw it along with the passport and weapon into the hole. His bicycle shorts, shirt, shoes bicycle helmet and gloves joined the wallet.

A change of clothes was in a large blue duffle bag packed the night before. The bag had was in the car's back seat. From it, he now retrieved jeans, a T-shirt and cowboy boots. After putting them on, he dumped the bundles of bills, from the money bag into the duffle bag and returned it to the back seat. The money bag, stained with guard's blood, now joined the other discarded items in the hole along with the bicycle.

He filled in the hole and carefully swept the sand over the burial ground with a soft bristle broom that he had bought for that purpose. All physical evidence of the robbery was buried. All that remained was a memory.

He climbed back into the Escalade, reached into the glove compartment and took out a wallet. It had been resting on top of a passport. He took the money that he had extracted from his now buried wallet and put it into this new wallet. It was Raymond Powell's wallet. The passport in the glove compartment was also Raymond's. He had taken them, the night he left Paris. John Cross was now dead and buried. Raymond Powell had risen from the dead.

John headed back along the dirt road to Highway 40 and continued to travel East. At Flagstaff, he turned South on Highway 17.

In the early evening, he reached the Spectrum Mall in South Tucson, off Highway 19. He found the McDonald's Restaurant he was looking for and parked the Cadillac as close as he could to the restaurant. John left the engine running with the keys in the ignition. He swung the duffle bag's strap over his shoulder and headed across the parking lot to Food City. He expected to find a taxi waiting there for a fare. Before he had reached the taxi, his Cadillac had been stolen by two young thieves. They hung around McDonald's every day, waiting for such opportunities.

John told the driver to take him to the Triple T Truck Stop on Highway 10. It was a short drive along East Valencia Road.

The truck stop was like a small town, with parking for over three hundred rigs. It was the largest truck stop north of Arizona's major border crossing at Nogales. Thirty billion dollars in Mexican exports pass through Nogales every year.

John got out of the taxi at the truck stop's restaurant. It was a typical North American diner. Truckers stoking up to prepare for a long night's drive filled the crowded restaurant. He found a booth and threw the duffle bag onto the bench seat across from himself where he could keep an eye on it. The waitress took his ordered for a cheeseburger and fries. For desert, he had peach pie with soft vanilla ice cream. As he ate, he scanned the room, looking for an easy-going, independent owner-operator who would be open to his proposal. Company drivers, in uniform, were ignored because they were forbidden to take passengers. A likely prospect was spotted, an older, overweight, balding trucker with glasses. He looked like he was getting ready to go.

John quickly gulped down his meal and ambled over to his target's booth. The trucker looked up at him with a hard, aggressive, don't-bother-me face. John gave him a warm smile and said, "Hi".

The trucker looked at him suspiciously, not smiling and did not reply. John ignored the rejection and continued, "I'm trying to hitch a ride east."

"Don't carry no passengers."

"I can understand that. You can't be too careful these days. I thought you might have wanted someone to talk to. It's long boring drive through corn country at night."

"You're right about that." The trucker paused, thought about it, checked John out and decided that John did not look like an axe murderer. He had taken the bait and now nibbled on it, "Where you heading?"

"The East coast. I grew up on the West coast. I want to see what I'm missing."

"Believe me, you ain't missing nothing. What you do?"

John noticed a baseball cap with the prestigious Pebbles Beach tree logo, lying on the seat beside the truck driver. He took that as his clue to an appropriate reply, "I used to teach golf."

"You're kidding. I love golf. What's your name?"

"Raymond, Raymond Powell."

"Mine's Hank. Ray, you're in luck, I'm heading for Philadelphia."

They shook hands. Hank waved at the waitress to get her attention, indicating he wanted both checks. Hank turned to John and said, "You got a bag? Let's get rolling."

John returned to his booth and retrieved his blue duffel bag. He indicated to the waitress that he was leaving enough money on the table to pay for the two meals. It would include a healthy tip. Hank protested John's picking up of the check, but not too much.

With his green and yellow Pebbles Beach golf hat now on his bald head, Hank headed towards the door. John followed Hank out into the parking lot. It was brightly lit by flood lights on high towers. The lights distorted the color of the trucks. The stench of diesel fumes, the screech of air brakes and the rumble of a dozen mighty truck engines, hit John and Hank like a wall. John followed Hank across the pavement to the rig.

It was one of the biggest truck tractors that John had ever been up close to. There was a shiny blue cube, the size of backyard shed, welded to the back of the cab. Chrome coated almost everything, the dual 150-gallon gas tanks, the massive bumpers, dual air horns on the roof and the side view mirrors. The tractor had a protruding long nose and a shiny, flat grill. It gave the truck an aggressive, intimidating look.

Hank hauled himself up by the chrome hand rails fixed to the long, shiny exhaust stack that extended a few feet above the cab. John hurried around to his side of the tractor and did the same. The blue duffel bag's strap was still slung over his shoulder.

Inside, Hank took the duffel bag from him, opened a door to a small closet. It already seemed jammed to capacity, but he pushed it in. Turning to John, he said, "Welcome to my home. Let me give you the ten-cent tour. Back here, you'll see we've got a bunk that folds up against the wall. A table folds up to where the bunk was. Above that first bunk is a second bunk. It folds into the wall. Over here, is my shower stall with a real toilet built into it. We've also got a stove, microwave, refrigerator, and a television. On the roof is an air conditioner and a generator. The generator runs all this equipment when the rig's engine isn't running."

"Incredible. What does a rig like this cost?"

"It's a 600 horsepower, 18 speed overdrive, Peterbuilt 386. I got it second hand with only 800,000 miles on it. A new one like this would cost in the area of $150,000."

"You own it?

Yeah, me and the bank."

"It costs as much as a house."

"True, but it's the only home I've got. I'm on the road over three hundred days a year. It saves me a ton of money on motels and restaurants. Usually I do my own cooking, you were lucky to catch me eating in the restaurant. This tractor is my money maker. When I bid on a haul, I'm competing with hundreds of others for the job. I've got to have my expenses under control, if I want to make profitable bids and survive. Now let me show you my office."

They stepped back into the cab. Hank turned on the truck's headlights. The wraparound dash lit up with a mass of gages. He pointed out the CB radio, satellite radio, cell phone, a transponder for crossing both the Canadian and Mexican borders and finally his laptop. It had a special stand, so, as he drove, he could easily receive and send bids to various brokers. When Hank extinguished the cab's harsh interior lights, subdued red lights under the dash came on, Hank said, "These are my night time travelling lights. I've seen similar red lights in submarines. Now let's get this show on the road."

The high backed, leather, Airride seats gave good back support. John commented on the visibility from his lofty perch. Hank eased the truck out of the parking lot and headed to Highway 10.

"We will take Highway 10 all the way to Deming, New Mexico, pick up Highway 25 north to Albuquerque and there we take 40 East to Oklahoma City. This a twenty-three-hundred-mile trip and I've got to get this load delivered to Philadelphia within four days."

"What're you hauling?"

"Wheel rims."

John made the mistake of asking, "You ever played Pebble Beach in Carmel."

"Oh yeah. The most expensive round of golf I ever played in my life. It cost me $495."

"For one round of golf?"

"Yep, for one round of golf."

"Was it worth it?"

"Well, let me tell you about it and you decide."

As they rolled across the United States, Hank called upon a lifetime of golf stories for his captive audience. John quickly came to realize that there was no such thing as a free lunch.

CHAPTER 9

SANCTUARY

Since there were no direct flights from Las Vegas to Taos, the two FBI agents had to fly to the nearest major airport, which was Albuquerque, New Mexico. However, to reach Albuquerque, they had to first fly to Phoenix, wait an hour and then catch a connecting flight. It took almost four hours to complete the eight-hundred-mile trip. Agent Tully was a big man; he had not appreciated being sardined into those narrow airline seats.

To prepare for their meeting with The Sanctuary, Agent Connors had tried to gather as much information on it as he could. Little more than an address and a phone number were found. Tax records disclosed that their full legal name was The Sanctuary of the Chosen.

The Internal Revenue Service in Washington confirmed that under the law The Sanctuary met all the criteria of a legitimate church. They were unable to provide any details on who or what The Sanctuary worshipped. Their unofficial assessment was that their church status was a tax dodge. When Connor asked why they allowed such a tax avoidance ploy, they said that top management in the Revenue Service had told the IRS to leave them alone.

In their annual review of tax returns the tax agents had seen the generous contributions The Sanctuary had made to both political parties. Connor's contact had concluded that The Sanctuary was being protected by New Mexico politicians.

When Connor asked, the IRS, what were the criteria that made The Sanctuary a church and thus exempt from taxes? They replied that they had to register as a church, and that they had to have a religious history. When he asked, what they meant by religious history, the tax people replied that it was a written record of what the church believed in and how they expressed their beliefs. They also had to meet to express these beliefs under a leader who had to be part of a defined hierarchy. The IRS pointed out that a church need not have anything to do with Christianity or any established religion.

The IRS agreed with Connor that almost any group could organize itself as a church if it followed those rules. Connor shook his head in disbelief.

An agent, from the FBI's Albuquerque office, was assigned to meet them at the airport and drive them to Taos. With Michael Asino's high political profile in the South West and the fact that the casino robbery was now a murder case, getting budget approval for the trip had not been difficult.

The Albuquerque special agent meeting them turned out to be a woman. She was standing holding a small sign with Agent Connor's name on it as they exited the plane. She introduced herself as Mary Beth Corrado. Since they were carrying no luggage, she used her FBI ID card, to lead them around all the normal security barriers. They were sitting in her car ten minutes later. Connors insisted that he had to sit in the front passenger seat. He said if he were not driving that he would get carsick if he sat in rear seat. Tully took the rear seat but was not happy about it.

Only twenty percent of the FBI's agents are female. Tully and Connors were part of the elite, chauvinistic, Criminal Investigative Division. They were surprised that the Albuquerque office had assigned a female agent to assist them with a murder investigation. Most of the female special agents worked in the Directorate of Intelligence or in the Cyber Division.

Mary Beth had learned to put up with the macho guys from Criminal Investigations. She knew what Tully and Connors were thinking.

She answered their unspoken question, "We're short staffed today. I was the only one available to drive you up to Taos. I work in Intelligence doing risk analysis and foreign language translations. I'm fluent in four. It's nice to get out in the field for a change. A great day for a drive."

Connors grunted a neutral response.

Mary Beth continued, "I wasn't given a chance to read anything on this case. All I know is that there is an organization in Taos that is connected to a killing in Nevada. What do you think you will find up there?"

Connors liked discussing the cases he was working on. Sometimes, fresh eyes caught insights into motives and behavior that he might have missed. Mary Beth seemed bright. Maybe her analytical background might raise questions that he missed. He and Tully filled Mary Beth in on what they knew. She listened and absorbed it all but said little. After they had exhausted the case, the three of them spent the rest of the two hours talking shop. They learned that the Albuquerque office suffered the same internal political frustrations that they encountered in the bigger Las Vegas office.

Mary Beth keyed in The Sanctuary's address into her GPS. It led them to a dirt road, on the outskirts of Taos. It stretched from the highway into the empty desert. Far off in the distance, they saw the white adobe walls of buildings surrounded by trees. One three story building, with a pyramid shaped structure on top of it, soared above the rest. There were no signs indicting where this dirt road led.

Halfway, between the highway and the buildings, they encountered a six-foot high, chain link fence. It seemed to stretch for miles. Where the fence crossed the road, there was a large rolling gate. A small guard hut sat next to that gate. As they came to a stop, a uniformed guard approached their car through a smaller pedestrian gate.

Another Albuquerque agent, not Mary Beth, had arranged for them to meet with the leader of The Sanctuary. She showed the security guard her ID and told him that they were meeting with Winston Hawkins. Despite their efforts to be anonymous, the plain, large, dark grey car fooled no one. It looked like a police car trying to appear inconspicuous.

The guard studied her ID against a clip board he was holding. He reached into his shirt pocket and extracted a shiny sheet with small white circles on it. Small numbers were faintly printed on the circles. Peeling one off, he indicated that Mary Beth should let him stick the small, round, flexible, plastic sticker in the area just above where her right thumb and her forefinger meet. At each of the car's windows, the guard checked their identification, wrote in his clipboard and fastened similar stickers to their hands. He told them they could now proceed to the only three-story building on the campus. He returned to the air-conditioned hut and a few seconds later, the large gate rolled open. The agents drove toward the pyramid rising above the trees.

As they approached the buildings, Mary Beth expressed her surprise at how large the campus was. Hundreds of young men, mostly teenagers, dressed in white shirts and black pants were scurrying between classes from building to building. She slowed to a crawl, to avoid hitting any of them. The students gave the car a curious, but polite stare. They made the FBI agents feel like aliens from another planet.

Above the main entrance to the three-story building, was a sign reading Hawkins Hall. The agents parked in a slot close to the entrance. They piled out and made their way inside to a reception area. An attractive, middle aged, woman seated behind a long counter greeted them.

Since Taos was in the FBI's Albuquerque jurisdiction, Mary Beth took the lead. She explained who they were. The receptionist checked a list. It confirmed their appointment. She then whispered into a phone. In a few minutes, an attractive, well dressed, young woman entered the reception area and asked them to accompany her.

Winston Hawkins' administrative assistant led them down a hall to an elevator which took them up to the third floor. The elevator opened into a small anteroom with a desk which the agents assumed was their guide's. She opened a door behind the desk and held it open for them. As soon as they entered, she closed the door behind them and returned to her desk.

The room they had ventured into was a large, private office. It took up the entire floor. The large, floor to ceiling windows, on all four sides, displayed endless stretches of desert underneath bright blue skies.

Winston Hawkins stood waiting for them inside the door. He was tall, thin, with a full head of white hair and a trimmed beard. He gave them a warm, friendly smile, shook their hands and led them to a large conference table in a corner of the room.

Seated across from Winston, the agents took out their notebooks and opened them. Connor glanced at the questions he had prepared. Mary Beth and Tully stared at agent Connor and waited for him to begin. As lead investigator, they expected Connor to start the questions.

Connor asked, "Do I address you as Reverend Hawkins, Doctor Hawkins or what?"

"No, no, no, I prefer just plain, old, Winston."

"Winston, we are here on a murder investigation. A few days ago, during the robbery of an armored truck, at the Cheers Casino in Laughlin, Nevada, a guard was killed. Perhaps you read about it or saw it on television?

"No, we get little outside news here. What possible connection could a robbery in Nevada have with The Sanctuary?"

"We believe it involves a suspect, by the name of John Cross. Our investigation has also led us to believe that there is a connection between him and The Sanctuary."

Before he replied, Winston Hawkins looked perplexed by this statement, "I know a John Cross. He was a student on this campus a few years ago, but I find it difficult to believe that he could ever kill and rob someone. The Sanctuary takes care of its own. If they have a need, they only need to ask for help. A mistake must have been made."

Connor knew that The Sanctuary had owned 15% of John Cross' company but Hawkins had not mentioned their share in FICA. Connor pursued that omission, "During our preliminary investigation, we also learned that The Sanctuary" owned a significant percentage of John Cross' collection agency."

He let that hang in the air, waiting to see how Hawkins would respond.

"That is possible. We own shares in thousands of companies. You should understand that the reason The Sanctuary exists is to develop entrepreneurs, capitalists. Capitalists create corporations. We have provided thousands of our graduates with their initial seed money in return for an equity position in their businesses. In addition, they pay us a tithe on their company's annual earnings. It is a legitimate charitable expense for them. This flow of revenue, from all our graduates, finances our saving of poor, deprived, abandoned orphans. We rescue them from a living hell and turn them into productive, successful members of society."

"I don't understand. Why do your graduates continue to support your church years after they have left the campus?"

"Because the church has given them a purpose in life. They too suffered as children, but we saved them. It is a way for them to repay The Sanctuary for what we did for them. They agreed when we first took them in that they would do it. Most of all, they do it, because it is the right thing to do."

"It seems like a lot to expect from them."

"We think it is a fair exchange. At our expense, for ten years, we prepared them and gave them an education superior to any other institution in the world. They were illiterate, starving and ignorant when we saved them. We fed them, protected them and prepared to them to be winners, in what is a harsh, challenging world. After those ten years, we send them on a two-year mission to find and save abandoned children, who are as ignorant and lost as they once were. They know that when they have fulfilled their mission that they will have qualified for seed money from the church to establish their business. Their only commitment is to transfer 15% of their corporate shares and 15% of their annual profits to The Sanctuary."

"How willing are they to pay this 15 percent tithe?

"Very willing. As a group, we have more millionaires per capita among our graduates than the graduates of any other educational institution in the world. Our graduates are capitalists. The Sanctuary has guided them to financial success. Our graduates assist each other in growing their wealth."

"Surely, every graduate who receives this seed money does not become wealthy? Very few new businesses survive for even five years."

"Our entrepreneurs have set backs, but they never fail. They can only fail if they stop trying."

"What happens when they do fail and you lose your investment?"

"You must understand, that to our graduates, The Sanctuary is their everything; their mother, their father, their identity and their family. We are the center of their lives and they are the center of our lives. We do not recognize failure. Our stake in their companies allows us to see what is going on and to step in and fix things. If a business was beyond salvage, we would look on that setback as a learning experience and would finance them on their next entrepreneurial venture."

"John Cross was one of these recruits?"

"We refer to them as Sanctuarians and yes he was one of us."

"Has he been on the campus in the last month?"

"To the best of my knowledge, he has not. It has been several years since he has been here."

"Is it possible that he is here now and you would not know of it?"

"No, that is not possible."

"How can you be so sure?"

Winston Hawkins smiled before he replied, "Have you wondered about the white patches that we stuck to your hands when you came in?"

"Yes, security badges would have seemed more appropriate."

"Well, embedded in those patches are microchips. Every Sanctuarian on this campus, or who has ever lived or worked on this campus, has a microchip injected in their right hands between their thumbs and forefingers. Scanners, throughout the campus, let us know where everyone is. That microchip can even let us know what they had for lunch if we really wanted to know."

Winston Hawkins stood up and walked over to his desk and picked up a small computer tablet and brought it back to table. He put it down on the table in front of them. He pressed an app that said "Campus" and then tapped in John Cross' name. The computer responded with "STATUS: NOT ON CAMPUS" and displayed the date of his last campus visit. It was three years ago."

"Would you contact us if he showed up here?"

"I would. The Sanctuary prides itself on keeping a low profile. We gain nothing by drawing attention to ourselves and having a murderer on campus would draw attention to us. We have lawyers, on staff, who spend a great deal of time steering us clear of any unfortunate exposures."

What Hawkins had deliberately omitted telling them, was that he was also able to scan for John Cross nationally. The large national alarm company, that had installed the microchip sensors on campus, had a network of sensors installed in a hundred thousand locations across the country.

"While we did obtain a search warrant, would I be correct in saying that you would give us complete access to all the records you have on John Cross. We are looking for clues that would lead us to him."

"By all means. On your way out, my administrative assistant will provide you a print out of the contents of the file we have on John Cross."

He picked up the phone and made that request. As he hung up Agent Connor asked, "Would it be possible for you to give us some background on The Sanctuary? For example, are you a Christian church?"

"No, we are not a Christian church but that doesn't mean we don't respect Christians. Our founder, my father, Jack Hawkins, was a World War II veteran. The war affected him greatly. After what he experienced, he no longer related to organized religion. He was one of the first soldiers to see the horrors of the German extermination camps. The plight of the refugees, after the war, especially the abandoned orphans, troubled him. It left him with a great desire to help them. He was not a rich man but providing limited help was possible. He started with one abandoned orphan. A twelve-year-old Polish boy, that my father got into the United States by claiming he was an orphaned nephew. Immigration laws then were not as strict as they are now. A few months later he brought in another. Soon he was taking care of ten of these kids."

"That would require a lot of money."

"Yes, it did. It turned out, my father was an entrepreneurial genius. Responsibility, for these children, gave him the incentive to make more money than he would ever have made working for someone. Just after the war, with all the servicemen returning, there was a huge demand for consumer goods. The economy was booming. My father worked out a deal with a Japanese electronics company that had built radios for the Japanese army during the war. They supplied him with the tubes and the parts that he assembled into cheap radios. The kids spent part of each day, after school, assembling radios. My dad would then go on the road, selling these radios out of the trunk of his car. The business took off and spread. Soon, he had to move the business out of the house into bigger and bigger facilities. Within a few years, he had thousands of employees. While the orphaned kids, he had first helped, showed gratitude for the food and shelter he had provided, what they most appreciated was being part of a successful business. As my father's business, had grown each of them had evolved into outstanding executives working for him. Each of them, had then established their own business."

Hawkins paused for effect, "This gave my father an idea. If he could help ten boys to become successful entrepreneurs, then he could help many others. If a percentage of the profits from each of his boy's future business was donated, he would be able to help thousands, of abandoned children. He recognized that he would have to find the brightest and the most aggressive of abandoned street children. They had to be able to appreciate the opportunity they were being offered and be willing to share their wealth with The Sanctuary for the rest of their lives. My dad visualized a result-oriented curriculum focused on entrepreneurship. What you are seeing today on this campus, results from his thinking. It worked."

Mary Beth asked something that had been puzzling her, "I saw only young men on the campus. Are there no women in your program?"

"No there aren't."

"Why would that be?"

"It isn't that we haven't considered it but to be honest, it would complicate things and increase our costs. Since our aim is to invest as much money as possible in saving as many children as possible, we were unable to cost justify saving girls."

Mary Beth's face showed she did not like the answer, but she did not question Winston's response. Connor asked, "Where does this, church thing, come into it and the Sanctuary name?"

"The name sanctuary is just another word for church. The church thing, as you referred to it, came about when my father learned that churches did not pay taxes. My father was no fool. He believed that the money he was paying in taxes would be better directed to helping abandoned children. A lawyer who saw the good work he was doing, helped him get the church legally recognized. My father found no problem in meeting the requirements of being an established, distinct, legal church entity with a religious history. A church, having a religious history, is open to interpretation. It is rather meaningless requirement. Capitalism filled the requirement for our recognized creed. Three outstanding books on entrepreneurship and investing were our bibles. We fulfil the requirement for a form of worship and having regular religious services by our Saturday luncheon meetings. Mind you, only those who have a real problem they want to discuss, show up for them. Our ordained ministers are the administrators and teachers we employ."

"What were the three books you mentioned?"

Currently, they are Jason Fried's, Rework; Charles Duhigg's, The Power of Habit and Benjamin Graham's, The Intelligent Investor. When Sanctuarians come across better books, then these three, then we consider substituting the new books. We like to be current and relevant."

The four agents wrote the names of the books and authors down. Connor asked, "No God is part of it?"

"Do you mean some kind of all-powerful, all-seeing entity, floating around on a cloud who sees little sparrows fall and controls everything that occurs?"

"Yeah."

"Because of his wartime experience, my father was unable to accept that an all-powerful God could exist. No God would have tolerated the extermination of millions of Jews, the dropping of the atomic bomb on Hiroshima and the starving to death of millions of innocent children. What he believed in was capitalism and that people pursue what is in their own selfish interest. He saw that entrepreneurs maximizing their profits benefit everyone. They do what is right for their customers so that the customers will keep on buying from them. Profits tell companies what is worth producing or abandoning. To him capitalism was the absolute motivator and the only true explanation for everything good and bad in this world. He selfishly turned abandoned street children into successful entrepreneurs. These kids selfishly pursued profits that they shared with The Sanctuary, who selfishly used these funds to save even more children."

This was too much for Mary Beth, she asked, "Wouldn't the ancient Ten Commandments be better laws to guide you than capitalism?"

"Whether you call them commandments, laws or rules, they are political tools meant to control the masses. All rules are open to interpretation by the powerful. Without power, laws are unenforceable. Politicians and capitalists use conventional religion to justify their questionable actions. Religious rules keep the masses obedient and compliant. The Sanctuary avoids running into conflicts with the law of the land but it is not afraid to dispute laws that it does not see as profiting mankind. You must understand, that these lawless, godless children were searching for meaning and security in a complex, hostile, insecure world. With us, they found a logical, tangible rule to guide them."

Mary Beth, with her ritual of going to church on Sunday, praying, singing hymns and reading the bible, saw that he was rejecting her Christian teachings. She was intelligent. She accepted that in the real world, any object that provides no hard evidence of its existence is imaginary. This did not stop her from believing that God's existence must remain hidden because if he proved his existence that would take away the need for faith.

It was impossible for her to let Winston's statement go unchallenged. She interjected, "I thought that the Ten Commandments are simple rules for anyone to live by?"

"Not all that simple, or your religion would not have fractured into a multitude of competing faiths. Sanctuarian's have only one commandment. They measure every decision in their life against it."

Surprised, she asked "What is that commandment?"

"All actions that profit mankind are good and all actions that do not profit mankind, are bad."

"That sounds too simplistic. I am not sure I even understand it. For example, is theft good or bad?"

"That depends on the theft. Money stolen from a constructive, positive project would be bad because mankind is not benefitting. However, money stolen, from someone who was not using it positively would be good if it benefited mankind."

"Surely selling heroin to junkies would be bad."

"Sanctuarians look beyond the obvious. If the profits, from the sales of heroin, fed thousands of starving children, it would be good. Why? Because saving people's lives is a positive. There is a net benefit to mankind."

"Well, if that is the case then surely murder would be bad?"

"Not necessarily, if through murder, you saved your own life or your loved one's' life or perhaps you murdered a potential terrorist destined to murder thousands of people. These would be a positive benefit to mankind. You must look beyond the obvious."

"Sanctuarians have reduced everything to the ends justifying the means. This can be very dangerous."

"Yes, it can be a challenge. Every Saturday, those Sanctuarians, who are facing such challenges, meet to discuss and debate the difficulties of living in a society where the authorities only superficially look at what is good or bad. Most people obey the law, like sheep. Sanctuarians don't. Unlike them, we know why we obey laws."

"So, Sanctuarians can obey or to not obey the laws of the United States?"

"As much as it is possible, they obey the laws of the United States but we have martyrs who will sacrifice their lives to profit mankind."

"Are you saying that Sanctuarians can act as judge and jury? That our nation's laws are for everyone but Sanctuarians? That all our laws are open to interpretation? Are you saying that Sanctuarians can decide that someone is standing in the way of profiting mankind and can then kill them?"

"As a last resort, yes. Is this any different from soldiers being sent to kill strangers, just because Congress has declared war against some poor, tiny nation, thousands of miles away. Democracy is a tyranny of the majority and the majority may or may not make a right decision. Sanctuarians make their own right decision, regarding whether someone is standing in the way of profiting mankind."

"Does this mean you have no heaven or hell?"

"No heaven. No hell. Any reward or punishment, that we receive for our decisions, will be in this world, in this life. The happy, successful people of The Sanctuary share their wealth. They help others. Why? Because they have true empathy. Every one of them, first suffered before a Sanctuarian saved them. They understand the marvels of receiving help. Helping is not a prerogative of just established religions. Sanctuarians understand that their ultimate purpose in life is to help the hardened, desperate children that society, and its traditional churches, have ignored and abandoned. All Sanctuarians die, knowing they have profited mankind. When they die, they accept that the only thing they leave behind is a disposable shell. Their spirit lives on, in the lives of those whom they have saved, just as those they save, will become Sanctuarians, and perpetuate the benefiting of mankind. This will go on forever."

Tully brought it back to the murder investigation, "How would you explain John Cross murdering this armored truck guard?"

"First, you don't need me, to tell you, that someone is innocent until proven guilty. However, if he did it, then it was an accident or some form of payback. Someone was standing in the way of profiting mankind. His motivation would not have been greed. This would not be a simple robbery. Something else would have had to have occurred."

The two agents from Las Vegas looked at each other and acknowledged that they had a motive. They now understood why John Cross had dared to strike back at Asino. He had stolen John's company, and that company was an important source of revenue for The Sanctuary whose commitment was to profiting mankind.

Connor suddenly feared for his safety. With his elbow, he nudged the butt of his hidden Glock with his elbow, for reassurance. He knew he should have no reason to fear this, harmless, white haired Sanctuarian, but he did not deny the fear of knowing that, if Winston concluded that these FBI agents were standing in the way of profiting mankind, they would never leave this compound alive. To threaten The Sanctuary was the same as threatening mankind. A thousand fanatical Sanctuarians on the campus would not hesitate to sacrifice their lives to remove a negative threat to mankind. Each FBI agent only had seventeen bullets in their Glocks.

It was time to escape the confines of The Sanctuary. To Connor, it was like swimming in a Louisiana swamp and learning that what you thought were logs floating around you, turned out to be man eating alligators.

Connor brought the meeting to an end. He now realized they had nothing more to gain here. If the Sanctuarians knew where Cross was, they would not see, telling the FBI where he was, as being of any benefit to mankind. The longer they stayed in this compound, the greater the chances were that the Sanctuarians would see these FBI agents as a threat to mankind.

Taking a business card out of his suit's breast pocket and placing it on the table Agent Connor said, "Winston, thank you, for your help in this investigation. If Cross shows up, please phone me at this number."

"Would you stay for lunch?"

"Thank you for your kind invitation but we have a plane to catch in Albuquerque."

The three agents stood and left. Before they had reached the car, all three had peeled off their hands and crumbled the round, white security patches. They threw them on the ground as if the patches were diseased.

On the drive, back to Albuquerque, they reviewed the meeting. All three agents agreed that they had felt intimidated in it. Yet, they found difficulty in explaining why they felt that way. As the embodiment of the most powerful government in the world, they expected to be the intimidating factor. Had they encountered something with a power beyond their comprehension?

As soon as the three agents left, Winston Hawkins searched for John Cross in the security company's national sensor system. If a Sanctuarian passed close to an automated teller machine or rested their hand close to a monitor in a bank, the security company's system would pick up their microchip. The last time a sensor had picked up Cross' microchip was at a truck stop in Tucson, Arizona, two days ago. He had now disappeared.

As the agents drove into Albuquerque to catch their return flight, Connor received a phone call from the Las Vegas FBI office. John Cross's Cadillac had been found parked on a street, a few blocks north of the Mexican border crossing at Nogales, Arizona.

Connor believed that this must mean that Cross was now in Mexico. With the three and a half million dollars in cash, he was carrying, Connor knew that in Mexico

John would be able to buy a new identity and protect himself from extradition for the rest of his life.

CHAPTER 10

PHILADELPHIA

As Hank's truck left the prairies; the trees got taller; the countryside got greener. The Peterbuilt 368 climbed easily over the Appalachian Mountains and started its descent to the coast. Traffic got heavier and heavier as they approached the densely populated east coast corridor.

The South West's big skies, wide open spaces, endless horizons and desert scenery were now just a distant memory. For John Cross, the four-day trip was a rebirth. He had slammed one door behind him and a new door stood waiting for him to open it. Having escaped death as a child, every day since then had been an unexpected gift. He had proven he knew how to survive.

Despite, how well-appointed Hank's Peterbuilt was, John was tired of being confined. He had two cravings. One was to leap from the confines of this truck and run for miles. The other was a long, hot shower. It had been four days since he had shaved. His beard was showing great potential. Once he got settled, he would shave off all the hair on his head and continue to let his beard grow thick and bushy. He hoped these two cosmetic changes, and the wearing of glasses, would change his appearance. He wanted to minimize the chances for someone from his past recognizing him. His life would be over if the FBI or Michael Asino's mob friends found him.

At home, in his own little world, Hank was as happy now as when he had started the road trip. Thanks to John Cross, his captive audience, he had managed to relive every great golf course he had ever played. John had been both amazed and appalled at Hank's fixation on golf. John asked Hank, "How far are we from Philadelphia."

"About two hours but I'm not actually going right into Philadelphia. I'm delivering this load to a factory in Trenton, New Jersey. It's a suburb of Philadelphia. What I figured I will do, is drop you off at the Trenton Transit Center. It's a train station. You'll be able to catch the North-East Line right into downtown Philadelphia."

"That sounds great. You got any suggestions on where I should stay in Philadelphia?"

"What kind of neighborhood are you looking for?"

"I'm not sure but it seems to me that being close to downtown would make the most sense."

"You know, the closer you are to the downtown area, the more it'll cost you."

"That doesn't surprise me."

"You should be able to find something in Washington Square. A lot of people your age live there. Washington Square is not that far from the main station. The Trenton train will take you right into it. Why don't you swing my computer around and see what kind of accommodation you can find there?"

After an hour of searching, as the truck rolled along, John found several suitable furnished apartments for rent. Some were too small, less than 500 square feet. He felt that an apartment would give him the privacy that he needed to remain as invisible as possible.

The leases being offered ranged from a few months to several years. Until he could figure out what he was going to do with the rest of his life, the shorter the lease, the better. Hank passed John his cellphone. John made an appointment for later that day with the rental agent of what seemed to be the most suitable apartment building.

Hank turned south onto highway US 1. This would take him past the Trenton Transit Center. When he got there, he brought the Peterbuilt to a stop. The truck was blocking traffic. John quickly thanked Hank, lied when he promised to keep in touch, and quickly descended with his large duffle bag slung over his shoulder. Although this took only seconds, the cars stuck behind the truck were already impatiently sounding their horns. John stood on the sidewalk and watched the truck leave with a mighty roar. Hank tapped his air horn once as a final goodbye. As the truck moved out of sight, John turned, passed a large multi colored abstract statue on his way into the station.

Inside, he purchased a one-way ticket to Philadelphia's 30th Street Station. A schedule showed the next SEPTA train would be leaving in half an hour. This gave him enough time to get a Big Mac at the station's McDonald's restaurant. He wolfed it down and made his way to the platform.

In less than an hour, the train had traveled the thirty-two-miles into downtown Philadelphia. It deposited John at the 30th Street Station. With his duffle bag's strap, slung over his shoulder, he crossed through the station's soaring, cavernous concourse and followed the signs to the 29th Street exit; Taxis were waiting there for fares. It was just a short cab ride to the apartment building on South 9th street.

Built in the nineteen-twenties, the ten-story apartment building had been recently updated. The modern glass entrance contrasted with the building's ornate, old fashioned, window frames. It was the least expensive furnished apartment he could find in the area. From their advertisement, he gathered they rented to medical students at the nearby Pennsylvania Hospital.

The rental agent was an older woman. She kept an eye on the tenants and visitors, coming and going from a small lobby office. She introduced herself as Mrs. Clark and took him, in a slow elevator, to the fifth floor. John was not impressed by the strange groaning noises the elevator made as it climbed between floors.

As he had expected, the apartment was small, but it was big enough for his purposes. The furnishings were better than expected. Everything smelled a bit musty as if the apartment had not been occupied in months. The glass in the living room's big bay window needed cleaning, but the window did make the room feel bigger and brighter.

Mrs. Clark told him that the $1,475 a month rent covered all the utilities, including an internet connection. John liked that. It would lessen his contact with curious, outside parties. The only negative he saw was that he had to sign a twelve-month lease, but he could afford it. He had been carrying a wad of fifty, one hundred-dollar bills, in his pant pockets, ever since he had closed his personal bank account in Las Vegas. When he told her that he was prepared to pay her the first and last month's rent in cash, if she would allow him to move in immediately, Mrs. Clark had no problem agreeing to this condition.

She returned to her little office and began to prepare his lease. It required that he provide her with photo ID. John had anticipated that this would be required, he handed her Raymond Powell's passport. Anxious to get her hands on the cash, she only glanced at it long enough to record his passport number. She carefully counted the bills he passed to her before she handed him the keys to both the apartment and the lobby door. In a final effort to separate more money from him and make an additional commission, she asked, "Mr. Powell would you be interested in having a cleaning lady come in every week?"

To keep, as low a profile as possible, a cleaning lady was the last thing Raymond wanted. He quickly replied, "No thank you."

"Are you working in the area?" she pleasantly enquired.

"Not too far away. Within walking distance."

"What do you do?"

"I'm a risk consultant. For the next year, I'll be predicting problems with a client's ongoing asset acquisitions."

With no idea, as to what this meant, she pleasantly replied, "Oh, that sounds interesting."

"It can be. I need to pick up some things. Is there a hardware store close by?

"Yes, about a five-minute walk away. Turn left. Go down to the next corner. Keep left and you will find it about four doors down."

With the duffle bag over his shoulder, John trudged down to the hardware store. As expected, he found a display of duct tape in a wide selection of colors. He chose a black tape, paid for it and deposited it in the duffle bag.

Back at the apartment building, he waved to Mrs. Clark and bid her a good evening, as he quickly strode to the elevator. His duffle bag had never left his grasp. Earlier, Mrs. Clark had suggested that he leave it in her office, while they looked at the apartment. John had ignored her, for several million reasons.

Finally, he had privacy. He locked the apartment door and put the duffle bag down. He could finally relax. He hooked the door's security chain to further secure the door and then walked over to the bay windows to close the blinds, so no one could see into the apartment.

The duffle bag was carried over to the kitchen table where he shook out its contents. Bricks of one hundred-dollar bills, wrapped in plastic, fell quietly onto the table. Each brick was four and a half inches high and was made up of one thousand bills. He piled the bricks in stacks of five. There were 35 bricks, worth a total of $3,500,000. He took $525,000 from the pile and shoved it back into the duffel bag. He placed another brick of $100,000 on the table.

He now took the remaining blocks of money and the black duct tape he had just bought and went into the kitchen and opened the cupboard doors beneath the big, deep kitchen sink. John lay on his back and proceeded to wedge twenty-nine money bricks into the cavity between the sink and the walls of the cabinet that surrounded the sink. He ripped off strips of black duct tape and fastened the bricks into the cavity.

Although it was not a perfect hideaway, it would do until he could slowly deposit all the money with an investment dealer. It was unlikely that anyone would ever choose to lie on their back and look at the gloomy dark bottom of his kitchen sink. If they did all they would see would be black plastic which, he hoped, they would interpret to be sealant or insulation.

From the $100,000 he had set aside, he extracted $5,000 and put it in his wallet. The remainder, he placed in the night table drawer. This money would be used to open a bank account, buy some food and new clothes,

The stress of knowing he was being hunted and the long trip across the country had exhausted him. He slowly made his way to the bedroom, carrying the almost empty duffel bag of money. He tossed it onto the double bed, took off his clothes and crawled under the sheets. He was in a deep sleep, almost as soon as his head hit the pillow, one limp hand rested on the $525,000 in the duffle bag.

CHAPTER 11

PURGATORY

Hunger woke John up at nine o'clock in the morning. The first order of business was that long, hot shower, he had been dreaming about. While his hair was still wet, he took scissors and hacked off as much of his hair, as close to the scalp as he could. Next, he put shaving cream on his head and shaved it clean. He looked in the mirror and checked it out. He hardly recognized himself. In another few weeks, his beard would be much thicker and further alter his appearance.

Before he could eat breakfast, he had to take care of the money in the duffel bag. With the duffel bag slung over his shoulder, he again returned to the hardware store. Here, he bought a sturdy, red plastic toolbox, big enough to hold the $525,000 in cash. He also bought brown wrapping paper, clear sealing tape and a marking pen. As he was paying for his purchase, he asked the cashier where the he could mail a package. He thanked her when she told him it was just a few doors away.

Back at the apartment, he took the $525,000 from the duffel bag and put it into the toolbox. He sealed it shut with the clear tape and wrapped it in brown paper; he addressed the finished package to Winston Hawkins in Taos, New Mexico. For a return address, he put FICA, 41 Boulevard Rochechouart, Paris, France. Winston Hawkins would know who had sent it. In large print, he wrote "PERSONAL & CONFIDENTIAL" on it. He was now ready to make the trip to the post office and then go across the street to the diner for his breakfast.

After his breakfast of bacon and eggs, he went to the nearest bank, the Shully Bank of Philadelphia. Raymond Powell's passport provided sufficient identity for opening an account. He had gambled that the French authorities had still not identified Raymond's body. Until he was declared dead, Raymond public records would only show that Raymond was still alive.

John deposited only three thousand dollars in cash in the bank account. Each day thereafter he deposited a few thousand dollars until the $95,000, in hundred-dollar bills, that he had set aside for his living expenses, was in the bank. As he had expected, the bank tellers after the first few deposits did not notice their frequency.

A high-end men's wear store was only a few doors away from the bank. There he bought two good quality suits, three white shirts, ties, dress shoes, underwear and casual clothes. The alterations took a day. The next day, dressed in a suit, he looked like all the other young professionals that inhabited the Washington Square neighborhood.

He was ready to open a stock trading account with a storefront investment shop. The nearest one was a ten-minute walk away. Within a few minutes of entering their offices an investment advisor was completing the paper work. When asked how much he intended to invest, John said $500,000. The advisor rubbed his hands with glee as he calculated his potential commissions.

For his employment and work history, John told the salesman that he was a self-employed artist who had been out of the country for many years. He added, that he had only returned upon the death of his aged parents. As their sole heir, he was now liquidating the estate. The investment advisor smiled when he realized there could be many more large deposits.

As planned, to further alter his appearance, John visited a neighborhood optometrist. He told the optometrist he needed glasses because things were no longer as sharp and clear as they used to be. He had noticed no change in his vision but the optometrist found enough wrong with his eyesight to justify selling him 2 pair of glasses, one with clear lenses and a pair of sunglasses. John thought his bald head, trimmed beard and glasses made him look older and very much like many of the university professors who lived in the neighborhood. The world would now see a self-confident image of middle-class respectability.

Over the next month, John increased the deposits into the investment account. Soon all the millions, he had hidden under the sink, were deposited. Since he had had no problem in depositing the $100,000 in expense money into the Shully Bank, John now opened an on-line, self-trading account with the bank's large investment division. He then instructed the Shully Bank to arrange for the transfer of all the money he had deposited with storefront investment shop to his new Shully Bank trading account. Since it was an electronic transfer and not cash, no one at the

Shully Bank questioned his receiving such a large amount. For greater flexibility, John wanted all his assets in an established financial institution.

John was ready to start investing. The Sanctuary's instructors had ground into him the principles of careful, value investing. The professors had viewed, with disdain, speculators who saw the stock market as a casino or slot machine.

John's aim was to find profitable, well established companies, with low price-to-earnings ratios, that paid better-than-average dividends. He would invest only five percent of his total funds in the shares of any one company. Out of the thousands of stocks being traded on the major exchanges, he found the best twenty stocks meeting his criteria. He expected to lose a small amount on three or four stocks out of the twenty he had purchased but to have an annual gain of at least ten percent on his total portfolio.

With a substantial monthly income being derived from his investments, he now had time to ponder what he wanted to do with the rest of his life. There was no going back. Those searching for him would not rest until he was dead or in jail. His future was indefinite.

H considered opening another collection agency but rejected that option. It is what the police and the mob would expect him to do. He concluded that whatever he did it would have to be something that would give him as much pleasure as possible, in the short time, he might have to enjoy it.

His stock portfolio required little effort. He now had time to enjoy his art. He bought paints, canvases and an easel and painted for hours every day. When he needed a break and to get out of the apartment, he explored Philadelphia. He visited The Philadelphia Museum of Art, The Barnes Foundation, The Pennsylvania Academy of Arts and all the private galleries on Second Street.

One day, a gallery owner, who was also an avid golfer, told him of a great golf course that had waived its initiation fees to attract new members. It was only twenty minutes away from John's apartment.

John took a taxi to the club. It was an elegant one-hundred-year-old private golf course. After a tour of the club, he joined. In the pro-shop, he bought clubs, a bag, shoes and golf clothes. These were all stored in his locker at the club.

It was on his third round of golf at the club that he realized of what he wanted to do with the rest of his life. He wanted to own a golf course. It was the original dream; he and Raymond Powell had shared. His days now became filled, with not only investing, painting and golfing but in searching the internet and golf magazines for a golf club he could afford to purchase.

He also researched everything he could find on acquiring and running a successful golf club. One expert recommended that buyers concentrate their search in states where golfing was possible year-round. Another recommended buying a course that could draw on a market with a population of at least twenty million. He also read that while it cost about six million dollars to buy a profitable golf course, for three million dollars, if you were careful, you could buy an unprofitable one with profit potential.

Even when he learned that more than half of America's seventeen thousand golf course were not making money, he was not discouraged. The younger generation were more interested in video games than golf. The older golfers were dying off. He arrogantly believed that having built a successful collection agency he could make any business profitable.

He also continued to do Google searches to see if there was any recent news about the Laughlin Casino robbery. He felt guilty and depressed when he read that the armored truck guard had died. It had been an unfortunate accident.

The subsequent posting of the FBI's $100,000 reward for information leading to his capture and conviction gave him a few restless nights. It served to increase his caution. He now restricted his public exposure to the golf course and the small diner across the street from his apartment building.

He golfed alone, not wanting to answer questions about his background from the club members. The waitresses, in the diner where he ate every day, knew what his tastes were. The result was a minimum of communication, beyond the usual greetings, at both the golf club and the diner. When he ate, he always made sure he had a newspaper to read. It discouraged interaction with the diner's other customers. The members at the golf club thought that he was shy or anti-social. They left him alone. This did not mean they were unaware of how far and straight he could drive a ball.

John soon realized that he was now in a prison of his own making. He thought moving to a smaller, more isolated community, could lessen his anxiety. The large city was making him paranoid. Every stranger he saw now made him nervous. He thought in a small town there would be fewer strangers.

John was not the only one doing searches. Each day Winston Hawkins checked their security company's national monitoring system for John's presence. He was relieved when the monitoring system, began registering John's frequent visits to the Shully Bank in Philadelphia.

Winston showed no surprise, a few days later, when he received a mysterious package, with a Philadelphia post mark and Paris return address. It contained an untraceable $525,000. It gave Winston that warm glow, a father feels, when a son does the right thing. He expected a great return from their investment in John Cross.

CHAPTER 12

BENJI

"**M**rs. Clark, here are the keys. Sorry, but I'm in a hurry, I've got my car double parked outside. Thank you for everything. I'll send you a forwarding address when I get settled. Take care."

He wondered why he told her that he would send her a forwarding address. For his own safety, he had no intention of leaving any clues, where anyone searching for him could find him.

"Are you sure you want me to rent your apartment? You've paid for two more months."

"That's OK."

Mrs. Clark came out of her office to say goodbye to John Cross. She walked with him through the lobby to the building's entrance. John liked her. He had found her to be a warm, friendly person. Often, she was the only one he would talk to in a day. At the entrance to the lobby, she stood watching him, as he hurried to the car, worried that he would get a parking ticket.

The five-year-old Nissan Altima with low mileage had been bought because it was an innocuous family car that he hoped would transfer him anonymously to a new life. He drove off and never looked back.

From Philadelphia, he took US 13 southwest until he reached Route 1, just south of Wilmington, Delaware. The highway then followed Delaware Bay to where it reached the Atlantic Ocean at Benji Beach. It took him over two hours. The small resort town was also an easy two-hour drive, from the two large cities of Washington and Baltimore.

Benji Beach had become these three cities summer playground. In July and August, its population exploded from a few thousand permanent residents to over forty thousand visitors. Hotels, restaurants and entertainment had developed to cope with the summer influx. Some came to lie on the beach but others came to play golf.

One of the Benji Beach golf courses was for sale. It had risen to the top of Johns' prospect list of more than a hundred golf courses that were for sale in south east.

The Benji Beach Country Club was closest to meeting everything he had been seeking. It was a semi-private club, close to a large population, affordable with an asking price of only $3,000,000. It included a fifteen thousand square foot clubhouse with a small private apartment. John thought he could live in that apartment until he got established.

Once prime Delaware pasture land, it was now an eighteen hole, six-thousand-yard golf course. From the longest tees, it was a par seventy-two. Spread over two hundred acres, the golf course lacked hills but there were three large ponds and a creek to make it challenging. The advertisement also said it had a large swimming pool, two tennis courts, a driving range and a chipping range. It contained everything that John thought golfers would want in a club.

The real estate agent had told him, when he first phoned, that the golf course's owner had been a heavy drinker who died of cirrhosis of the liver. He had left no heirs. The bank holding the mortgage on the property had seized the club when it went into default. They had been trying to get this nonperforming loan off their books for over a year.

John saw Benji Beach as being just far enough off the beaten path that he could live a quiet life there, well hidden from the FBI and any other Las Vegas connections. Yet, it was within a two-hour drive of a market of over twenty million people. A population big enough to provide enough golfers to make the business prosper.

The climate was ideal. On the coast, the Atlantic breezes kept it cool in the summer and warm in the winter. When John checked, historical weather records he found that it rarely got below freezing. The average winter snowfall amounted to only two inches. Golfers could play the course all winter. It surprised him when he read that despite being this far north, the coastal area was classified as semi-tropical.

A golf course is a big investment in real estate. John had considered the possibility of building a housing development built around the golf course. The east side of the golf course bordered the Atlantic Ocean. His research revealed that the average price of a beach front home in Benji Beach had soared above a million dollars. Wealthy northern baby-boomers were leaving the big northern cities and retiring to rural areas with temperate climates. If he ever wanted to subdivide the course into housing lots, it would be worth many times more than the three million dollar selling price. He could not imagine how he could lose on this purchase.

Benji Beach's potential as an ideal corporate conference destination had not escaped him. A quick check of hotel room rates had confirmed there was a good choice of accommodation. It was far enough from the three major cities to be an attractive out-of-town destination while still being an easy drive. The fact that Benji Beach had already attracted an annual major beach volleyball tournament which attracted thousands of players from the Atlantic seaboard states only confirmed the potential John saw in front of him.

He turned off Highway 1 onto Benji Beach's Main Street. He rolled through a retail strip until the road stopped at the beach. The last building was a two-story retail stores with a giant sign on its roof advertising a fudge. A low, concrete wall blocked vehicles from driving out onto the beach. With a season only three months long, John wondered how a business could make a profit just selling fudge.

John parked vertically, in front of the real estate office, across the street from the fudge store. Even though this was the off season, and the street was deserted, there was still a parking meter to contend with. He got out and tried to insert a coin into the meter. The meter was out of order and wouldn't accept his quarters.

He walked to the low concrete wall and looked across the wide beach to the Atlantic Ocean. The fresh, salty made him realize how unhealthy large cities were. To the north and the south, the wide beach stretched for miles. A wooden board walk bordered much of the immediate beach area. Ocean waves slid up the beach and receded. It wasn't New Mexico, but he got the same sense of big skies and space. In Philadelphia the buildings always seemed to be pressing in on him.

It felt like he belonged here. He turned back to the street and walked over to the real estate office.

The real estate office was small and cramped. Old fashioned, oak, wooden desks failed to impress him. An elderly receptionist, behind a low counter, sat staring at a computer screen. She looked up and peered at John through her bifocals. John suspected from her apparent surprise at seeing him that he must be the first customer of the day, even though it was now past noon.

"May I help you?" she asked in a gravelly, quavering voice.

"My name is Raymond Powell, I have an appointment with Peter Sprackman."

The receptionist nodded and picked up her phone and tapped in an extension number. John could hear it buzzing in an office just ten feet behind her.

"Mister Sprackman, a Mister Powell is here."

Without the benefit of the phone, John heard Sprackman reply, "OK, I'll be right out."

There was a pause, she hung the phone up and stared at John before she said, "He'll be right out."

John wondered, if using the phone instead of just turning around and telling Sprackman he was here, was meant to impress him. The next sound was the creak of a wooden swivel chair as Sprackman got up. John was forming mental images in his head what Sprackman would look like. As expected a wiry, white haired, intense, little man popped through the door. The real estate agent gave John that full, empty smile that sales people give prospective customers who they have never met. He mumbled cheerily, "Mister Powell?"

"Mr. Sprackman?" John replied, as he shook Peter Sprackman's hand.

"I've got it all set up. The loan officer is expecting us at the bank in half an hour. He's been the acting general manager of the club since they took it over on the mortgage default. He'll give us a tour of the property and answer your questions. It'll only take two minutes to walk to the bank. Why don't you come into my office and we can have a coffee in the meantime?"

The office was just big enough to seat Sprackman and two thin visitors around his small desk. They exchanged pleasantries about the weather and what a nice place Benji Beach was. Soon, a dragging noise was followed by the elderly receptionist who crept in carrying two coffees in white Styrofoam cups. She also had sugar packets, tiny cream containers and wooden stir sticks. John prepared his coffee and tasted it. It was watery instant coffee and was already less than hot. He had anticipated nothing better.

Peter Sprackman slurped his coffee, smacking his lips, enjoying the cold instant coffee. It established that he was not a coffee connoisseur. Putting down his coffee he laid out the essentials for John, "They want three point two million, but I expect they'll take two point nine million. They're eager to sell. How much of a mortgage they will take back is another question? They will want to lend you money. The place needs to be spruce up, but nothing that a little paint can't fix. You can point out the less than pristine condition to them. That should get them in the mood to negotiate. How soon do you want the closing date?"

John recognized that this question was a feeble attempt to determine how hot a prospect he was. He baited Sprackman, "As quickly as possible, I want to move into that apartment in the club house as soon as I can. I've given up my apartment in Philadelphia. I'll be staying in the Benji Beach Grand Hotel until the deal closes. I don't like hotels."

Sprackman beamed at this revelation. They finished their coffees and walked up the street to the bank. The loan officer, who would drive them to the golf course, was standing in front of the bank, waiting for them. A blond, red faced man with a long neck and a large Adam's apple. John could not help staring at it as it bobbed. It took less than ten minutes to drive to the golf course.

John sensed that Sprackman was already savoring the large commission he would receive as both the listing and the selling agent. John sensed that this would be the first solid offer the bank had received for the golf club and probably the biggest sale Peter Sprackman had made in some time. As the listing agent, Sprackman was supposed to be working in the best interest of the seller but he had already dropped the seller's price before negotiations had even begun.

CHAPTER 13

CLUB

During the short drive to the golf course, there had been some idle chit chat. From their comments, John Cross believed they thought they were dealing with a business neophyte. John Cross was anything but a neophyte. He knew what he had taken on. Buying a golf course was like acquiring a small city populated by golf club members, casual customers, employees, suppliers, neighbors and bureaucratic civil servants. The bureaucrats monitored licenses, permits, water rights, environmental issues, operational contracts, federal laws, state laws and local bylaws.

The clubhouse was on a long circular driveway. It reminded John of those large classical, white clapboard, two-storey houses he had seen driving through rural Pennsylvania. There were a dozen cars parked close to the entrance. The banker pulled into a handicap parking spot, next to the entrance. Rank has privilege.

John stood for a few seconds staring at the building. He agreed with the sales agent. The building could do with a coat of paint, the salty sea air is hard on paint, otherwise the clubhouse looked in good repair. The roof shingles were fine, no broken windows, no potholes in the parking lot, the grass was cut, and the flower beds weeded.

When they entered, through the main entrance, John found himself in a long hallway running from one end of the building to the other. On a wall, placed, so you could not miss it as soon as you entered, was a bill board detailing the club's rules. Most of the rules were the common-sense sort of prohibitions that John wondered why they had even bothered posting them. The others were so old fashioned and conservative that John wondered if the club was deliberately trying to discourage new memberships.

He recited the offensive rules to himself, "Shirts with collars and sleeves must be worn, and must be tucked in, at all times. Slacks or golf shorts (mid-thigh or longer) must always be worn. Short-sleeve mocks are permitted, if meeting the golf industry standard. Mock necks must measure 1 1/2" high. Caps shall be worn, bill forward, on club property. Tank tops, athletic slacks, halter tops, tee shirts, bathing suits, sweat pants, athletic shorts and denim shorts are not permitted on the Main Floor of the Clubhouse. Denim is prohibited unless specified. Hats are allowed until 5:00 pm and will not be permitted in the dining room unless there is a private party or a club golf function."

These archaic rules would be a problem in attracting new members. As expected by such rules, John learned the average age of the golf club members was sixty-five and that memberships had been shrinking for the last ten years. The older members were dying off or becoming too incapacitated for golf.

To his right, were double doors that opened to a large banquet room, with a bar-lounge area, close to the entrance. French doors at the back of the banquet room appeared to open onto the golf course. John estimated that the room's capacity would be two hundred golfers.

To his left, was a large pro-shop. It was full of all the brightly colored golf clothes and the expensive golf equipment, you expect to find in a golf pro-shop. Everything appeared to be on sale. There were no customers. He looked for sales staff but there were none in sight.

At the end of the hallway was the kitchen. When he pushed that door, open and peered in, a cook looked up, gave him a quick glance and then returned to stirring something in a large pot. John thought the kitchen's fixtures looked well maintained, but they did not look new.

They made their way down stairs to the basement to view a small gym and a change room. John could smell that damp, cedar odor of a sauna when they were in the men's change room, but he never saw it. They did not enter the ladies change room.

They took the staircase up to the second floor. Here was the club's office, two small meeting rooms and the apartment that John wanted to live in. After inspecting them, John took out a small notebook and listed changes he would make to the club house.

Back downstairs, they took a rear entrance and made their way, down a slight incline, towards a   swimming pool. Behind it, was the driving range, chipping area, tennis courts and a snack bar. Six customers were sitting at wrought iron tables on the snack bar's fieldstone patio. John estimated that the patio could seat fifty people. The tennis court's surface, white lines and net looked faded and worn.

It was a longer walk to a large metal equipment shed. When they pushed the shed's sliding door open, they found fuel tanks, compressors, sprayers, lawn mowers, pumps, generator, tractors, trucks, trailers and all the other expensive machinery needed to runs a golf course. John estimated that there was at least half a million dollars' worth of equipment in the shed.

They strolled back to the snack bar and sat down. The banker bought them coffee. John sat there enjoying the pleasant warmth of the sun shine. The sun skipped off the ripples in a pond that golfers had to hit over to reach the 18th hole.

John wanted this golf course. The banker, sensing John's mood, tried a trial close, "I noticed you making notes. What changes would you make to your golf course?"

John smiled at the blatant attempt to test his hunger to buy. He replied, "Let's not get the horse in front of the cart. I've just started my evaluation."

"How would you like to proceed?"

"I noticed when we were on the second floor of the club house that that there was a small board room next to the office."

"Yes, there is."

"Would it be possible for me to use that meeting room for the next three days? I want to go over your records?"

The banker looked like he couldn't believe that a buyer would ever want to peruse their records. He responded, "What records?"

"I'd like the year-end financials, for the last three years, along with this year's figures to date, budgeted objectives and tax records. Also, I want to look at the membership statistics, rounds summaries and a list of all the club's fixed assets with their depreciation schedules. I'll want to work out revenue and expense projections. Oh, yes, I'd like to review all the club's contracts, so I can figure out which ones I need to assume."

"Anything else?"

"Yes, all the employee records. I want to see job titles, salaries, years of service, reporting structures and annual reviews."

The banker realized that Raymond Powell was not the neophyte he had hoped they had found. This would not be the quick, easy sale he had hoped for.

"This will probably take a while to put together. Perhaps you could you arrange a tee off time for me, tomorrow morning? I want to play the course and get a feel for all eighteen holes"

"This time of the year the club opens later, at 8 A.M. Do you want me to set you up in a foursome?"

"No, I'll play alone. I want to play it with as few distractions as possible. When I finish, which should be in the early afternoon, I then want to start going over all the club's financial records that you've been able to gather."

John Cross wanted to analyze the trends and determine if it was possible for the club to make money or not? On average, golf courses, net out a profit of about 15%. However, John knew government statistics stated that a third, of all golf courses were losing money. If this one wasn't making money, he wanted to understand what it would take to get it up to at least 15%.

For a year, it had been without a manager. With this banker managing it, he would be a surprise if it were making money. He expected that the banker would do his best to hide its poor performance from him but the Sanctuary had spent years preparing him to do this kind of analytical work.

The ride back to the real estate office was more subdued than the drive to the golf club. The real estate agent and the banker, each considered various strategies to salvage the sale. They knew, what John would find.

Back in Benji Beach, they pulled in next to John's parked car. It had a bright yellow parking ticket shoved under its windshield wiper. "Welcome to Benji Beach," John mumbled under his breath.

The Benji Beach Grand Hotel was a few blocks away. It was four stories high, backing on the beach. A curved driveway lead him through landscaped grounds to an impressive entrance.

With no bellboy in evidence, John took his own bags out of the trunk. He left the car in the driveway and made his way into the hotel and across the impressive marble lobby to the front desk. There was no one behind the desk. With his bags at his feet, he stood waiting for someone to appear. He coughed to get attention. It worked. He heard the scrape of a chair through the open door behind the counter. A tall, young man peeked around the corner, smiled, and came out to check him in. He upgraded John to a suite at a discounted price. This didn't surprise John since it was the off season and the hotel was almost empty.

He deposited his bags in the suite, took the elevator back to the lobby and left the hotel to explore the town. Two blocks away he found a fake Irish pub called, The Leaping Leprechaun where he had a Guinness with his Irish stew.

The next morning, John arrived at the golf club a little after seven o'clock. He was hoping to have breakfast before he teed off. The club house dining room was closed. He walked over to the snack bar and found it was also closed.

In the pro shop, a young kid greeted him. John introduced himself, explained why he was here. He asked him if he could tee off earlier than eight o'clock. The kid could not find John's name on that day's player list. He looked confused. When John told him that he was a potential buyer of the golf course and that the banker was supposed to have arranged for the free round of golf, this only made matters worse.

Since it was too early to reach the banker to confirm his story, John paid cash for the round of golf. The kid allowed him to tee off early.

John knew that you judge the quality of a course by its layout, playability, aesthetics, condition and amenities. The best way, to understand each hole, was to walk the course. The first three holes would have made good cow pastures and did not excite him. He considered several ways to make them more challenging.

When he got to the fairways that ran beside the ocean, he found spectacular views but several houses were too close to the east side of the course. He wondered how many windows got broken and made a note to check the club's insurance policies for such coverage. Further on, he came to an area of undeveloped woodland separating the fairways. He contemplated building several houses there.

On the green closest to the ocean, was an area that indicated a lack of oxygen in the soil. John wondered why the grounds keeper were not aerating and top dressing the greens. The fairways could become unplayable. Cancellation of future tournaments were a possible consequence of poor green maintenance.

It had been a long time since John had carried a golf bag but a cart would not have given him the same understanding of the course. After each hole, he stopped to make notes. In the early afternoon, he finished all eighteen holes.

At the club house, he showered and changed. As he dressed, it hit him that he was starving. He had not eaten all day. The thrill being able to walk his own golf course had distracted him.

In the club house dining room, he ordered a steak sandwich. It was over cooked, dry, tough and fibrous. The soggy, limp French fries did not complement the meal nor did the flat draft beer.

A belly, full of greasy food, left him as lethargic as a python that had swallowed an elephant. He made it upstairs to the main office. He let them know he was ready to review the financial data that he had requested. The accounting clerk was not happy. She wondered how many of the staff John would fire when he discovered how poorly the golf club was doing and whether she would be one of them.

When John entered the board room and saw the foot-high piles of paperwork on the large mahogany table, he wondered how he would ever get through it. He searched through the piles until he found the previous three years of financial statements. He pulled up a chair to the middle of the table and started to make notes of anything he found unusual.

Soon, he was looking at the current year-to-date figures and comparing them to the historical accounting figures. Under the bank's supervision, the course's revenues had dropped like a stone throw into a deep pond. Net earnings were just above break even, hovering around $100,000. This would suggest a reasonable purchase price of $1,000,000 for the club not the $3,000,000 the bank was looking for.

John's wondered if this golf course was worth buying. However, what was valuable was the land. His research had shown the price of land in Benji Beach had been climbing. If he couldn't turn the golf course around, it would be a good real estate investment, providing he could get it at the right price. Based, on what he had seen, this golf course could generate substantial profits.

For the next two days, he started reviewing the financial data early in the morning and finished late in the evening. When he completed his review, he arranged to meet with the banker and real estate agent at nine o'clock, the next morning.

The banker opened negotiations, "Well Mister Powell, since you are still here, you must have seen what a great opportunity this golf course offers for someone with your abilities."

John stared at the banker and thought about an appropriate reply and then edited it, "The golf club has potential but since it isn't making money, you should pay me to take it off your hands."

This response took the banker by surprise. He was not use to such bluntness so early in the negotiation. He chose his next words, suspecting that, this buyer, now knew more about the golf club than he did, "Perhaps the golf course has slipped but some smart owner will turn it around and become rich. The land, the course is on, is worth a fortune."

"I can buy a farm, a mile away with more acreage than this golf course, for less than half of your listing price."

"True, but the golf course has great beach frontage which makes it precious."

"With global warming and rising ocean levels, beach front property in a state like Delaware where land is only a few feet above sea level, may not be the best long-term investment."

That took the wind out of the banker's sails. He said, "Mister Powell, you've had three days to study this investment, what's your offer?"

"A million dollars, cash."

"That's ridiculous. The selling price is three million."

"You usually pay ten times earnings for a golf course. This golf course is earning almost nothing. A million dollars is more than generous."

Although the banker said nothing. He did not disagree with John. For several seconds, he pondered the offer. The hundred thousand that the bank had just put into the golf course to keep its doors open was only the latest money they had been shoveling into this bottomless money pit. He also considered that there had been no other offers. Putting more money into the property, for real estate development, was not something he wanted to have to propose to the review committee. He had hoped that some wealthy fool would come along and give them something close to the asking price. His experience had taught him that the first offer in real estate is often the best offer. It was time to sell. He replied, "A million dollars is out of the question. I think the bank would consider two million."

"Well, I tell you what. If it isn't worth a million, it sure isn't worth two million, but I'll gamble and meet you half way. A million in cash, up front, and I will take a half million-dollar operating loan at one percent over prime. The golf course will continue to be your security."

The banker calculated that the million would more than cover their loss on the previous owner's mortgage. A loan would keep the golf course as a banking client. This new owner seemed to be more than capable. He responded, "Two percent over prime."

"Okay, two percent over prime it is. How quickly can we close this sale so I can move out of the hotel?"

"Give me a day to get everything drawn up."

"I'll need a copy that I can take to my lawyer."

"I should have one ready by for you by four o'clock tomorrow afternoon. Here are the forwarding directions that you will need for your bank. Let's schedule the signing for Friday, at nine."

With that, John stood up and shook the banker's hand. He returned to the hotel to phone his bank about transferring the million dollars and to lay out a long-term business plan for the golf course. He phoned the hotel's manager and asked him if he could recommend a local lawyer who would meet with him on short notice. The manager referred him to the hotel's lawyer.

CHAPTER 14

SUCCESS

After signing the sales agreement on Friday, they agreed that the official transfer of ownership would take place on the following Tuesday. This was the golf course's quietest day. To prepare for a smoother ownership transition on the Tuesday, John requested an immediate introduction to the club's four department heads. He was sure that they would want to know the sale was completed. John wanted them to stop worrying about their future employment.

The banker, eager to end the bank's responsibility for the golf club, thought such an introduction was a great idea. He said he would arrange it for later that afternoon.

Just before four o'clock, John and the bank manager drove out to the golf club in separate cars. They met with the four managers, in the same meeting room, where John had reviewed the club's financial records. The banker introduced John as the new owner. After saying some nice things about the managers and John, he exited the meeting. He had done his duty. The golf club was now someone else's burden.

The first thing John did was to tell the managers that he needed their help in implementing all the changes that he envisioned would benefit the club's sales and profits. The four managers exchanged worried glances. Changes suggested employment risk.

To them, the new owner looked too young. He was at least ten years younger than they were. They wondered how he could have accumulated enough business experience to even recognize the mess they were in. As they sat there, showing their best poker faces, what was going through their minds was, could they work with him or should they start an immediate job search?

John stared at the four of them. He wondered if they could enthusiastically accept the changes he planned to make and if they were smart enough to recognize the benefits that he envisioned.

The human resource files that he had read described the job functions of the four managers. The Golf Course Superintendent oversaw the grounds and all building maintenance. The Golf Pro's responsibilities were the pro shop, gym, change rooms, tennis court, driving range, golf carts and tournaments. The Food and Beverage Manager's were the banquet room, bars, kitchen, dining room and the snack bar. The Office Manager 's were accounting, the computer systems and record keeping.

John asked if there were any questions. The managers stared at each other but remained mute. They all had questions, lots of questions, even dangerous questions, if misinterpreted, could get them fired.

To get them talking, John asked them who had responsibility for marketing and sales. The four managers, again, looked at each other. The Office Manager knew it was not his responsibility. He replied that the pro shop, and the restaurants were the money makers. The golf pro responded by saying the deceased previous owner was the only one active in sales and marketing. John had hoped to hear them say that they were all responsible for sales.

Their response gave him his chance to present proposed changes. "This golf course is in real trouble. It has had no organized sales effort, for a year. This has left revenue in a precarious position. It is teetering on the edge of insolvency. I have no intentions of allowing it to go bankrupt. Until we can afford a sales and marketing manager, I will add that role to my general management responsibilities."

No one, as he expected, had objected to him accepting responsibility for sales management. It was showing them that he would not be an absentee owner but would be an active part of the team. He continued, "As best, as I can estimate, it will take us six months to build sales momentum and get monthly profits to where they should be. To get expenses in line, with existing revenues, as quickly as possible, I need each of you to put on your thinking hats. Tell me how, in your department, we can reduce expenses by 15% and where are the opportunities for revenue gains. On Tuesday, when I take over, the first thing I want to do is meet with each of you, so you can show me what you've come up with."

The golf course superintendent interrupted, "I see no way that we could reduce grounds keeping expenses by 15%."

John had expected push back and was prepared, "On average, this golf course's labor costs are running at 55% of our revenue. In a well-run golf course, per government statistics, labor costs should be running at closer to 35%. That is a 20% difference, not 15%. While sales and membership have been shrinking for the last three years, staffing has stayed the same. Fewer customers, means less work for your staff. Reducing our labor costs, is the first place, we should adjust to regain lost profits."

The food and beverage manager, who looked very unhappy, responded, "We are a family. Several of our staff have been here twenty or more years. I don't see how can we maintain our high level of service with fewer people?"

"I've got a business to run and I'm the one who has just sunk a million dollars into this golf course. I don't intend to lose my investment. When we meet Tuesday, I want to see which employees you will let go. To avoid the iceberg of insolvency, we need to turn this ship around."

John paused and looked at each of them. He recognized that there was a thin line between inspiring managers to function at a higher level and demoralizing them, so much, that they gave up.

He continued, "If your department is not adding to our profits, then we have to try something different. Our downsizing will not be for ever. It's only until we work our way out of this hole. When our revenues get to where they should be, we will be employing far more than we are now. Until then, the remaining staff need to put out more effort, to cover for those 15% who are leaving. It isn't just staffing. Look at all expenses. From now on, I will be looking at every purchase order, every bill and every check being issued. I'll be questioning every expense that will not help us increase our revenues. With your help and support, in six months, this golf course will be in the best financial shape it has ever been."

John looked at the four of them. Their eyes were open wider, and they were breathing harder than when they had entered. The four managers knew that what John had said was true. They had been going through the motions, operating at half speed, long before the previous owner had died. Their vacation was over. It was time to get back to work.

Whether they realized it or not, they felt inspired. Everyone likes a challenge and for the first time, in a long time, they were being challenged to think and to plan. They all wanted to be part of a successful operation.

They needed their salaries. None of them, could just quit. They agreed to go along with the new owner for now. It was the easiest path to follow for the immediate future.

John said, "Okay, that's enough for today. Let's get back to work. I'll meet with each of you, Tuesday, to go over the changes to your operation."

Before this meeting, John saw the office manager to arrange for his move into the empty apartment on the second floor. Not only would the apartment become John's new home but also his office. When the meeting broke up, John used the key he had obtained to let himself into the apartment.

He did a quick inventory to see what he would need. The second bedroom was an office, with a large desk, filing cabinets, bookcases, telephone and even a desk top computer. He needed a password to operate. He made a note to get it. The small kitchen would not get much attention from him. The dining room downstairs is where he expected, he would take all his meals. In the bedroom, sheets and blankets were on the bed. Someone must be cleaning the apartment because it was shiny and dust free. A linen closet contained extra blankets, sheets, pillow cases and towels.

On the drive back to the hotel, he started to lay out his plans for the golf course. On Tuesday morning, he checked out of the hotel and made his way to the golf course. He made one stop at a supermarket to buy snack food: cheese, eggs, jam, peanut butter, instant coffee, soft drinks, beer and wine.

CHAPTER 15

MATTEO

The first thing Tuesday morning, at the golf club, John started to do research. He needed a better understand of the golf course's market and how to approach it.

First, he Googled all the competing golf courses within a hundred miles. On a spread sheet, he recorded their fees, what they offered golfers and what the golfers had to say in their reviews about the courses. It was important that he understand his competitors. On another spread sheet, he recorded all the hotels, with over a hundred rooms, within an hour drive of his golf course. He wanted them to refer their guests to his course. In a third spread sheet, he recorded all large businesses, associations and government departments within a two-hour drive of the golf course. The next step would be to contact each and determine whether they held annual golf tournaments for their employees.

At noon, he stopped his research. It was time to meet with the managers. The greatest potential for increased revenues and effective cost cutting, was in the restaurants. John started with the food and beverage manager. He phoned and asked him to come to his office.

The manager's name was Matteo Dafina. John heard his gentle knock on the apartment door. When he opened it, Matteo gave him a big smile. He was short and corpulent, in his early forties. They made their way to john's office. When they sat facing each other across his desk, John asked him, "If you owned those restaurants down stairs, what changes would you make?" He then stared at Matteo.

Matteo started off enthusiastically, "Mister Powell."

John held up his hand to stop him and interjected, "Mister Powell was my father. Please call me Raymond or Ray. We will be working together as a team."

"OK Ray. I thought about it over the weekend. To cut down the number of employees, I propose that we close the snack bar. It hasn't made money in years. On each of its two shifts, we employ a fast order cook, a helper, a cashier, two waitresses and a busboy. Not being in the same building, it has always been hard for me to supervise them."

"How will the members react?

"The women are all health conscious and don't eat the greasy French fries and hamburgers being offered there. They also give their husbands a hard time about eating such unhealthy food."

"Where will the golfers now go for lunch?"

"Into the main club house. What I propose doing, is creating three restaurants, inside the main building, all served by one kitchen. Where the bar is now, I now propose we add in steam tables and refrigerator tables. We will serve the food cafeteria style."

"That seems a bit basic?"

"Not the way I want to do it. My speciality is fine Italian cooking. Each day the hot table will offer three types of pasta, a risotto, grilled fish, chicken, pork, veal and vegetables. The cold table will offer salads to which we can add a choice of sliced chicken breasts, tuna and mixed seafood. My objective is to provide healthy delicious meals for less than ten dollars. Beverages and deserts would be extra. With a little advertising, we will attract more than golfers. Oh, yes, I almost forgot, we will also need a pizza oven. Everyone loves pizza."

"Pizza's aren't very healthy."

"True, but I can make them so delicious that they will forget that they aren't good for them."

"The golf course now advertises itself as being restricted to members. How do you get more customers in your three restaurants?"

"Yes, the membership restriction turns off any potential customers who might want to come here just to eat. While this Italian eatery would be open to the public, I propose that we also have an exclusive, up scale, dining room - just for those willing to commit to the annual membership. That would keep our existing members from cancelling."

"Would that be one of the three dining rooms you propose?"

"Yes, while the Italian restaurant would be nice, it would not be special. The member's dining room would be special, with its steak, lobster, white linen table clothes, crystal, fine silverware, flowers on the table, candles in the evening, tasteful paintings on the walls and thick carpets. Only a member's key card would allow access to it. The snobs will love that you must be a member to get in. It will increase golf membership. Some will join, just to gain access to this restaurant and never set foot on the golf course."

"What about the third room?"

"This would be the large room where we now hold the golf banquets, large meetings and weddings. I also propose building a large patio, just outside the banquet room that can be entered through the French doors at the back of room or from the banquet room. It wouldn't cost much to build."

"Wouldn't the two new restaurants you propose cut into this banquet's floor space? Don't we need the banquet room to be as large a possible to get the big golf tournaments?

"We do but we might have to sacrifice having large tournaments."

"Maybe not. I've got an idea that will open more space for you. Let me get back to you later this afternoon. Oh, yes, that sign in the hall way, seems like something left over from the dark ages. It is almost insulting. Can you get someone to take it down? We want to attract new members not chase them away."

"Some of the long-time members many not renew their membership if we take it down."

"How many elderly members have died in the last year?

"A dozen."

"How many members in their twenties have joined in that year?"

"Two or three?"

"Why is that?"

"Well, taking out a membership is expensive for a young person. The initiation fee, the annual fee and the monthly minimum food charges, are significant. Younger players raised on video games find golf too slow. It isn't much fun with all its rules and its chauvinistic atmosphere. I read somewhere, that for these younger players, it is the wife who makes the final major purchase decisions. You would wonder what selfish incentives; she would need to have before she would approve a golf membership for her husband. The old fogies have their clique. They aren't very accepting of new members. I understand that few new members, renew for a second year."

"Now, do you see why that sign must come down and why we need to make changes that will make this club attractive to young couples? Your ideas on the restaurant changes are great. I can see the wives, of the younger new members, enjoying lunch in the Italian restaurant and dinner in the exclusive dining room. Can you put it all in writing and give me some preliminary costing? Could you also let me know when we could start and how long it would take to make the changes? How much time do you need to write it up?"

"I'll work on it for the rest of the day and finish it tonight when I get home."

John stood. This was Matteo's signal that their meeting was over. John phoned the golf pro and asked Andrew Brown to join him.

CHAPTER 16

ANDREW

The golf pro was tall, lean and athletic. John thought he looked to be in his early forties. His tight, black golf shirt, with the club's crest on it, showed off his well-defined biceps. He exuded confidence and had an almost cocky condescension. John greeted him with, "Andrew, you're a long way from home."

"Was it my accent that tipped you off?" He smiled, revealing uneven teeth, yellowed from smoking.

"That and the unmistakable attitude of an Englishman slumming in the colonies. Where did you go to school?

"Rugby."

"Did you go on to university?"

"No, I went into a British army officer's training program. From what I have seen, I got a far better education from Rugby and the army, than any of the university graduates I've met over here."

"You're probably right. Where's the golfing come from?"

"My father was a keen golfer. He owned a large Renault car dealership in Manchester. When I was quite young, he bought a house that backed onto a golf course. Whenever, I was home from school, I would hit hundreds of golf balls every day and play as many rounds of golf as I could. I came to America to join the tour and ended up here. I had had enough of trying to make a go of it on the pro circuit."

"Were you aware that you are the highest-paid employee in this club?"

"No, but I suspected that I was. It doesn't surprise me. Golf clubs do not pay employees well."

"Why is your operation not making a profit?

John saw that this had brought Andrew down to earth. The pleasantries were over. Unclear how much John knew about his operation, Andrew took his time in answering. He was trying to construct, the answer, he thought John might expect and one that would justify his high income. That John, might even be thinking of firing him, had also occurred to him. It would be a quick way to bring down the club's overhead.

Andrew responded, "Our problem is a loss of revenue. With a shrinking membership, we can no longer offset our fixed costs. A significant number of members died in the last three years. The other challenge is the increased competition in equipment sales. I've had our member take out their mobile phones and check our prices, right in front of me. They can buy the best clubs, on line, cheaper than what I pay for them from the wholesaler. The same goes for balls, gloves, shoes, shirts and pants. They even get next day delivery. As well, to match the prices at other clubs and to get tournaments, we've even had to reduce charges on green fees, golf carts and buckets of balls for the driving range."

John had suspected as much. He quietly said, "We can't do much about the cut rate prices the manufacturers are selling in bulk to internet retailers. Some of these, on-line golf shops, are buying ten thousand clubs at a time. However, my plans will increase membership and take business away from other golf courses. These plans require your retail space on the first floor. Any objections?"

"Well, I do get a percentage of every sale in the pro shop. How do I get compensated for giving up this revenue stream?"

"Nothing, but you will make it up on increased revenues from golf lessons, cart rentals, green fees and other things that you get a piece of. Which as you mentioned is an ever-shrinking source of revenue. You'll also get to keep your job and save me the time and expense of finding a replacement. I intend to be very busy building up traffic to this club."

Andrew smiled as he said, "I didn't come to this country to be a bloody shop keeper. It has been an area of frustration for me. I won't miss it. But we need somewhere to sell the basics that members always need at the last minute, like balls, gloves and tees."

"I agree. That wide hallway connecting the locker rooms and the gym is a good place to set up a small retail space. We can reduce the clothing down to hats and golf shirts with the club's logo on them. It will also allow you to make easier contact with members who come to golf. The store upstairs is too far away from the change rooms."

"Yeah, that could work."

"Good, can you give me a plan for the new space? We'll get contractors in as quickly as possible. How many employees can we remove from the store upstairs? Also, I need your ideas on how we can get the best price for unloading in bulk all that golf merchandise on the first floor."

"We'll be able to let go two employees. We will still need two down stairs to handle the two shifts. I will get some bids on buying the inventory."

"I also noticed that there seems to be six locker room attendants on staff. For a club this size, four would be more in line."

"I suppose two on each shift could work, especially if we could contract out the cleaning at night and remove our existing cleaner. An outside cleaning crew could do that job in two hours."

"Why didn't you propose this before?"

"I did but the club owner and the cleaner were close."

"Your assistant. Is he necessary?"

"Yes, when I am out giving lessons, someone has to be in charge here, to help members and keep an eye on things."

"Couldn't an employee in the new pro shop take that job on?"

"I'm not sure."

"Well let's try it. It will be temporary, until we get things rolling, but we need to cut now until it hurts."

Brown couldn't argue with that, so he kept silent. John waited and then continued, "Any questions? What else should I know?"

"Yes, I watched you playing a few holes on Friday. Where did you learn to play like that?"

"At a small business college. They believed that a well-rounded executive needed to play golf well. Like you, I spent most of my spare time, as a young teenager on a golf course."

"I look forward to playing a round with you?"

"Yeah, I'd like that too, but first let's get this club back on its feet. I look forward to seeing how you want the new retail area laid out."

Brown shifted his long, lanky frame out of his chair and headed out of John's apartment.

⊠CHAPTER 17

DWAYNE

A soon as Andrew Brown had left, John picked up the phone and asked Dwayne Dix, the Golf Course Superintendent to join him. A half hour later, he heard a loud knock on his apartment door. He got up and opened it. Dwayne stood there, shifting from one foot to the other. He was a giant of a man, about forty-five years old, at least six feet, five inches tall and close to three hundred pounds. Dressed in his khaki colored work clothes, he looked like a displaced army tent. John ushered him in. Dwayne stepped in and waited to follow John.

Seated in front of the desk, Dwayne stared at John, who asked, "Remind me, how many people you've got working for you?"

"Twenty-one."

"How many can you lay off?"

"This is the quiet time of the year. I suppose I could get along with two fewer greens keepers. It's all related to how much wear and tear there is on the greens. I'm reluctant to let anyone go. We've spent years training them in fairway maintenance and on the green mowers. It's hard to find reliable people willing to get here by six in the morning. They aren't making a fortune."

"Do any of them have a driver's license that would let them drive a bus?"

"That's a strange question but I know at least one of them does. Why do you ask?"

"I want you to buy two buses that can hold twenty people and their golf equipment."

"What are we going to do with the buses?"

"I've got a plan to work out a relationship with the five largest hotels in the Benji Beach area. Our buses will do a circuit of these hotels, every half hour, to pick up and drop off golfers. This locks the hotel guests into our club and gives the hotels something extra to offer their guests. The golfers won't have to worry about drinking and driving. The second bus will be a backup. I need you to get me some prices on what two buses would cost and how quickly we can get delivery."

"New or used?"

"A good used one would be fine if you can find one. Any idea where we can find someone to paint them? They will be our mobile billboard. Every visitor to Benji Beach will know of our presence every single day that they are here."

"A special advertising paint job would probably have to get done in D.C. I'll do the research."

"I'm planning on turning the snack bar into a baby-sitting area so we can make the club more attractive to women. Water attracts kids. I'm worried about some kid drowning in that pool. Does anyone swim in it?"

"A few hot days in the summer, you will see some someone in it. The old people don't use it. It costs a fortune to heat that thing in the colder months."

"How long would it take to bury the pool and cover it with sod?"

"Jeez, the old people will not like that being done to their junior, Olympic size, swimming pool."

"I thought you said they didn't use it?"

"They don't but it looks impressive. They like to show it off to visitors."

"It's a hazard waiting for a law suit. Let's get rid of the threat. When could you have, it buried?"

"Next Friday."

"Good, do it. What do you think makes this course exceptional?"

"The five sets of tees to accommodate any level of player and the layout of the water hazards on the sixteenth and eighteenth holes."

"That's it?"

"Yeah, that's about it."

"Are you getting any complaints about the course?"

"I am not really getting any complaints."

"Well, I have a few. I noticed a few things when I played the course. There was no hole-by-hole map on the scorecards and no hole layouts at each tee box or GPS co-ordinates posted, so that golfers could get an aerial view of the holes on their iPhones. Now, they guess how to play each hole. What can you do about it?"

"That is something for the golf pro. I'll see him about it."

"I also saw lots of divots not replaced and too many unrepaired ball marks."

"It could have been an off day. I'll make sure the greenkeepers get on top of it. You won't see it on your next round."

"I know you've got a tough job. It's ten hours a day, seven days a week, maintaining what is a small city. You're responsible for all the equipment, irrigation, cart paths, mowing, weeding, fertilizing, plumbing and trimming. Without you and your staff's dedication, we would have nothing to sell. If you do your job well, no one even notices your existence. Listen, I'm not about to tell you how to do your job. All I want is for you to make this the best damn course in Delaware."

"Ray, all I can do is my best. I'll get busy on finding those buses."

Dwayne Dix left, feeling that he could work with John and that John was no fool.

CHAPTER 18

NORMAN

Norman Booshard, the office manager, was the next one invited to John's office. He had to knock twice on the apartment door before John heard him.

Born and raised in Benji Beach, he was short, bald and thin with a comb over. The job was his life and his identity. The thought of the golf course failing, and being out of a job, was something he feared to even contemplate.

He had started at the golf club as an accounting clerk shortly after finishing high school. When Cecil Smith, the office manager, had left, for greener fields ten years ago, they had promoted Norm, as the most senior clerk in the accounting department, to office manager. Since then, the only change to the accounting system was to automate the monthly membership billings.

John was an unknown quantity. This made Norm feel insecure. When John said, "The accounting clerks seem to be doing tasks that we could automate."

Norm could only answer, "The computer system we installed ten years ago, seems to work just fine."

"It will not be able to handle the changes,"

Norm nervously asked, "What changes?"

"I want to change the golf club from a membership club to a pay-as-you-use club. Portable, high speed, credit card and debit card processing will be essential."

"Our accounting system can't handle those kinds of transactions. It would be expensive to buy a system that can handle them."

"I also want to give golfers internet access, so they can book their own tee times and pay us in advance. Instead of billing them for their purchases at the end of each month, I want everything charged to credit cards. That way we will get paid faster and remove the possibility of any bad debts. From what I could see it now takes almost two months to get paid for something a member purchased at the beginning of a month."

Norm nodded his head in agreement because what John had said was true but it had always been that way. He waited for John to finish.

"Food, beverage, gasoline, fertilizer and seed inventories also need to be tracked for statistical purposes. From time to time I also want to be able to email special promotions to everyone who has ever played our course."

"Do you know who supplies these systems?"

"No, it is a system that you, not me, know you can work with. You need to ask around, do some internet searches, check out any references with other golf courses already using such software. A supplier who can give us good customer support and training is essential. When you find one that you think can provide what we want, let's meet with them."

"How much should I budget for this new accounting software?"

"More important than the cost, is will the system do, what we want? The right system will allow us to reduce accounting staff and receivable cost which translates into big, long term, savings."

"When do we need it?"

"As soon as possible. Within a month would be good. It'll take time to get it installed, get all the bugs worked out and for your people to get up to speed on it. Do you think that is possible?"

"As soon as I leave here, I will start researching what is available."

"OK, keep me posted on how things are developing. Let's sit down and review your progress in five days."

Norm was up and heading for the door with more of a spring in his step than when he had entered. He felt important. The future success of the golf club was now, as much in his hands, as any of the other managers. His terror of not having a job at the golf club had evaporated.

CHAPTER 19

PROFIT

Over the next six months, everything fell into place. The new member's private dining room became the most elegant eating spot within sixty miles. Its separate entrance, with a discreet brass plate on the door, stating, "For Member's Only" provided an air of exclusiveness. This appealed to the insecure and the social climbers. The club sold dozens of new memberships because of it. Excellent steaks, fish and lobster had the members wanting to eat there several times every month.

When everything at the club was functioning as John had imagined it would, he visited the owners of the four largest hotels in Benji Beach. They were told about the new bus service that, every half hour, would take their guests back and forth to the golf club. To cement his working relationship with the hotel managers, he lay a free golf club membership down in front of each of them. The hotel owners not only became his new best friends, but their hotel guests could now be classified as guests of a club member. This would entitle them full access to all three restaurants and to special club discounts. This symbiotic relationship would now enrich both the golf course and the four hotels.

Benji Beach became accustomed to seeing the brightly colored buses promoting the golf course and its Italian restaurant. For political and motivational reasons, John had decided to call the restaurant "Matteo's". It was busy from when it opened at eleven in the morning until it closed at eight o'clock in the evening. The customers raved about the excellent quality of the Italian food and the low prices.

The low prices at Matteo's were deceiving. To get them in the restaurant, they had priced many entrees at what the locals paid elsewhere for a hamburger. However, once the customers added a delicious soup, a healthy salad, a slice of pizza, a cappuccino and a homemade gelato; they were lucky to leave for less than twenty dollars. No one complained. They recognized that they were getting good value for their money.

Shrinking the pro shop, to a token presence, gave the club twice the banquet space. Larger weddings, golf tournaments and company meetings now filled the banquet room almost seven days a week. Many of these new bookings arose from a customer having first visited the club to eat at Matteo's. They liked the food, the location and the ambiance.

Many of the weddings were destination weddings for clients who lived in the Washington, Baltimore and Philadelphia areas. Benji Beach was just far enough away from those cities to make the location a special event. The hotels that had memberships in the golf club were quick to give discounts on rooms to guests attending a wedding at the golf club.

The golf course never looked better. Dwayne Dix had risen to the challenge. Complaints about hole maps, unraked bunkers, torn up courses and missing beer carts ceased.

The club was now so automated that there was little waiting to check in, or for tee offs. Their new website displayed each hole's statistics with hints and configurations. Golfers could study the course, days before they played it, or even on their cell phones as they were playing it.

If there were open tee times during the day, Andrew could email a special reduced-price offer to golfers who lived in the area. Now the course was always busy.

In the seventh month, when John received the financial results for the previous month, he asked Norm if there had been a mistake. They were showing an operating profit of just over $300,000. Although John had said that they would have respectable profits within six months, he had had doubts about such an aggressive target. Norm showed off his knowledge of the new accounting system by detailing where all the sales gains and cost savings had come from. John shook his head in amazement. He booked a dinner, for the following night in the member's dining room, and invited the four managers and their wives to join him.

At the dinner, he told them how proud he was at what they had achieved. He then presented each of them with a check of $5,000 as token of his appreciation. Much fine wine was downed with their steaks. Every time they reached a new operating profit record, John repeated these celebratory dinners.

The next morning after that dinner, John went to the bank and took out 15% of the $300,000 in cash. He inserted the $45,000 into a padded envelope. Since mailing it at the post office in Benji Beach was too public. He drove north to Dover, Delaware to mail it.

The envelope was addressed to Winston Hawkins at the college in Taos, New Mexico. Once again, John put the return address of FICA, 41 Boulevard Rochechouart, Paris, France on the envelope.

For John to hide his location from The Sanctuary, was unnecessary. The day he had first walked into the bank in Benji Beach, Winston's monitoring system had picked him up. It now recorded all his frequent trips to the bank.

Winston had been wondering when payments to The Sanctuary would begin but he had never lost faith that they would begin. When the $45,000 arrived, it came as no great surprise to him. It was John's role in life to generate revenue for The Sanctuary. He had already proven that he was an outstanding revenue producer.

When John left the post office, he had a smile on his face. Once again, he could start payments that would save children from dying a miserable death on the mean streets.

CHAPTER 20

HEIRESS

Mid-morning, two years after John Cross purchased the golf course, he stood in the club's small pro-shop with two corporate executives. They had travelled from D.C. to see whether the Golf Club would be a suitable for their next sales meeting. Fifty of their employees would be coming. With the kickbacks, the Benji Beach Golf Club got from the local hotels, the three-day event could bring in more than $150,000 in revenue.

The executives had told John that, for the three days, they would like to hold their meetings in the morning and play golf in the afternoons. Eager, to show them, how great the Benji Beach Golf Club could be for their sales meeting; John had asked them to drive down from Washington and join him for a round of golf and lunch.

A third executive who was to join them had to attend to some disaster. As they stood, listening to Andrew Brown, the golf pro, selling the virtues of the course, an attractive woman entered the pro shop. She waved at Andrew who smiled and waved back. The two prospective customers looked her over.

"Who is that?" whispered the taller executive.

"That," Andrew replied, "Is Miss Naomi Green, the heir to the Greenline Engines fortune."

John's back was to her. He had missed her entrance. He turned, to see what had captured their attention. She flashed him a big smile.

That she had obviously got their attention amused her. All four of them smiled back at her, convinced that her smile had only been meant for them, and them alone. Andrew asked, "How are you today, Miss Green?"

"I'm fine, Andy, but I hoped that I could get in a round of golf this morning. Will anyone be needing a fourth?"

The executives did not miss this opportunity. The taller one responded, "We're missing a fourth. Why don't you join us?"

John, amused at this added club feature, could see it helping him close the sale. He was not about to object to his guests' fantasies about playing golf with a beautiful woman.

"Are you sure?" She coyly replied.

The two executives abandoned John and Andrew and moved closer to Naomi.

"Oh, we would be more than pleased to have you join us." They introduced themselves. She shook their hand and was obviously enjoying their drooling attention. John glanced at Andrew, who gave him a nod as if to say she really is something. The short, white, golf skirt did an excellent job of showing off her long, tanned legs. Naomi Green appeared to be an excellent example of good health. She was neither thin nor fat. With her blond hair tied back, it emphasized her high cheek bones and hazel eyes.

John was more than just attracted to Naomi. That bothered him. He had always seen himself as an island, a fortress. Not needing anyone. Totally focused on only growing his business for the benefit of The Sanctuary.

Andrew and John joined the two grey haired executives. They were monopolizing Naomi's attention like a couple of high school kids.

Andrew interjected, "Naomi, I've got someone I'd like you to meet."

John Cross smiled at her. Naomi smiled back.

"This is Raymond Powell, the owner of the golf club. Raymond, this is Naomi Green. Her Dad's been a member here long before I showed up."

"Glad to meet you Mrs. Green."

"It's Miss Green. Pleased to meet you Mr. Powell."

"It's just, Raymond. Can I get your clubs for you?

"My, my, my - such service. Why thank you Raymond."

The foursome teed off. Naomi joined John in his golf cart. The two executives shared a cart. They would have preferred to have ridden with Naomi.

John admired her swing. The ball soared straight and true. She was a great golfer. The executives were more intent on watching her than concentrating on their game. After watching her execute a beautiful shot on the tenth hole, he nodded to her and said, "Very nice. You are very good." It was his turn. He teed off. The ball landed a few feet from the hole.

Naomi laughed after his shot and said, "Thanks for that last compliment. After your shot, it is a real compliment. I believe I'm looking at our next club champion."

"No, that's not about to happen. I like to keep a low profile. Will you join us for lunch?"

"You're winning. I'd be glad to join you for lunch but only if I pay."

"That's nice of you to offer but it's my club and you, and the other two gentlemen, are my guests. You can help me convince them to hold their sales meeting at Benji Beach."

During lunch, the two executives kept checking their watches. John had advised Matteo Dafina to prepare a special meal that would impress his guests. They raved about the food but were anxious to get back to Washington before rush hour turned its streets into one big parking lot. They skipped dessert. Thanked John for a great day and assured him that they would complete things in the next few days.

After they left, John and Naomi sat sipping their coffee and enjoying a plate of fresh fruit and imported cheeses. Naomi told him how much she enjoyed the elegance of the member's private dining room. John smiled and said, "It pleases me to hear you say that. With all the changes, I made to the club that I expected to lose the long-standing members."

"Quite the contrary. You've breathed life into this club. It was dying before you took it over. The ladies especially like the little touches you've added. Those with children, especially appreciate the babysitting service. Since they all worry about their weight, they've also rave about the low calorie, low sodium, healthy lunches that you've made available at Matteo's. When they are having a busy day, and don't want to cook, they appreciate being able to bring home your great food for their kids. The kids like your pizzas. So, do their husbands."

John laughed as he said, "Enough! I'm getting a swelled head but I'm disappointed that you didn't mention the new wine list."

"Oh, I noticed the wine list, monsieur. *C'est tres elegante.*"

What wine is your favorite?"

"Yesterday I had warm Hakutsuru Junmai Ginjo sake to go with my miso-rubbed roasted chicken breasts and sushi rice pilaf."

"My God, that rolls off your tongue like liquid honey."

"The women members, were so glad to see you getting away from steak and more steak."

"Hey, we do great steaks too."

"You do, but a choice is nice."

"Tell me about yourself."

"Not much to tell. I'm thirty-one, spoiled, independent, selfish and like playing golf. Oh, yeah, and I've got an MBA from Harvard."

"And what do you do with your MBA from Harvard?"

"What do you mean by, do? Do you mean where do I work?"

"Yeah."

"I don't work."

"That's interesting. You must share your secret with me. It sounds like a great trick if you can pull it off. You don't look like you are starving."

"What? Now you're telling me I'm fat?"

John smiled as he said, "Oh, you are far from fat. I would say you are perfect."

Naomi laughed as she responded, "Oh, I am far from perfect. I don't work because I am the only grandchild of a wealthy man. He provided for me in his will. My father taught me how to invest that money in the stock market and I live off the income of well diversified stock portfolio. The MBA was to get a better understanding of the business world, not to get a job."

"Beautiful, smart and rich too. Here's a toast to Naomi Green, may the wind be always at her back."

They raised their glasses and clinked them. As they did, John couldn't help comparing her aristocratic life of privilege to his escape from dire poverty. A background, that never let him escape the nagging fear of being dragged back into poverty. He felt he should let her know, they had something in common, so he said, "Although I didn't get an MBA from Harvard, I did get an MBA from a small, obscure, university in the South West."

"Why am I not surprised? Are you from the South West?"

"Yeah, I was born in Los Angeles. When I was twelve, I was orphaned. After that, an institution in New Mexico took me under its wing and educated me. They prepared me for a life in business. I was lucky."

"Was this a religious institution?"

"Not as you would see it."

"Are you religious?"

"Do you mean in the conventional sense, of a belief in some ancient, omnipotent being, flying around in the heavens, controlling everything?"

"Yeah."

"No, I am not religious. I am not able to conceive something that is so powerful that it is inconceivable. An omnipotent being, is too far removed from my reality. Even if such a being might exist, I saw too much horror as a kid that I cannot believe that anything, other than myself, is in control of my actions and my destiny. What I do believe in, is random luck and coincidences. People do get hit by lightning bolts. Just like I had the good luck of being plucked off the streets of Los Angeles as an abandoned child. I would probably have died on those streets and never have had the good fortune of meeting you."

"That sounds heavy. What are these horrors you have seen?"

John caught himself. He was from Los Angeles. Raymond Powell was from Phoenix. He chastised himself for getting sloppy and letting his guard down. Such a lapse, with the wrong person, could cost him his life. All it would take is one mistake like that at the wrong time and either the FBI or the Las Vegas mob would have him. He had better lay off the wine.

For several, uncomfortable seconds, all the raw memories, from his youth and his flight from Las Vegas, washed over him. He responded, "Sorry, but I don't talk about the past. What is past, is in the past. I gain nothing but depression by dredging it up. I live in the present, and I look to the future."

Naomi knew when to retreat, "Raymond Powell, you are an interesting man. I have never met anyone quite like you. You are not like the boys I grew up with."

He replied, "You should run for the hills. I could be dangerous."

"True, but I like to live on the dangerous side."

John laughed and replied, "I've never met anyone quite like you either. I want to know you better."

"I would like that."

"I don't feel like working and you don't have to work. Let's drive up the coast? We'll see a movie in Dover and then get dinner?"

"That sounds like fun but I need to change and freshen up. Could you pick me up in an hour?"

"Great. Where do I find you?"

From her purse, Naomi, took out a small note pad and wrote her address and phone number on it. She slid it across the table to John. He picked it up, looked at it and smiled.

"I know where this is. It must be in one of those exclusive, giant, beach houses north of town."

John pulled her chair out and walked her to her car. It was a silver, BMW 650I convertible. He had expected nothing less. It gave a throaty growl as she pulled out of the parking lot. He went upstairs to his apartment to shower and change.

CHAPTER 21

NAOMI

Having prospective clients to impress, he had long ago sold the Nissan Altima, that he had purchased in Philadelphia. He now leased a Range Rover. This is what he drove to Naomi's beach house. It was in a gated community, only a few minutes' drive away.

Each house was on at least an acre of land. Before the guard would open the gate, he phoned Naomi for clearance. As he pulled into the driveway of the beach house, John estimated that it was probably worth more than double what his golf course was worth.

It was two hundred feet from the road and backed onto the beach. John thought it would be best described as Italian modern. If had lots of glass and terraces on two levels. He spied a covered garage, for at least six cars, underneath the house. A long circular driveway led to the wide steps that wound up to the first level entrance. The pink stucco and the rounded arches gave it a very Mediterranean look.

John left his car at the base of the stairs and made his way to enormous double doors. He rang the doorbell. Its chimes announced his presence.

He gave a start when Naomi's disembodied voice came out of hidden speakers, "I'm almost ready. The door is unlocked. Come in and make yourself at home. I'll be right down"

He pushed the door open and entered an impressive marble lobby. It would have done justice to the head office of a mid-size bank. An elaborate, wooden spiral stair case floated up to the upper level. He noticed an elevator beside it. From a skylight, forty feet above him, sunlight poured into the lobby. The interior was wood with contrasting soft pastel walls and furniture.

Someone, with taste and money, had amassed a huge, eclectic, collection of paintings that covered every wall. He walked over and admired them. They were originals, by artists that he was familiar with, but had only seen their work in photographs or in art museums. He was always looking for new ideas that he could incorporate into his own paintings. Like a kid in a candy store, he drank in the collection.

Before he saw her, he could hear Naomi's high heels tapping towards him on the marble floor. He turned and marveled at the transformation, from golf jock to understated elegance. She took his hand and led him towards the back of the house. A wall of glass opened out onto a spacious deck where a hundred people could have easily mingled. The sea view stretched, unobstructed, over the beach to the horizon. The deck surrounded an oval swimming pool with a hot tub adjoining it. A long wooden bridge, stretched from the deck, over the dunes, almost to the water's edge.

"Impressed?" she asked.

"Yes, but rather over the top, isn't it?"

"It was very important to my grandfather that no one fail to recognize that he was a man of means. I loved this place, and he knew it. He left me fifty percent of this beach house and fifty percent to my father. I've got great memories of the summers spent here with my grandparents."

'It's worth a small fortune."

"True but it was just this magical place that I loved. While I grew up in Baltimore, it was never home. Within days of my grandfather's death, I moved here, and I've been here ever since.

"You live here by yourself?"

"No. There is a cleaner, Joe the maintenance man and Margaret the cook-housekeeper. My parents often come over for the weekends. In the summer, they will spend several weeks here."

"What does your father do? Is he retired?"

"No, Howard Green has always done whatever he wants to do. He was an only child who inherited most of his father's investments. As a major shareholder in several companies, he either chairs or sits on their board of directors. That keeps him busy. He and I own the controlling shares of Greenline Engines. He is Chairman of that board."

"Ready for your drive?"

"Sure, let's go. It's such a nice day, why don't we take my convertible. You can drive. Park your car in the garage out of the sun."

They made their way to Highway 1 and drove north through the flat, swampy, Delaware countryside. The only, real hills in the entire state are on its northern border with Pennsylvania. Even those hills, are only a few hundred feet high.

The dullness of the countryside encouraged conversation. They compared the courses they had studied at university and the places they had visited. Naomi was surprised to learn that he had lived two years in Paris and that he spoke fluent French. She was even more surprised to find that he had a greater love for art than he did for golf. She said that she wanted to see his paintings. To give him the incentive to show her, his paintings, she told him that she had bought all the paintings, that he had seen in the beach house. This led, to her telling him how boring she found the constant demands of investing her, ever growing, dividend income.

She confessed, that being on the Greenline's board was a farce. It had not taken her long to realize that Howard selected directors to rubber stamping any action he wished to see carried out. None complained. Their compensation for attending board meetings was generous, and each year they received generous stock options.

Before they knew it, they had reached Dover. The multiscreen movie theatre was just off Highway 13. Not having any specific movie in mind, they chose the first one at the top of playbill. It was a farce about a depressed young woman intent on committing suicide. She is first delayed by a lawyer wanting to write her will, then a funeral director wanting to sell her a coffin and later by a life insurance salesman intent upon selling her a policy before it was too late. The woman becomes so angry and disgusted with these vultures that she refuses to commit suicide.

After the movie, they sought a sea food restaurant that John had knew, called Denny's Hideaway. On its patio, they ate a grilled skate and sipped champagne as they watched a fiery red sun fall below the horizon. John sipped his wine and stared at Naomi.

"Why are you staring?"

"This morning I woke up to a day, that was just like any other day, and then you entered it. I don't think my life will ever be the same."

" I thought only I felt that way."

"You're kidding me?

"No, you're something else. Raymond, your determination and fearlessness, scares me. Yet, it attracts me. I scare away most men. They recognize that I don't need them and that they can't manipulate me or dominate me. Why aren't you scared of me?"

"Scared? Why? Because you could buy me and sell me with your pocket cash? You inherited your money. I got mine the hard way. If you lost your money, what would you do? If I lost my money, I know how to get it back. No, I don't envy you, nor am I intimidated by you. I suppose, in a way I am sorry for you. You will never truly appreciate what success is until you have come from nothing. You can never realize the joy of knowing that everything, is an opportunity. I stare because I wonder where we go from here?"

"I haven't got a clue. I think we play it by ear. Whatever will be, will be."

John smiled and raised his glass to toast her, as he repeated, "Whatever will be, will be."

On the drive, back to Benji Beach they were quiet, both lost in thought as they considered their pasts and their futures. When they pulled into Naomi's driveway, she asked, "Raymond, can you come in for a drink?"

"Sure," John replied, as he pulled her convertible into a parking spot in the garage beside the elevator. In the elevator, Naomi pressed the button for the second level, not the first. She grabbed John's hand and led him across the hall to her bedroom. She closed the bedroom door and melted into his arms. They undressed each other and took their time exploring each other's bodies with their mouths. John picked her up and carried her over to the bed.

They never closed the drapes. Hours later, the red ball of a morning sun climbed out of the Atlantic Ocean. It woke John with a start. Naomi had curled her body around him. Her breasts were deliciously warm and soft against his back. He wanted to just lie there, but he had responsibilities.

As gently as possible, he extricated himself from the comfort of the bed. Without opening her eyes, Naomi murmured, "Don't Leave. Stay. I want to remember this morning for the rest of my life."

"Okay, a few minutes longer, but running a golf courses is an early morning job. I like to impress upon the troops that the boss is out there slaving away at sunrise, just like I expect them to be."

"But you are slaving away at dawn. You have a very important customer to satisfy."

John laughed before responding, "You are a smart ass aren't you." He drew her close to him and kissed her.

Later, lying there sated, he saw Naomi lean over and pick up the phone beside the bed. He next heard her say, "Margaret please bring breakfast for two up to the dressing room."

There was a pause then she said, "The usual, fruit, scrambled eggs, toast, orange juice and coffee."

John laughed. Naomi sat up, looked at him and said, "Why are you laughing?"

"You have got to be kidding. I get breakfast too. This is a new experience."

Naomi just smiled and said, "You'll find a robe inside your dressing room. It is through that door."

She pointed to a door on John's side of the bed. He got out of bed and opened the door. A large dressing room led him to a private bathroom.

In a drawer, next to the sink he found a razor, shaving cream, deodorant, toothpaste, a toothbrush and shampoo. After a shower and shave, he put on the terry-cloth robe he had found in the dressing room closet and returned to the bedroom.

Naomi wasn't there. He heard water running. He tapped on the door on her side of the bedroom. She told him to enter.

Naomi's dressing room was even larger than his. It was not only her dressing room but her study. There was a desk surrounded by floor to ceiling bookcases. A desk top computer and a scattering of correspondence indicated that this was where she did her paperwork.

On a round mahogany table, two silver warming domes were keeping their breakfast warm. They sat down to eat.

John's thoughts raced back to a night when was twelve years old. Late at night, he and his gang lingered in the shadows behind the local McDonald's waiting for it to close. They knew at closing time the restaurant dumped its unsold hamburgers in the dumpster. The back door to the restaurant opened and a tray of hamburgers disappeared into the dumpster. Moments later the hamburgers were being devoured by the hungry children. To them, it was a feast fit for a king. They could not imagine that they would every experience a greater culinary joy.

After his breakfast, John kissed Naomi goodbye and hurried to his Range Rover. It was important that he set an example for his employees. He felt guilty unless he was the first one at the golf course each morning. To compound his guilt, Naomi had made him promise that he would join her for lunch on her cruiser.

Her cruiser's slip was at a yacht club a few miles south of Benji Beach. It took less than ten minutes to drive there from the golf club. There was a security presence at the marina. Since Naomi had registered his name with them, as soon as he identified himself, the gate rolled open.

John found a spot, in the large parking lot behind the club house. He made his way to the walkway that led to the marina's network of floating docks. It was like a small city, thousands of feet of inter-connected docks spread from the one main dock over acres of water. He did not count them, but he was sure it sheltered hundreds of boats.

He saw Naomi, a hundred feet away on the main dock way, hurrying towards him. She was wearing a red bikini that caught more than John's eye. When she waved, he waved back and walked towards her. When they met, she embraced him, kissed him and grabbed his hand.

Naomi led him through the labyrinth of floating docks to her boat. He hadn't known what to expect. The cruiser, like her house, was big and impressive. John calculated that the vessel to be at least sixty feet long. He had read somewhere that when a vessel was over fifty feet it got classified as a yacht.

As they boarded, Naomi asked him, "Have you spent much time on boats?

"Small boats, yes, but I have zero experience with boats this size."

"Well, before I finish with you, you will be an expert sailor. You are my crew. I'm going up to the bridge. I need you to undo these lines when I yell." She pointed to the lines, "You'll start with the bow line and then the stern line." She then added, "The bow is the front. The stern is the back."

Naomi climbed aboard and made her way to the bridge. John heard the deep throaty rumble of a diesel engine. She yelled at him to undo the bow line. She powered the boat snug against the dock bumpers as John moved to the stern line. He released that line and then leaped from the dock onto the boat.

Skillfully, Naomi backed the boat into the channel. She then shifted the boat into a forward gear guided it out of the marina, careful not to raise a wake. Once she reached the river, she opened the throttle more but was still careful about her wake. In ten minutes, they had exited the river and were moving away from the coastline at full throttle. Her blond hair streamed out behind her.

Below deck, John changed into his bathing suit and then climbed up to the bridge, to join Naomi. She flashed him a big smile. This was something she enjoyed. The boat was shooting a rooster tail of spray into the air as it planed over the waves. John smiled back at her and said, "When you asked me if I wanted to go for a boat ride, I had not expected the boat to be quite this large. How many bedrooms does this boat have?"

"There are four state rooms with double beds and the two benches in the dining area make up into single beds. I haven't been in some of those state rooms this year?"

"Who taught you how to handle a big boat like this."

"My father, in his youth, much to my grandfather's horror, did his two-year conscription in the Coast Guard. He has always loved boats. Thanks to him, I've been around big boats all my life."

"Where are, we are heading?"

"There's a deserted cove, up the bay where I love to anchor. It is remote and quiet. Nobody bothers you there. Romantic, is how I would describe it."

When they reached the deserted cove, Naomi cut the engine. John listened to the anchor chain rattling out. When it stopped, the sudden silence, for a few seconds, was oppressive. Soon their ears adjusted to the subtle lapping of the gentle waves caressing the hull.

They almost believed they were the only two people left in the world. John took Naomi into his arms and kissed her. She led him below to the largest stateroom. In seconds, they had shed their clothes and lost themselves in the joy of each other's bodies.

Later, naked, they jumped hand in hand into the ocean. After their swim, they climb back on the boat to lie on the deck and soak up the warm sunshine. Hungry, Naomi got up and put together a simple meal of salad, cold cuts and fresh croissants that she had bought on her way to the boat.

They revealed their dreams and aspirations. Naomi told stories of growing up in the affluent Baltimore ghetto of the rich and privileged. John side stepped all Naomi's subtle probing on his childhood. As the sun fell, and the shadows lengthened, Naomi started the engine and the boat made its way back to the marina at half throttle.

Over the next six months, John budgeted, as much time with Naomi, as he could take away from running the golf course. Naomi fit herself into his schedule. She had decided that she wanted to marry this unusual man. Subtly, she told him what she wanted.

Not being able to draw upon the experience of growing up in a real family, with functioning parents, John had never considered marriage as something that would ever be part of his life. Naomi had changed that.

He recognized that he now wished to spend every free moment he had with her. Sometimes, he stared at her, drinking in her presence as if it were a fine, exquisite wine. If his infatuation with her is love, then he accepted, that he must then love her. If marriage is a natural progression of a relationship, then he should marry her.

He was not blind to the fact that   Naomi had much greater wealth and that he had. There was nothing materially that he could offer her that she either did not now have nor could afford to buy. All he saw that he could do for her was to take on the responsibility of growing her wealth. He felt confident that he could do it faster and safer than she could. She had told him she found the investing to be a both boring and a burden. Unlike her, John loved the challenges of investing. It gave him pleasure to watch investments grow because of his analytical skills.

He finally justified marrying Naomi, by concluding that not only would he relieve her of the burden of investing but with access to her wealth, he could save far more street children, from a short life, than if he did not marry her. John proposed. Naomi accepted. This required that her fiancé now meet her parents.

John liked Howard Green. He found him to be a no nonsense, wealthy, capitalist, who was the son of a wealthy, no nonsense, capitalist. Howard assumed a life of privilege just like his daughter did. He didn't think he was better than others. It had never occurred to him that anyone could be more entitled to such a privileged station in life than himself. He also had never questioned why there were poor, starving children in the world. He accepted that it was the natural order of things, just as monarchs had once believed in the divine right of kings.

Her father found real pleasure in the game of golf. When Naomi told him that she was marrying the new owner of the Benji Beach Golf Club, Howard was not pleased. He had expected her to marry a man of great wealth, someone like himself. Not someone, involved in actually running a business enterprise.

Men like Howard earned their money, by choosing when to buy, sell and hold shares in companies that employed men, like John. It was the skills and hard work of men, like John, who generated the profits, captured the markets and created the capital gains and dividends for the privileged, wealthy elite.

Naomi arranged for her father and John to meet for a round of golf early one Saturday morning. Their love of the game forged a quick bond between them. As they talked, Howard, realized just how much hands-on experience he lacked and how much practical experience John had. It also impressed him that John had achieved what he had without family wealth. Not only had John survived but thrived in a world full of surprises and dangers. Howard gave the union his blessing. In John, he saw a strong man. A man who would protect and grow the family's wealth for future generations.

Naomi's mother, just wanted to see her daughter married, while Naomi was still young enough to give her grandchildren. She smiled and greeted John but, after thirty-five years of marriage, she had no illusions about men. John was no better or worse than a dozen other men her daughter had dated. It pleased her that Naomi had committed herself to establishing a permanent relationship. If the marriage to this poor boy did not work, her daughter would just move on. The mother-of-the-bride began planning the wedding.

The wedding took place on a warm weekend in June, at the beach house, instead of in Baltimore. This had been Naomi's choice. Hundreds of well moneyed friends and relatives filled the hotel rooms in Benji Beach. The ceremony and the reception took place on the beach house's deck. The wedding pictures had a backdrop of sparkling waves.

A local judge, to snag an invitation to the wedding, had begged Naomi's father to officiate. He performed the ceremony with the proper reverence. The wedding pictures took full advantage of the beach. An impressive orchestra played all the standard wedding songs. Some of Naomi's relatives drank too much and embarrassed the family. Bored young cousins, playing tag, shrieked and darted in and out among those on the dance floor.

Matteo Dafina, the golf club's food and beverage manager agreed to be John's best man. The other golf club managers were his ushers. When guests made whispered enquiries about John's relatives not being present, the smug cognoscenti's whispered reply, was that John was a penniless orphan from the West Coast who was marrying Naomi for her money. They gave the marriage a year at most.

As the sun set and the party was still in full swing, the bride and groom left the reception. They drove to Washington to spend their first night, as a married couple, in a luxurious suite at the Ritz-Carlton Hotel. The next afternoon, they flew first class to Los Cabos, Mexico. Naomi had insisted that they book a magnificent one-bedroom suite, on the beach, at the famous, Palmilla Hotel.

From their private patio, they had a magnificent view of the Sea of Cortez. The suite's price stunned John. The honeymoon cost him as much as the pickup truck that he had just purchased for the golf club.

☐

⊠CHAPTER 22

FALL

O n returning from their honeymoon, John and Naomi settled into that day-to-day routine that all marriages fall into. John's apartment at the golf club continued to be his office. Each morning, he made the short commute between the beach house and the golf course. Now, besides his workload at the golf club, he found more and more of his time was being spent managing Naomi's affairs.

With enough of a cash flow to meet all her desires, Naomi had little motivation to manage her surplus funds. John found, that over the previous twelve months, she had accumulated over two million dollars in dividend income. It was just sitting in her bank account, not making enough interest to offset inflation.

When a small private zoo came up for a quick sale on the outskirts of Benji Beach, he pushed Naomi to buy it. The large tract of land it sat on was worth far more than they were asking for the business. It was one of the few amusement destinations that existed within twenty miles. Naomi had no interest in managing it. John found a competent manager to run it for her under his Supervision.

A few months later, the largest bar along the Benji Beach tourist strip came up for sale. John met with the bar's owners and did a complete analysis of its potential. It was losing money but John could see an opportunity. He recommended that Naomi buy it. When she did, he arranged for Matteo Dafina to supervise it.

Matteo upgraded the bar's fixtures and its menu, just as he had done with private dining room at the golf club. He applied the golf club's food and beverage supplier discounts to its purchasing. When Benji Beach Golf Club members found that they could use their membership cards to get a 10% discount at the bar, the bar's sales and profits soared. It was one more reason to buy a golf club membership.

The reality of marriage changed John. A careful planner, he did not believe in leaving any loose ends. Although Naomi would never need his fortune, he still felt that as his life partner, he needed to show his total commitment to her. Under the warm afterglow of the honeymoon, he set up an appointment with his lawyer and to draw up a will that named Naomi as the beneficiary of his estate, less, the fifteen percent, The Sanctuary would receive.

He saw the two of them getting old and grey together. When he revealed this expression of love and total commitment to Naomi, she insisted that she must do the same. A few weeks later, in the same lawyer's office, she signed a will that named Raymond Powell as her sole beneficiary.

Like Naomi, John had also set up a small office in his dressing room at the beach house. Late one evening, as he was reviewing bills and approving payments, Naomi appeared at his dressing room door. She waited until he looked up and noticed her. When he did lookup from his computer, he smiled and greeted her, "Sorry, I guess I haven't been much fun. The zoo and that bar have taken longer to settle than I expected. What can I do for you?"

"Let's get out of Benji Beach. It's spring time. Paris is beautiful in the Spring. Why don't we go?"

"We will, but not right now. I've got some fairway reshaping to do and I want it done right. There's also that real estate development company, I want to buy into. They have contracts and plans and I have to review before we meet. Maybe next month, we could go to Paris."

"Money. Money! Christ, Ray, there's more to life than chasing money. Money's for enjoyment, to provide comfort, new experiences. I swear making money, to you, is like some kind of religion."

Ray looked up at her and realized that their relationship was not as deep as he thought it was. He wondered if there was a meeting place, between their two expectations of life. He paused before he answered her, "Naomi, you've always had money. You can't believe that within seconds it can all disappear. Unless you are on top of things, you can lose it all, just like that." John snapped his fingers loudly before he continued, "I lost one business because I was over confident. I was certain that I was too smart to make a mistake. Well, I'm wiser now, and I sure don't intend to lose another business because I was negligent or unprepared."

Naomi did not appreciate his response. She interpreted it to be a suggestion that she was both spoiled and negligent. She replied, "Funny, but I seemed to have got along just fine before I met you. Let me tell you, that unlike you, I do not intend to sit around counting my money all day. If you want to sit here and count your money, then have fun doing it. I'm going to Paris."

"Naomi, I can't go to Paris right now. You are free to do whatever you want. Go to Paris. I will keep an eye on things for you. If I can get this deal closed sooner, I'll join you in Paris."

Naomi, angry that she could not bend John to her whims, turned and stomped off down the hall to the master bedroom.

As she left, John muttered to himself, "Spoiled Bitch" and then felt badly for having even thought it. Disappointed in her attitude, he returned to the analytical work that he had been doing. It was after midnight when he finally finished.

Quietly, he made his way to the matrimonial bed. Naomi curled away from him, feigning sleep. Let sleeping dogs lie, John thought. Tired, he turned his back to Naomi and was asleep with minutes.

The next morning, he was up before sunrise and on his way to the golf club. Naomi usually opened one eye and wished him a good morning, as she heard him preparing to leave. This morning, she did not acknowledge his departure. As he backed his car out of the garage, he thought to himself that the honeymoon must be over. He assumed that she would be over her pique by the time he got home, later in the day.

When he got home late in the afternoon, Naomi wasn't there. On his desk, she had left a note that said she was on her way to Paris and, if he wanted to join her, then he would find her at La Reserve. John took the note, crumbled it into a ball and tossed it into the wastepaper basket.

The next morning, he dropped by his lawyer's office and signed a new will. The sole beneficiary of his estate would now be The Sanctuary in Taos, New Mexico. He had reached the conclusion that Naomi neither needed, deserved or appreciated his money. The Sanctuary would invest it to benefit of thousands of children.

Naomi returned home two weeks later. When John got home from work, she greeted him with a kiss. He put his arms around her and held her. She told him how she had missed him and was so disappointed that he had not joined her in Paris. John did not want to justify his behavior, so he said nothing. They made love that night but John could feel that their relationship had changed. That special spark was no longer there.

They carried on, both aware of their disappointment in each other. They accepted that relationships were never perfect, and people do not change. John continued to invest her money and his own, buying more and more businesses and properties in the area. With ever more income to invest and more enterprises to manage, he worked even longer hours. Ever greater amounts were being forwarded by him to The Sanctuary. Unbeknownst to Naomi, income from her investments were being included in the cash shipments being mailed to New Mexico each month.

The only selfish pleasure he now indulged in, was painting seascapes. He did these in his office at the golf course, late at night. Naomi knew of it. She concluded, by his absences, that painting now satisfied him more than she did. Naomi was often asleep when he returned at night.

He tried to make Naomi happy. They took a Baltic cruise. John had to end it in St Petersburg, Russia when one of his deals started to fall apart. He flew home and left Naomi on the ship to complete the cruise.

Naomi could not believe he had left her. She could not understand, why the more money John made, the more John worried about losing it. While his wealth was a small fraction of her wealth, he had enough invested that he no longer needed to work. If he should ever need money all he needed to do was ask her for some. She would never have hesitated in providing him with anything he might want. Watching him get into the taxi, taking him to the St. Petersburg airport, she had felt rejected and angry.

That evening, the ship left St. Petersburg for Helsinki. Abandoned and depressed, she drank too much wine at dinner, followed by too many vodkas at the floor show. When later that evening she reached the nightclub, on the top deck, she continued to drink. A six-piece band was playing slow, romantic music. Couples were dancing and laughing, enjoying life to the fullest. This made her feel even more sad and lonely.

As she sat at the bar, a tall, well-dressed man approached. He paused and took the stool next to her. She could feel his eyes on her but she ignored him. He leaned towards her and enquired, "Naomi Green?"

"Yes?" Naomi responded, surprised that this stranger knew her name.

"I thought it was you. You probably don't remember me. We were in the same economics class at Harvard."

Naomi peered at him and hesitantly replied, "Bob, Bobby Hollander? You look older."

Bob Hollander laughed and in a pleased voice said, "You do remember me. Yes, I am older. How would you like to dance?"

She held him tight as they danced. He liked being held tight. Unlike John he didn't want to leave her. If she couldn't be John's center of attention, then she would settle for the first person who would give her the undivided attention, she craved. It was close to two in the morning when Bob Hollander walked her back to her suite. She invited him in for a nightcap. One thing led to another.

She woke up in the morning, curled naked, next to Bob. It turned out that Bob also had his challenges. His wife had left him two months before they were to leave on the cruise. He was on the cruise because he had paid for it and couldn't get a refund. Until the cruise ended in Copenhagen, the two of them were inseparable.

Naomi learned that Bob had completed a law degree after his MBA and was now a lawyer for a large corporation in Washington. The company managed a restricted database for the federal government.

When they parted at the airport in Washington, he suggested that he could be down to Benji Beach in a little over two hours. The idea excited Naomi. It made her feel alive. She thought about how she could arrange it.

The weekends were John's busiest time. Naomi rarely saw him from Thursday until Tuesday. Sometimes he would sleep in his apartment at the golf club. For Naomi, weekends were her time to indulge in her selfish love of being on the water. She would take the boat out and make her way to some quiet, deserted cove. Sometimes by herself, but often she would invite friends to join her. Few people turned down a chance to spend a pleasant time on a yacht, drinking and eating the yacht owner's food and drinking her fine wine.

While she had schooled John in operating the boat, and he was a quick learner, he had no passion for the water. She accepted that he was from the dry South-West and only accompanied her on the boat to keep her happy. On the boat, he would pace the deck, like a caged animal, expressing his eagerness to get back on dry land to manage their money.

When Bob phoned her a few days after they got back, she asked if he wanted to spend the weekend with her. Bob responded that he would love to. The first time not want tongues wagging about her at her own yacht club, she met him up the coast at the Nanoose River Yacht Club.

They fell into a routine. Bob would leave his office late on Friday afternoons and drive back to Washington early in the morning on Mondays. As Naomi's affection for Bob grew and the weekend liaisons became more and more routine, she no longer cared what the boating people at her own yacht club thought. Naomi had reached that point, where she did not care whether Raymond learned about her affair or not. Being wealthy and privileged, she felt divorce had become an attractive option. She did not need Raymond Powell in her life.

About ten, on Monday morning, Naomi got a call on her cell phone. It was Bob, "Hi Darling."

"Good morning lover. How was your drive home?"

"No problem. I was sitting at my desk by eight o'clock."

"You were just great last night."

"Not as good as you. Unfortunately, I've got to go to a meeting Friday evening, but I can leave early on Saturday morning. Would you like that?"

"Oh yeah, we could take the boat up to the cove. There is something I want to explore. If you know what I mean."

"What about Raymond?"

"Don't worry about Raymond. A gallery in Dover is having a show of his paintings this weekend. He's going up Friday afternoon and won't be back until late Sunday.

"Doesn't he wonder what you do on that boat by yourself?"

"As long as I stay away from his business, he doesn't give a damn what I do on that boat, or anything else. Sometimes, he forgets I even exist. Thanks to you, I realize what a mistake I made in marrying him. I emailed my lawyer this morning. He is setting me up with the top divorce lawyer in the state. I should have listened to my father and got a prenuptial agreement. That bastard may walk away with half of what I've got."

"I can't say that I'm surprised that you will finally divorce him. Too bad about your investments."

"Mind you, he's invested my money well, so I probably won't lose much. He's put it into some weird investments, but they have certainly paid off. Did you know, he bought that small zoo on the edge of town? Raymond says the land is worth a fortune. Got to go. Love you, Bobby. Meet me at the boat by seven, Saturday morning. Can you get there by then, so we can leave before the wind picks up?"

"No problem, I'll get to bed early enough on Friday night and leave D.C. at four in the morning. That way I'll miss all the traffic on the Chesapeake Bay Bridge. See you Saturday morning. I love you."

⊠CHAPTER 23

DISCLOSURE

That same morning, in his office at the golf club, John Cross was concentrating on the previous month's financial figures, when his phone rang. He answered it with, "Hello, Powell here."

"Hey Ray, it's Wally Martin here. How's it going?"

When John had expanded beyond his original investment in the golf course and bought more businesses in Benji Beach, it got the attention of the local business leaders. Soon they had him on the Tourist and Accommodation committee of the Chamber of Commerce. Several times they asked him to run for president of the Chamber. He rejected such overtures because he was worried that a higher profile might come to the attention of those who were still searching for him. He believed that the interested parties in Las Vegas would never give up their hunt.

It was important that the local businesses leaders have a good relationship with the local constabulary. Walter K. Martin was the local Chief of Police. This sounded impressive until you learned the police force comprised Wally and ten other permanent employees. In the high season he added another fifteen temps. John, like other business owners, had gone out of his way to establish a friendship with Wally.

The golf club employees understood that Wally's was not expected to pay for anything at the club. They were to treat him like royalty. Wally wasn't stupid. He did not take advantage of John's generosity. He made sure the police force turned a blind eye to minor infractions. John never got a parking ticket or a speeding ticket. Late night noise complaints by the club's neighbors were ignored. Wally looked for every opportunity to ingratiate himself with the town's power structure. The townspeople considered John to be the richest and most powerful businessman in Benji Beach.

John responded to Wally with, "Catch any murderers today?"

Wally just laughed at John's humorous dig, like good buddies do when they tease each other. He replied, "Ray, this place is so dead tonight that I think it's time I raided the bootlegger and got some booze for the weekend."

John knew that Wally was only half kidding about how he got his free booze. He wondered what nugget of information Wally had for him. His calls were not frequent, and he usually had confidential information that no one else was privy to. To speed thing up, John asked, "To what, do I owe the pleasure of this call?"

"I'm afraid I've got some bad news for you Ray."

"Yeah, what's that."

"You ever hear of a friend your wife, by the name of Bobby?"

"No, can't say I have."

Well, I happened to overhear a conversation between him and your wife on my scanner, while I was staking out a drug dealer."

John knew there was no drug dealer. Crime in Benji Beach was boring. Wally relieved his boredom by listening in on private cell phone conversations. He responded with "Yeah."

"I don't like being the bearer of bad news and, I'm not sure if I should pass this onto you, but if it were me, I would want to know." Wally paused, leaving the bait hanging in the air, waiting for a cue from John before he continued.

"What news Wally?" His voice had become flat and hard. All the humor had evaporated from it.

"Apparently, Naomi will be meeting with a divorce lawyer."

"Really."

"Yeah, and she is meeting this Bobby guy Saturday morning at seven at her boat. They are going up to some cove. Apparently, you've got an art show up in Dover and you will not be back until Sunday."

There was dead air. Wally wondered if John had hung up. He asked, "Ray, you still there?"

"Thanks for the heads-up Wally. I owe you. What night are you off this week?"

"Tomorrow."

"Make sure you and Trish drop around to Matteo's for drinks and dinner. Try one of those giant steaks. I've reserved it right now."

"You don't have to do that. We're friends."

"I do, because we are friends. Would a seven o'clock reservation be good for you? If I can't treat my friends, then what is the point of my hard work. I'm sure I can show Naomi that she is making a big mistake."

"Thanks a lot Ray. That's really generous of you."

"I appreciate you keeping an eye out for me. You take care, Wally. Bye."

John placed the phone in its cradle. In the quiet stillness of his office, he faced this sudden threat. He felt he was back on the mean streets of Los Angeles where disrespect called for retaliation. His dedication, to saving thousands of lost children, was too important to allow for such obstructions. Too many children depended upon him saving them. While Naomi was frivolous and selfish, without a real purpose in her life, her money could save thousands of children. He was not about to allow her to pursue a divorce.

First, he had to verify what Wally Martin had just told him. Wally had always supplied him with accurate information, but this was too important to act on without verification. How might he do that? He looked at his watch. It was eleven-thirty. This was Naomi's bridge day. She would soon leave the house and would not return until late afternoon.

At noon, John left the golf club and returned to the beach house. In the beach house, he went to Naomi's dressing room and switched on her computer.

Naomi lacked John's systematic patience to solving problems with a PC. It seemed every month John would have to re-establish her connection between the computer and her laser printer.

He entered her password. The computer opened, and he started to read her email.

Not only was Naomi careless, but she rarely filed or deleted anything. It took John only seconds to find the email confirming her appointment with the divorce lawyer in Wilmington. He skipped over several affectionate emails from Bobby.

Having confirmed Wally's information, a plan took shape in his creative mind. He crossed through the bedroom to his own dressing room and turned on his own computer. He clicked onto the Craig's List app and entered a search for motorcycles in Washington, D.C. Within an hour, he had appointments with two sellers for the next day.

The following morning, carrying a small gym bag containing a black sweat suit and black canvas shoes, he walked over to the golf club's equipment garage and got the keys to one of the half-ton pickup trucks. In a pile of discarded lumber, at the back of the hut, he found an eight-foot long, sturdy, plank that he threw in the back of the pickup. He put the gym bag on the seat beside him.

On the drive to Washington, all he could think about was how Naomi's leaving him would diminish the monthly flow of money he was sending to The Sanctuary. Children would suffer and die because of her decision. She had given him no choice. He had to remove this threat to the survival of thousands of street children. His motivation was the guilt, he would feel, if he did not do everything possible to maintain the flow of funds to The Sanctuary. John could not allow her to end the marriage by divorce.

The first seller with a motorcycle for sale was in a row house just East of 16th Street North West in Washington. John parked the truck out of sight more than a block away. He walked back to the house, climbed the porch steps and rang the doorbell. A squat, middle aged woman answered the door. She scowled at him. She didn't look like a biker. John wondered if he had the wrong address. He asked, "You've got a dirt bike for sale?"

Without answering him, she turned towards the interior of the house and yelled out in a grating, thick, Italian accent, "Vittorio, it's a for a you."

She went back into the house. A few minutes later, a bearded brute appeared at the door. He was devouring a bright green Granny Smith apple that hid in the palm of his huge hand. It looked like he was eating his fist. He was wearing a blue work shirt, like mechanic's wear in garages, with "Vitto" embroidered on the pocket. John judged him to be at least six foot four and over three hundred pounds. His greasy, brown hair was long and shaggy. He looked down at John and mumbled," Are you the guy who phoned about the bike?"

"Yeah."

"It's around back in the garage. Come in. You've got to go through the house."

He led John through a living room stuffed with ugly upholstered furniture, covered in clear plastic. Past a crowded dining room into the kitchen. The mother was stirring something in a pot that smelled sweet and of tomatoes. They stepped down three steps to an outside door. It opened to a walkway leading to the garage, flush to an alley way that ran from one street to another, behind the row houses.

The brute opened a door into the old, red brick garage. A shiny Honda CRF25OOL motorcycle was in the center of the garage. To John it looked in good condition. He checked it for any cracks or dents. The chain and sprockets weren't corroded or worn. When he sat on it and compressed the forks, they gave firm resistance.

He asked if he could take it for a test run. The brute reached into his blue jeans, fished out a key and handed it to John. He then pushed up the garage door and watched John climb unto the motorcycle, kick up the stand and push it, with his feet, to the open door. He then engaged the motor. It started with a roar and settled into a gentle purr. , John took it out into the alley. He circled the block and came down the alley from the opposite end. The Brute waited for John's buying signal.

John smiled and said, "I'll take it."

The brute replied as if expecting an argument "It's $4,500 dollars' cash?"

"Yeah, I know, I saw the ad."

Reaching into the zippered left pocket of his jacket, John took out a roll of one hundred-dollar bills and peeled them off. He made stacks of ten, on top of a forty-five-gallon drum, that was in a corner of the garage. The brute gathered up each pile as John started the next pile. John wondered if the brute might try to rob him of the rest of the roll after he had finished laying out the whole $4,500.

John had put his small, PM9, 9 mm, Kahr in the other pocket of his jacket. The zipper was down, so he could retrieve the weapon if needed. You could never be too careful.

The brute smiled. He had perfect teeth and his wide smile showed his pleasure with the transaction. With the money counted, he stuck out a gigantic paw and shook John's hand. John waited a few seconds to see if the brute would bring up transferring ownership of the bike but he just stood there smiling.

John climbed on the bike and returned to his truck. He took out the plank and used it as a ramp to wheel the bike into the truck's cargo box. As he pulled away from the curb, he concluded that the bike must have been stolen.

The second motorcycle, that John wished to buy, was on a street off Pennsylvania Avenue, south of the Anacostia River bridge. It was a quiet, leafy, residential street of century old, run down mansions converted into rental units. The house he wanted was on a corner with a four-foot chain link fence around it. Once again, he parked the truck out of sight.

He walked back to the house and opened the gate. The walkway led to a small covered porch. There were two door bells. He pressed the one for apartment two and waited. He heard footsteps thumping down a set of stairs inside the house. The door opened and a tall, thin, long haired man, who looked like a college student, was staring at him.

"I phoned you earlier about the motorcycle you have for sale?"

"A lot of people phone and say they are coming but they don't."

"Yeah, well I'm here."

"The motorcycle is around back."

He led John to the back of the house. The motorcycle was under a blue plastic tarpaulin, tied down with a bright yellow rope. The seller undid the bindings. It was a Yamaha V-Star 250.

John went through the same inspection routine as he had with Honda except this time, he remembered to lift the seat and checked the battery for corrosion. He wheeled the bike down the walkway to the street, climbed on and rode it down a block and returned. It met his requirements.

"You want $4,100 for it?", he asked the vendor.

"I'll take $4,000."

"OK, $4,000 it is."

Once again, there was no mention of changing the Department of Motor Vehicle's registration. John wondered if all the motorbikes on Craig's List were stolen. He counted out the $4,000 and then rode the bike back to the truck. Once loaded it into the box, he tied it down beside the other bike. Anxious to beat Washington's afternoon traffic he headed back to Delaware.

⊠CHAPTER 24

PREPARATION

The 595 Expressway led John north and east out of the Washington. The Chesapeake Bay Bridge took him across the bay to Stevensville, Maryland. In the steamy hot summers, it can sometimes take hours to cross the bridge when thousands of Washington and Baltimore residents want to escape to Delaware's cooler east coast beaches. Across the bridge, the two-lane roads meander across fields and through small Delaware towns.

Two hours later, he reached an army surplus store on highway 8 just outside Dover, Delaware. He hoped to find two dark green tarpaulins. Something better was found, light-weight, nylon mesh, camouflage netting that snipers used. They were just large enough to hide the motorcycles and were a bargain at fourteen dollars each. Two motorcycle helmets were also bought. His purchases were thrown onto the seat beside him as he drove to a nearby sporting goods store to purchase two, fifty pound, dumbbells and two small gym bags to put them in. It took him two trips to carry the weights to the truck.

With his purchasing completed, he headed for the Blue Buoy Hotel on the outskirts of Dover. This was where his gallery had arranged for a special showing of his paintings. There was to be an opening reception on Friday night and viewing Saturday from eleven in the morning until nine at night. The gallery owner had assured him that the show would make money. She expected to sell all twenty of John's latest seascapes.

John role was to be one of smiling and greeting potential collectors as they arrived. Most of them, he suspected, were more interested in the free wine and canapes than his paintings. Not that this bothered him. It wasn't about making money. It was more the pleasure any artists get when someone, other than themselves, see the magic in their paintings.

He pulled off the North Dupont Highway at the entrance to the hotel and checked his mileage. Back on the roadway, he drove past the hotel until he found a dirt road leading into a wooded area. It was a half mile from the hotel. He drove in far enough that the thick, foliage, hid him from the highway. At a small clearing, he got out, let down the tailgate and used the heavy plank to unload a motorcycle. He pushed it into a thicket. Next, he fetched a sniper veil and a helmet. He placed the helmet on the motorcycle seat and draped the sniper veil over the bike. He raised each wheel and used them to anchor the veil in place. Unless someone tripped over the motorcycle, he believed there was little chance that anyone would discover the motorcycle before he came back for it.

With a single motorcycle now remaining, in the back of the truck, he headed south from Dover on Coastal Highway One. Just south of Milford, he took the Fowler Beach Road east into the Prime Hook National Wildlife Reserve. The road terminated, at a deserted beach, with not a building in sight. Miles away, on the ocean's horizon, he could see large ships passing.

In the parking lot, he unloaded the second motorcycle and rode it down the beach, keeping on the hard-packed sand, just above where the waves lapped on the beach. At a large thicket, he pushed the bike into the middle of it, draped the sniper veil over it, the helmet and a plastic bag containing a black sweat shirt, pants and black canvas shoes. As he walked back to the truck, he noticed the incoming tide had already washed away the tire marks he had left in the sand.

The hard part was over. He relaxed and stayed within the speed limit as he headed south to Naomi's yacht club. His entry card opened the club's gate. He drove in and parked the truck.

John walked past the club house, down to the docks. Here, he found the carts; the boaters use to transport supplies between their cars and their boats. He pushed a cart, loaded with the two gym bags containing the dumbbells to Naomi's boat.

Due to the size of her boat, it was in one of the furthest slips from the club house. This allowed her to enter and exit without having to maneuver in the narrow channels between the docks.

John climbed on board the boat, with one of the gym bags. He used the key, Naomi had insisted on giving him, to enter the cabin and make his way to a small stateroom. Naomi had not set foot in that stateroom for months, possibly years. He hid the first dumbbell in a small closet. When he returned with the second dumb bell, it joined the first. With both stowed, John made his way back to the truck and returned to the golf course. At the golf course, he did paper work and returned phone calls as he waited to complete the last piece of his plan.

Late in the evening, when he felt confident that the small zoo, he had purchased for Naomi, was closed, he drove over to it. A hundred yards from the zoo, on a side street, he parked behind a row of trees that gave him cover.

There was watchman, in a hut at the entry gate in front of the zoo. John knew he was old and arthritic. He rarely left the hut.

John made his way through the trees to the back of the zoo and climbed its chain link fence. He crept over to the back door of the zoo's administration building. With his access key, he entered the building. He switched on a small flashlight. In the veterinarian's office, he found the air pistols and a box of tranquilizer darts he knew were stored there. Putting them in a plastic shopping bag, he left. A lion's roar pierced the silence of the night as he made his way back to his car.

It took only a few minutes to drive to the beach house. He entered the house, made his way to the bedroom and climbed into bed. Naomi did not wake. She snored without a care in the world, unaware of what John Cross had planned for her.

⊠CHAPTER 25

RECKONING

Friday morning, John, made sure, he was up, showered and out of the house before Naomi was out of bed. He didn't want to see her. On the refrigerator door, he left a note for Naomi that he would be back in the late afternoon to pack before he left for the Dover art show reception. If she wanted to attend the reception, she should phone him. John knew she had no interest in attending.

When he came back in the afternoon, Naomi was out. She had scrawled on the note, "Thanks for the invitation but I have other plans. See you on Sunday when you get back. Hope you sell all your paintings."

He checked the garage to see which of their six cars she had taken. It pleased him that she had not taken the Mercedes Benz E350 convertible. A flashy, memorable car was important for the next step in his plan. After putting the top down, he threw his small carryon bag in the tiny trunk.

To reach Highway One, took longer than expected. The Friday afternoon migration, from Washington and Baltimore had already begun. Benji Beach was a popular destination in this summer.

There was very little northbound traffic, but the southbound traffic was bumper to bumper and would remain that way until late in the evening. John expected the flow would reverse on Sunday afternoon when he was supposed to be on his way home. He was in no big hurry to get to Dover.

An hour later he reached the Blue Buoy Hotel and found a parking spot in front of the reception area. When he signed in, he made a point of saying to the desk clerk, "Is my Mercedes safe out front?"

He pointed to the car. The desk clerk, thinking he was a pretentious jerk, looked where John pointed and politely replied, "There should be no problem, Mister

Powell. We will keep an eye on it for you. A security camera scans the parking lot. However, I would recommend that you put the top up because it may rain tonight."

As the clerk was processing his credit card, John left his bag at the reception and went back out and put the top up on the car. When he came back, he received the electronic key card for his room. He noticed the room number, on the little envelope the card was in, and enquired, "This isn't on the ground floor, is it?"

"No sir, it is on the top floor."

"I reserved a room on the ground floor?"

"No problem, Mister Powell, your request did not come up when I looked at your reservation."

The clerk checked his computer and said, "We do have a suite on the first floor available, at the end of the hall. It has a very nice patio that looks out on the woods. Would that be suitable?"

"That would be perfect. Could I get a wake-up call at nine-thirty tomorrow morning?"

"No problem. Is there anything else we can do for you?"

"Where would I find the Green Lantern Room? Apparently, that is where we are holding our reception, this evening."

"It's at the opposite end of the first-floor corridor from your suite."

With his new access card in hand, John trudged down to the end of a long corridor. The suite had a sliding glass door that opened to a small patio with a low privacy hedge around it. A lounge and a table with two chairs were on the patio. There were no houses behind the hotel. He would have no problem with anyone seeing him when he exited by the patio.

The gallery owner, who was managing the show, had invited him to dinner. John changed into an open neck shirt, dress pants and a sports coat. He then made his way to the dining room that was off the lobby.

Hazel was already waiting for him. She was a thin, middle aged, blonde with a face like a hatchet and hair color from a bottle. Her husband, and business partner, had died a few years ago, but she had carried on. Like most galleries, hers had seen better days. With artists able to make direct contact with collectors, through the internet, physical galleries had lost an advantage.

John did not have the time to direct market his paintings via the internet. Hazel took fifty percent of any painting she could sell. She was expecting at least two hundred people, most from within an hour's drive, to come to the viewing. The show would close by ten o'clock that evening and open again at eleven in the morning on Saturday. She hoped most of the sales would be made at this evening's reception.

At seven o'clock, they opened the exhibition. Two clients were already waiting by the door. Hazel greeted them with hugs and kisses. John smiled politely and answered their questions about his seascapes. The hotel had prepared trays of inexpensive cheeses, stale crackers and fruit. A cheap California wine provided the necessary lubrication.

It seemed the early arrivals had brought their appetite with them. They descended on the refreshments that Hazel and John were splitting the cost on. After gorging themselves, the free loaders began a slow tour of the room, pausing in front of each painting and staring at them. John wondered what they were thinking or if they were thinking at all.

Much to John's surprise, before seven-thirty he had sold one medium sized painting for $4,000. This sale would cover their expenses for the show. At ten o'clock, they called it a night. John locked the exhibition room and told Hazel he was tired and was going to bed. The agreed to meet for breakfast and open the exhibition room just before eleven the next morning.

After placing a do-not-disturb sign on the outside door knob, John undressed and got into bed. He set the bedside alarm clock for three-thirty in the morning. With all the things that could go wrong with his plan playing out in his mind, he had trouble falling asleep. When the alarm went off, it woke him out of a deep sleep. Wide awake, he washed the sleep out of his eyes before he opened his carryon bag and dressed in a swim suit, black hoody sweat shirt and black sweat pants. He pulled on black socks and his soft soled, black canvas shoes. In the pocket of the sweat shirt he inserted the tranquillizer gun and four of the tranquilizer darts that he had taken from the zoo. With the lights off, he opened the patio door, crossed the patio and went through the hedge. With the hoody covering his head, he disappeared into the shadows at the back of the hotel.

It was the dead of night, even all the party animals were asleep. While he could not hear any traffic on the highway, he still kept well away from it. When he was out of sight of the hotel, he returned to the roadway and walked along its shoulder until he reached the dirt road a half mile south of the hotel. No cars had come by, in either direction, during the ten-minute walk.

At night, things look different from what they do during the day. There was just enough reflected light from the clouds for him to make out where he was going. In his eagerness to find the motorcycle, he twice went looking for it in the wrong bushes. On the third try, he found the bike by banging his knee on it. He pulled off the sniper veil that had covered it and left it draped on the bushes so he could find it later. The helmet that he had left under the veil fit tightly. In a few seconds, he had rolled the bike out to the dirt road. It started it with a mighty roar that shattered the silence of the night. He flicked on the headlight and drove out to the highway, turned right and headed south.

With the bike vibrating between his legs, he twisted the throttle and blasted down the highway, anxious to reach his destination before the sun came up. In forty-five minutes, he was approaching the last bridge, just before Naomi's yacht club. He slowed down and steered the bike to the side of the road. In the far eastern horizon, the sky was turning from inky black to the first grey hints of dawn. With the headlamp turned off, he rolled the bike to the bridge's concrete footings and gave it a shove. There was a mighty splash when the motorcycle hit the water. By the light from a street light he saw it float for a while before the incoming tide, coursing through the narrows, pushed it westward. Soon, the bike sunk into the depths, well beyond the bridge.

Under the cover of night, he crossed the bridge and climbed the marina's chain link fence. Everything was quiet. When he reached the main dock, his footsteps thumped loudly on the wooden deck. He slowed his pace and moved more quietly.

On reaching Naomi's boat, he swung onto it, took out his key and opened the hatch door. He entered the cabin and locked the hatch behind him. With a small flash light to guide him, he made his way through the dark passageway to the cabin where he had stowed the weights. With his boots, still on, he lay down on the bunk and waited for Naomi to arrive. An internal mental battle was being fought between fulfilling his duty, like a good soldier for The Sanctuary, and his fear of the consequences, if caught. He had not expected to sleep but the soft bed, the darkness, the gentle rocking of the boat and the quiet of the night was too hard to resist.

⊠CHAPTER 26

OVERBOARD

When Naomi arrived at the boat at six thirty, her footsteps on the deck above, woke him, with a start. It took a few moments for reality to rush in, then he was awake. A half hour later he heard heavier footsteps on the deck and a muffled conversation between Naomi and, he presumed, Bobby. The diesel engine roared to life. John could feel the engine's vibration as he lay on the bed.

The cruiser slipped its moorings and made its way out of the marina. When the vessel was clear of the Marina, Naomi pushed the throttle forward and John could feel the boat's bow lift, slapping the waves, as it sped north into Delaware Bay.

John knew it would take almost an hour for Naomi to reach the quiet cove she liked to go to. A half hour into their journey, John loaded the tranquilizer gun and stuck it into his belt. He crept out of the cabin into the open cockpit. The roar of the engine and the waves slapping against the hull masked the sound of his approach.

Naomi and Bobby were sitting side-by-side on the bridge, in the twin captain's chairs, staring straight ahead. Naomi, at the helm, was concentrating on the boat's course. They were oblivious to his presence five feet behind them. John aimed the tranquilizer gun. The gentle pop of the air gun was not heard above the roar of the thousand-horsepower diesel engine. Bobby's hand reached up, to slap at his neck, where the dart had embedded, as if a mosquito had just stung him. As the drug coursed through his body, he reached out to grasp the dashboard, as he slowly collapsed to the deck.

Naomi, still staring through the windscreen, for several seconds did not notice the drama taking place beside her. When she noticed that Bobby had collapsed onto the deck beside her, she pulled back on the throttle. This brought the boat to a stop with the engine idling. John fired a dart into her neck.

Before she too slid, unconscious to the deck, she swiveled around in the captain's chair. Her eyes opened wide with the terror, at seeing him standing there with the air gun in his hand. Her mouth opened, and she tried, but never could ask John, why.

John was concerned that the effects of the tranquilizer might wear off in a few minutes. He quickly returned to the cabin where he had left the weights. Carrying the first weight, he returned to the two unconscious lovers. Using a heavy cord, he had brought with him; he tied Bobby's legs together and then dragged his body to the stern. Here he fastened the weight to the ropes around Booby's legs. The body hardly made a splash when he pushed it overboard.

It wasn't until he had completed this task that he considered the possibility that he might be under observation. He scanned the ocean in all directions. It was still early in the morning. There were no other boats nearby. He estimated that they were at least two miles off the Delaware shore line. The idling boat was being rocked by a rising morning breeze.

He went down to the cabin to fetch the second weight. Returning, he removed the life vest that his wife was wearing. It would have inflated as soon as she hit the water. He threw it overboard, watched it inflate and float away. Next, he tied Naomi's legs together, just as he had tied Bobby's. Dragged to the back of the boat, he tied the weight to her feet and pushed her limp body overboard. When her body hit the water, he could have sworn that he saw her eyes open wide with horror.

John now moved to the helm and checked the GPS. Using the automatic pilot, he plotted a course that would take him up the coast to the Prime Hook National Wildlife Reserve. He put the engine in gear, pulled back on the throttle and the boat followed the course.

It was just after eight in the morning when the boat reached the wildlife reserve. As it idled and rolled on the swells, a hundred feet off shore, he shed his sweat pants, shirt and shoes and threw them overboard. This left him in only the bathing suit he had been wearing underneath the sweat pants.

The boat's automatic pilot was set on a new course that would take the boat south east, down Delaware Bay into the Atlantic Ocean. He set a moderate speed. As the boat began to move; he dived into the water and swam ashore. A few minutes later, he was staggering out of the water and crossing the beach to where he had stashed the second motorcycle. Pulling off the sniper's veil, he put on the black sweat pants, shirt and shoes he had left on the seat. With the motorcycle helmet on, it would be impossible for any passerby to identify him.

When he hit the starter, the motorcycle roared to a start. The bike was guided along the hard-packed edge of wet sand, until he got to where the road met the beach. Roaring west up Fowler Beach Road he headed to Coastal Highway One and then followed the highway north until he was a half mile south of the Blue Buoy Hotel. Taking the same dirt road off the highway, that he had exited from a few hours ago, he hid the bike under the sniper veil that he had left hanging in the bushes.

He walked back to the hotel, staying away from the road as much as possible. With the sweatshirt's hood pulled over his head, it would be impossible for anyone, he might encounter, to identify him. He entered his suite through the unlatched patio door. It was just before nine o'clock.

It took him twenty minutes to shower and shave. He was ready for the front desk's wake-up call at nine-thirty. Finishing that call, he dressed in a hound's tooth sports coat over a black turtle neck and black slacks. He was aiming for an artsy image, to match the expectations of the prospective collectors, who were coming to see his seascapes. Doing a final check in the full-length mirror, he made his way to the dining room for breakfast.

As he passed through the lobby, the desk clerk bid him a good morning and earned goodwill for the hotel by telling John they had kept a close eye on the Mercedes all night. John thanked him. It pleased him that the hotel had helped establish his presence at the hotel.

In the dining room, he found Hazel, the gallery owner, sipping a coffee.

"May I join you?", he asked playfully.

"You may. Did you sleep well?"

"No. I had a hard time getting to sleep."

"You look tired."

"Oh, I'm okay. It is not my first restlessness night."

"It is probably excitement over the show that kept you awake."

"Yes, that must be it."

The waitress came and took John's order. Hazel kept on looking at her watch. John ate quickly and paid the bill. They made their way to the Green Lantern Room.

It was close to three o'clock in the afternoon when John looked up and was surprised to see Wally, Benji Beach's police chief, enter the Green Lantern Room with a very serious look on his face. He made his way to John. Everyone turned to stare at the uniformed police officer.

"Hi Wally, I didn't know you were an art lover."

"Sorry Raymond, but I've got some bad news."

"What news?"

"The coast guard found Naomi's boat dead in the water in the two-way traffic corridor south of Cape May."

With great horror, John responded, "Is Naomi Okay?"

"We don't know. There was no one onboard. The Cape May coast guard station had received calls from ship traffic that it was a danger to shipping. The coast guard phone me as soon as they determined where it was registered. They've told me they are assuming she has been lost at sea but they are out looking for her. I went by your house, just to verify that Naomi wasn't there. Not finding anyone there and knowing you had this art show, I drove up, to let you know."

Billy paused before he asked John, "Do I assume you know nothing about her disappearance?"

"No nothing, she wasn't there when I came home in the afternoon yesterday. I packed and left, maybe twenty minutes later. She had left a note on the refrigerator door, wishing me well. I'm sure it is probably still on the refrigerator door. The yacht club should know when she took her boat out. I assume it was this morning." John lowered his voice and leaned closer to Billy, "I know you told me her friend Bobby was coming to visit her, but believe me, I've got nothing to do with her disappearance. The hotel can confirm that I haven't left the here since I arrived yesterday afternoon."

"I wasn't suggesting anything, but I had to ask. She's a wealthy socialite. You should expect to be under a microscope. I phoned her father and let him know. He said he was leaving immediately for the Coast Guard station"

"I need to get down there too."

"If you leave now, you should be able to catch the 4:15 ferry across the Bay."

"I better go get my stuff and check out."

"Can I do anything for you?"

"Nothing that I can think of."

"OK, then. I've got to get back to Benji Beach. You'll soon know more about what is going on with the search than me but if I do hear something, I'll contact you. Sorry that I was the bearer of such bad news."

"Wally, thanks for coming and telling me in person."

They shook hands. Wally left.

Hazel approached John and asked him what was going on. He told her the bad news and said that he had to leave. She told him that she understood. In ten minutes, he had packed, paid his bill and was driving down the highway to Lewes, Delaware to catch the ferry to Cape May, New Jersey.

Wally waited, in a remote corner of the parking lot, until John had left the hotel. He then went back and nosed around. The desk clerk confirmed that Raymond Powell's car had been under constant observation, since the previous afternoon, and it had never moved until the departure a few minutes ago. He also told Wally that he had made a wake-up call to John, at nine-thirty, and had seen Raymond Powell go into breakfast a few minutes later.

Wally asked for the key to John's room. He searched it but found nothing interesting. The room had not been cleaned. The bed was still unmade. He went back to the art gallery's rented exhibition room. Hazel was still in it. She told Wally that last evening John had said he was tired and had returned to his room around ten o'clock.

Wally returned the room key to the desk clerk and asked to see the video from the hallway security cameras. The cameras covered the area between the reception room and Raymond Powell's suite. Watching the video, he saw Raymond go into his room around ten at night and emerge in the morning on his way to the dining room. Satisfied that Raymond Powell had never left the hotel, Wally got into his police care and headed back to Benji Beach.

John arrived at the ferry just as it was being loaded. He paid the fee and joined the line of cars entering the ferry's parking deck. Once the ferry got under way, he left the car on the parking deck, and climbed the steps up to a lounge full of noisy tourists. He bought a beer and sat by a large window, looking out over Delaware Bay.

Lost in thought, he considered the events of the last twenty-four hours. He wondered if soldiers, sent into battle, to kill those who threatened the assets of the nation, felt the same conflicted remorse that he now felt after they had won the battle.

It took more than an hour to make the seventeen-mile crossing. As they approached the flat, low New Jersey coast, a bell rang followed by an announcement that the passengers should now return to their vehicles and prepare to disembark.

The Coast Guard station wasn't far from the ferry terminal. It was a large installation. He learned later that hundreds of coast guard officers did their training here. The guard, at the gate, directed him to the station's commanding officer

The commander brought John up to date on what had so far been an unsuccessful search. John asked whether it was possible that Naomi might have stopped to rescue someone, fallen overboard, and then been unable to get back on the boat?"

"That's possible," the commander replied then speculated that the vessel could have drifted miles beyond where the actual accident might have taken place.

John was invited to wait in the base cafeteria. They would come and get him if they found anything.

John sat drinking a strong coffee in the sterile, quiet cafeteria, looking very much like the bereaved husband. The door to the cafeteria opened and Naomi's mother and father joined him. Saying nothing, John embraced his mother-in-law who gently cried on his shoulder. He did his best to comfort her and then shook his father-in-law's hand. This hard, tough executive looked broken. Howard Green feared the worse for his missing daughter and was trying hard not to show it. All the power, his money gave him, mattered little right now. He feared that nothing could bring her back.

As the sun set, the commanding officer came into the cafeteria and informed them, for safety reasons, he had had to call off the search until six the next morning. He suggested John and Naomi's parents seek lodging at the nearby Bedford Inn, just a few blocks away from the base.

As they drove towards the base's gate house, they could see a large crowd gathered around several large white trucks, on the other side of the gate. A guard stepped out of the gatehouse. He waved John over to the side of the road. John lowered his window and asked, "What's going on?"

"Mister Powell?"

"Yes?"

"The media showed up two hours ago."

"Media?"

"Yes sir, your wife's disappearance was reported by the networks. They arrived shortly after. If you like, I can phone the local police to come and escort you to where ever you are going."

"We were just on our way to the Bedford Inn. I understand it is close by."

"It is, but there will be no hotel rooms left at the Bedford or at any other hotels for miles around."

"What would you recommend?"

"When the hotels are full at graduation time, a widow, just outside of town, opens her place to a few guests. It's a nice place. If you like, I could phone her. She's got a long driveway into her farm house that should keep the press away from you. I'll get the local police to escort you to her farm and make sure no one bothers you while you are there."

"Let me talk to my wife's father. He's in the car behind mine. I'll get right back to you."

John got out of his car and went back to talk to Howard, who had his car window down and was peering at John. John described their predicament. Howard agreed that all they wanted was somewhere to sleep and that a farm house would be fine.

As John approached the gate house, to tell the guard, the reporters on the other side of the gate started to shout questions at him. He ignored them. It was a feeding frenzy. The portable flood lights of a television station snapped on. It bathed him in a harsh white light. John stood and waited while the guard phoned Mrs. McGrady, the widow. She agreed to open her farm house to them. The guard assured John that it was only ten minutes away. On a scrap of paper, he drew John a quick map of how to get there.

The guard also phoned the local police. In a few minutes a police cruiser arrived. Its red flashing lights cleared the way to the guard house. The guard raised the gate to allow the cruiser on the base. The constable joined them in the guard house. His plan was to allow John's and Howard Green's cars to leave the base first. The policeman would then drive behind them which would block the press from following them. It was unlikely that any of the reporters would try to pass a police car. Once, John and Howard where out of sight, the constable stopped and waited for the reporters to abandon the chase. He then proceeded to Mrs. McGrady's farm and parked by her gate.

The plan worked well. Howard staying close, behind John's car, followed him up the long driveway. Mrs. McGrady's farm house was old and large. It had an old fashioned, wraparound porch, encircling the lower floor. The clapboards were a sparkling white and the shutters, that frame ever window, a dark, bottle-green. Yard lights, flooding the front yard, indicated that they were welcome and expected.

They went back and forth, between the Coast Guard base and the farm house, for the next three days. At the end of the three days, the base commander told them he was calling off the search. He told them that that they had done a thorough search of Delaware Bay and fifty miles out into the Atlantic. They had concluded that there had been a horrific accident and Naomi Green was now considered lost at sea.

The press made a meal out of Naomi's disappearance. They speculated on sea monsters, pirates and rogue waves as an explanation for it. Exaggerated rumors that Raymond Powell was to inherit hundreds of millions of dollars fueled the story's interest.

Comparisons, to disappearances where husbands paid to have their wealthy wives disposed of were made. The reporters made sure their inferences were vague. They wanted to avoid any legal action by a wealthy, litigious Raymond Powell.

Some reporters went as far as interviewing the staff at the Blue Buoy Hotel. Like the police, their investigation only confirmed John's alibi.

For months, the story got national and even international coverage. The business press reported on it because Naomi was a director of Greenline Automotive, a major corporation, traded on the New York Stock Exchange. The tabloids reported on it because Naomi was rich and photogenic. They displayed pictures of Naomi in provocative bikinis to entice shoppers waiting in line at the supermarket.

As much as John Cross did his best to avoid photographers, most of the stories contained a picture of him. With his shaved his head, beard and glasses, he was confident that no one could match photos of Raymond Powell to the pictures of John Cross in the FBI wanted posters

⊠CHAPTER 27

INHERITANCE

Two weeks, after the coast guard had declared Naomi lost at sea, her parents held a memorial service in Baltimore. On the day before the memorial service, the agent in charge of the FBI investigative team assigned to her disappearance, met with Howard Green. Howard had used all his influence to put pressure on the Director of the FBI to investigate his daughter's disappearance. The agent gave Howard Green, an off the record, unofficial review of their investigation.

He seemed to take pleasure, in telling her father the FBI believed Naomi had had a lover on board the boat with her when she disappeared. They had found his prints when they dusted two half full glasses they found in cup holders on the boat's bridge.

Her father's immediate response to this information was, "Could he have been her killer?"

"It is unlikely. When we ran those prints against our national fingerprint database, we got an unusual hit. The prints belonged to a lawyer by the name of Robert E. Hollander. He was the legal counsel for a contractor that operates one of the government's top-secret databases. He was responsible for approving anyone who wanted access to it. When we contacted his employer, our investigators found they had reported him missing to the Washington police. This led us to visiting your daughter's yacht club. We found Hollander's car in their parking lot. His job demanded such a high security clearance that he was almost always being vetted. When we reviewed his records, we found nothing. His record was remarkably clean, not even a traffic ticket."

The investigating agent established Hollander's connection to Naomi. He told Howard, how both had been, MBA students at Harvard, taking many of the same courses. Rather than being a possible murder suspect, the FBI had concluded Bob Hollander met the same fate as Naomi Green.

Being a frequent visitor on the yacht, it was not surprising the FBI found John Cross' finger prints all over the boat. Prior to starting their investigation, the FBI had taken his prints, so they could eliminate them from the investigation. This avoided the expense to run unnecessary prints against the national fingerprint database. If they had run his prints against that database, they might have discovered the person, they believed to be Raymond Powell, was John Cross, a murderer wanted by the FBI in Nevada.

The FBI agent told Howard Green they had found no blood stains or any other indications of foul play on the boat. Their interviews with Naomi's friends and acquaintances disclosed no conflicts or threats. They also found no evidence that she had chosen to disappear. The only unusual thing their investigation disclosed was this secret relationship with a Robert Hollander. Her friends all reported she had appeared to be happily married to Raymond Powell.

Any sympathy, Howard had for his son-in-law's loss, evaporated after he heard the FBI's conclusions. As he saw it, if his wonderful daughter had taken a lover, then her husband was responsible for her being unfaithful. His sympathy turned into a suspicion that, somehow, John Cross was responsible for her disappearance. When he voiced his suspicion to the FBI agent, the agent assured him witnesses had confirmed that John had never left the hotel where he was exhibiting his paintings. The security cameras, overlooking the hotel's entrance, showed his car had never moved until after the Benji Beach police chief had arrived and informed Raymond Powell of her disappearance. Cameras in the hallway, even showed him going into his room, after the art exhibit closed, late in the evening. They next showed him coming out of his room for his breakfast, in the morning. The staff at the hotel had reported no unusual or suspicious behavior by Raymond Powell.

Howard was more than surprised when he learned from the FBI agent that John was the sole beneficiary of Naomi's will. Until that moment, he had not known Naomi even had a will. This meant John would become the second largest shareholder of Greenline Automotive, second only to him. His daughter had always voted her shares in total harmony with his interests. Now, he saw a threat that John might align with other shareholders. He might even challenge Howard for control of the board of directors and the company.

This was an unforeseen business risk. It would not be to his advantage, to have Naomi declared dead, until he had worked out a solution to this threat to his power. He was confident control of her shares could not be voted until she was declared officially dead and that had to wait until seven years had passed. With no immediate threat, he felt he had plenty of time to resolve any threat to his control of the company.

Howard had a flawed understanding of the law in Delaware. On John's behalf, his lawyer, three months after Naomi's disappearance, applied to the county's probate court to have John appointed conservator of her estate. This application detailed the circumstances under which she went missing, what attempts had been made to locate her and the reasons she would have communicated with John during these last three months if she were still alive. A list of her considerable assets accompanied a statement explaining why John was the petitioner. Within sixty days John was directed to provide a written report that outlined the condition of Naomi's estate. After filing his application, every week, for a month, a notice had to appear in the local newspaper announcing a hearing to be held about the alleged deceased.

Howard Green's lawyer told him what John was doing, was legal and unless Howard had evidence that showed his daughter was still alive there was no point in attending the hearing. As for Howard Green's suspicions that John had somehow caused his daughter's disappearance, his lawyer warned him, if he ever voiced it, defamation charges could be laid against him.

After reviewing the evidence, the judge issued an order that for the next four weeks, his ruling that Naomi was deceased, was to be published in the local newspaper. Three months after that, if there were no challenges to the notices brought before his court, the judge would declare her dead. John as the conservator and only heir would then assume full control of all her assets, including her Greenline Automotive shares.

Seven months later, John moved from being a common, multi millionaire, to joining the ranks of the super rich. He now controlled assets of more than a hundred million dollars. While he had thought that he had had a full knowledge of all of Naomi's assets, he was surprised to find there were multimillion-dollar investments that she had never discussed and may not even have known she had. Managing these investments would require far more effort than he had expected.

After several months of managing her money, it gave John great satisfaction to give his lawyer a locked titanium suitcase. Unbeknownst to the lawyer, it contained a million dollars in cash. He instructed the lawyer to find a trusted courier to deliver the suit case to an address in New Mexico. To avoid going through airport security, the courier would have to drive to New Mexico and back. For arranging this, John advanced $20,000 to the lawyer for the courier and $2,000 for the lawyer's effort in arranging the shipment. Although curious, the lawyer knew better than to question what was in the suitcase.

The lawyer's son, Brent, was home from college and had a few weeks free. When asked if he wanted to make some money for two weeks of work, his son was surprised to find out it would involve driving to New Mexico and back. Two weeks of staying in hotels and seeing the country seemed to him to be a great adventure. His father said he would receive $5,000 for this chore plus all his travel expenses. John's lawyer knew how to make a profit.

Driving on I-70, across the country, it took Brent only three days to reach Taos. He had strict instructions that the suitcase was to be handed to Winston Hawkins and that he was not to disclose who he was nor where he had travelled from.

Winston Hawkins had received a postcard, the day before Brent arrived. It contained six numbers in two groups of three "8-24-3" and "9-21-6". Below the numbers was a one-line message that read, "Greetings from 41 Boulevard Rochechouart, Paris". Winston knew who had sent this card and its importance. He put the postcard in his desk drawer and waited.

The next day, his administrative assistant, looking flustered, interrupted him. She told him that there was a young man in the reception area who said he had a delivery to make but it had to be handed to Winston Hawkins. Winston was not surprised and told her to show him in.

Clutching the suitcase tightly, Brent entered Winston's office. They shook hands and Brent handed him the suitcase. Winston asked him if he had eaten. When he replied that he had not, Winston said that one of his aides would take him to lunch. Brent found the cafeteria to be very much like his own college cafeteria, but the food was better.

When Winston unlocked the combination locks on the suitcase, using the codes John had mailed, he found a short unsigned note from John Cross. It read, "This is the first of many millions. The Sanctuary saved me, and I want to save hundreds of lost children just like I was saved."

Although John was not aware of it, Winston had been monitoring John's circumstances for years. He was very much aware of Naomi's mysterious disappearance and John's inheritance. With so much money at risk, he realized that the time had now come to assign a guardian angel to John Cross. It would have to be someone who would not hesitate to sacrifice his own life to protect The Sanctuary's investment in John Cross. He asked his secretary to fetch Gabriel LaChance.

Gabriel had been a street-smart kid in Paris. In Taos, he showed that he was academically gifted. He had caught up to his age group and moved through all the high school grades in two years. At eighteen he had completed an undergraduate degree. It had then taken him two more years to complete legal studies, do his clinical field placements, externships and pro-bono work.

With John Cross' circumstances in mind, Winston had arranged for Gabriel to complete his five-month clerkship at a prominent, corporate, law office in Wilmington, Delaware. After the clerkship, Gabriel had written the annual Delaware Bar Exam and passed all the required screening procedures. He was now admitted to the Delaware Bar.

That afternoon, Winston met with Gabriel and directed him to proceed to Benji Beach. He was to open a law office and then contact John Cross. Gabriel's bank account received finds to cover the expense.

With the law office in place, Gabriel approached John Cross, early one morning, at a lobster restaurant that he knew John owned and where he knew John usually had his breakfast. Gabriel walked into the restaurant, pushed his way through the swinging doors that led to the kitchen and took a seat in John's private booth in the passageway between the kitchen and the dining room. John was sitting in his booth, reading the local newspaper. Startled by the intrusion into his private space, he put the newspaper down and frowned at the young stranger who was smiling at him. He looked like someone that he knew, but not as he remembered that person. John said indignantly, "Can I help you?",

Gabriel leaned close and whispered, so that only John could hear him, *"Mais oui, Monsieur Cross."*

It was like a slap in the face. Raymond Powell's mask had been torn off his face. John Cross stood there, a naked fugitive. He whispered, "Do I know you?"

"Mais, oui, on the streets of Paris you saved my life."

For several seconds, John was silent, as his past unraveled in his mind. The panic in his eyes disappeared. He smiled and said, "Gabriel? My God, Gabriel, is it really you?"

"C'est moi."

"My God, you were just a kid. Look at you, all grown up. What are you doing here?"

"I was sent to help you, just as you were sent to help me."

"But why?"

"Our leader does not want unknown couriers arriving in Taos with suitcases full of money. He feels that we must establish a more professional arrangement to shelter you and The Sanctuary."

"What does he have in mind?"

"Can we go somewhere, where we can speak freely?"

"Of course, I'm finished. Let's go."

They left the restaurant by the rear entrance and climbed into John's green Porsche. John drove out of town. He pulled, off the highway, into a deserted parking lot by the sea.

They left the car, walked down to the beach and sat on a large log that had washed up during some long-forgotten hurricane. The wind, the cries of the seagulls and the waves lapping onto the sand were the background chorus to Gabriel's message. Far away, from all possibility of their conversation being overheard

Gabriel started the conversation by saying, "You are a fugitive with a large price on your head. Sooner or later, the odds are, someone will determine that you are not Raymond Powell. It is important we do our best to avoid that happening. However, every time you send funds to Taos, you are increasing the possibility that your delivery will be intercepted, and someone will trace it back to you."

John nodded. He had always understood that possibility existed. Gabriel continued, "I am now a qualified, Delaware, lawyer. Anything we now discuss is privileged and falls under the laws governing lawyer-client confidentiality. You and I, see that our purpose in life, is to save lost and abandoned children. Through your business acumen, you have provided The Sanctuary with millions of dollars. It has saved thousands of children. Despite your wealth having grown to over a hundred million dollars, you are still a fugitive. If something were to happen to you, it is important that your millions continue to go towards saving children. We have to make sure these millions are never seized by the government, under their assets-acquired-by-crime laws."

"What are you proposing?"

"I want to create several, interlinked, offshore companies. The Sanctuary will control them, but it will be impossible to connect them to The Sanctuary. I'll make sure this ownership is so well buried only you, me and Winston will understand how it all works. After they are established, you will sell all your assets to these corporations for a nominal fee. It will then be easy for me to funnel all future income from your businesses to these offshore corporations and, from there, to Taos. Thus, if you should ever be identified, you will know that what you have created will survive to save the street kids."

"What will it mean to my day-to-day activities?"

"You will now be an employee with no legal ownership of the assets you are managing. As chief executive of the corporations, you will continue to receive a salary and benefits. It will more than take care of all your needs. There will be no change in your life style. For legal and tax purposes, you will now pay rent to these offshore corporation for all your residences, automobiles, boats and other toys."

"My life style will not change?"

"No. Nothing will change."

"Good, it seems that I now have a new lawyer."

John held out his hand. Gabriel shook it, before he said, "I've been doing a lot of thinking about your safety."

He reached into the breast pocket of his suit and removed an odd-looking cell phone. He put it in John's hand and explained what it was, "This is a military grade cell phone, with an amazing number of apps built into it. It is water proof and just about indestructible. Besides a built-in flash light, a laser and much more. It is always emitting a signal that allows me to see on a map, on my duplicate cell phone, where you are. From now on, carry it with you. It could save your life. If you get into trouble, you press this red panic button on the side and it alerts me. I will see where you are and immediately come to your aid wherever you are."

John picked up the phone, looked at it and then put it in his pocket.

Gabriel continued, "If, you feel the game is up, the safest most reliable route, out of here, is by sea. You kept your wife's boat, but we need a backup. One of the new corporations will purchase a second one. I'll register it as my boat and berth it close to your boat at the yacht club. Then, if you need to get out of Benji Beach fast, and there is some problem with your boat, you'll always have the second boat as an alternate. Two boats, reduce our risk in handling an unforeseen situation."

"Don't you think this is overkill? I think the chances of me, being discovered, in place like Benji Beach is remote."

"Perhaps you are right but there is nothing wrong with being prepared for any eventuality. We can afford the second boat but the Sanctuary can't afford to lose your contributions. I'll make sure both boats are always fueled and stocked, ready to take you across the Atlantic. Both of us will have keys to the boats."

Gabriel became quiet. He had covered all the points he had rehearsed.

John smiled and said, "I feel you have lifted a great weight off my shoulders. It feels good, to have someone, I trust with my life, watching out for me."

"The only thing left to do, is to inform your current lawyer, that from now on, I will be handling your legal affairs. I want them to send me all open files. Here is my office address."

Gabriel reached into his pocket and handed John his business card. They stood and made their way back to John's car.

☐ PART 2

THE FALL

CHAPTER 28

COLD

In a small barbeque joint, called "Blowing Smoke", on Highland Drive, in Las Vegas' seedy, strip club district, FBI Agent, Connor, had, with great ease, separated the pork meat from a rib. He dipped it in the smoky, blood red, Arkansas BBQ sauce and transferred that perfectly cooked morsel to his yawning maw. He was ever so careful not to drip sauce onto his tan, lite weight, summer suit. A bottle of ice-cold Corona finished off the meal.

Blowing Smoke was a hangout for the local and state cops. It was also frequented by employees from nearby businesses and a few white-haired pensioners. It did not cater to the tourist trade. This was not a fine dining establishment.

The two FBI agents were sitting at one of the grease stained, picnic tables, in a dark, back corner. The other clientele ignored them. Despite the heat, they had kept their suit jackets on. The coats hid the Glocks in their shoulder holsters.

Agent Tully, turned to Agent Connor, who was devouring a well-oiled corn fritter, and said, "Do you realize that it's ten years since John Cross killed that guard at that Laughlin casino?"

"Why in the hell would you bring that up? The chances are Cross is dead and buried, in a shallow Mexican grave."

"True but the file has come up for its annual review. We haven't received a lead on it in five years. Isn't it time that it was classified as dead and sent over to the cold case guys?"

"No can do."

"Why not?"

"Did Washington tell you that you could close the file?"

"No, but..."

Connor held up his hand like a cop holding back traffic and said, "Cross is still on the radar screen of some very well-connected people. They think we continue to look for him every day under every rock in the South West. We want them to continue to think that. The case stays open until we either find Cross or his body."

"This case is getting to be like that old Monty Python skit where the pet store owner tries to convince the customer that the dead bird nailed to the perch is just sleeping."

"Listen to someone who has been doing this a lot longer than you. The senior senator for Nevada, the director of the FBI and the great governor of the wonderful state of Nevada have told the casino owner, and noted Republican party donor, that we will spare no effort in solving this murder. So, until Mike Asino gets knocked off, or the world comes to an end, this will be an open file in the FBI's Las Vegas office."

"I have better files to work on."

"So, do I, but until I win the lottery, to keep my job, I will continue to do what is politically correct and since, I'm the senior member of the team, so will you. Just spend a couple of hours on it. Do some computer searches. Phone some of Cross' contacts and see if they've heard from him. Contact Asino's people, see if they've heard anything. They'll probably find him before we do, anyway. If they do, we won't have to worry about the expense of a trial."

"The mob may still be looking for him but The Sanctuary isn't. My Taos informant has told me that big bundles of bills keep arriving anonymously, in the mail. She thinks they are coming from Cross. No one has confirmed that they are, but it seems he is still alive in their books. Perhaps we should let the mob know that we think Cross is being selective in his cash payments. That ought to piss them off and get them out there beating the bushes. As for me, I haven't got a clue where to even start looking for him or his body."

Agent Connor tilted back his bottle of Corona and drained the dregs.

⊠CHAPTER 29

WASHINGTON

Washington is a steam bath in the summer. On hot, hazy, Friday afternoons, all anyone wants to do is escape the office.

Steve handed his administrative assistant a contract defaced with cross outs, scrawled notes, arrows that shifted paragraphs, yellow hi-lighting and coffee stains and said, "Lisa, if you can put this contract back together and email it to Joe before you leave tonight, I would appreciate it. He wants to get it into next month's projections."

Lisa looked at the old-fashioned mahogany desk clock on Steve's credenza. It was five after five. She was not happy. It would take her another hour to make it presentable.

As Steve was putting on his suit jacket, the irritated administrative assistant stomped out of his office. Her husband would already be waiting for her downstairs.

When he stepped out of the air-conditioned office building, the heat hit Steve as if he had just opened the door on a blast furnace. He jay-walked across the busy street to the parking garage, dodging the stop and go traffic. For someone, six foot six inches tall, he moved like the athlete he was.

Packed with excited, smiling commuters anxious to get home to start their weekend, the garage elevator stopped on every floor. Finally, it was Steve's turn to exit. That morning, he had thought he had been very lucky to find a parking spot on the garage's top floor, close to the elevator. Starting his BMW, he turned the air conditioning on full blast, for a few minutes, to push the hot stale air out of the car before rolling the windows back up.

When he exited the garage, he forced his way into the slow-moving traffic by intimidating some white-haired woman in a red Honda. After travelling for six blocks, he swung over to the curb, without signaling, in front of an office building that had seen better days.

A tanned, fit looking blond, who had been pacing up and down in front of the building's entrance for half an hour, staring at the approaching traffic saw Steve's car approaching. Every few minutes, she has been pulling out her cellphone to check the time and see if Steve had phoned to explain why he was late. People rushing by on the sidewalk ignored her. There were lots of pretty girls in Washington. The faint smell of exhaust fumes, the heat and the roar of the traffic were making her feel faint.

As soon as she saw Steve's BMW approaching, she stopped pacing and stood still, as if she had nothing better to do, then stand on sidewalks looking at the passing parade. Steve got out of the car, popped his trunk open and put in her suitcase. He leaned over, pecked her dutifully on the cheek and said, "Sorry, Sue Anne but the traffic was a killer. I left long before five o'clock."

"Oh, that's OK. I only got down here a few minutes ago."

Sue Anne climbed into the passenger seat next to Steve. He forced his way into the traffic, despite being aware that even a tiny scratch on a BMW could end up costing him thousands to fix.

"One more pick up and Benji Beach here we come," he said enthusiastically. Sue Anne faked a half smile and said nothing. This was not a good start to her weekend.

Another half dozen blocks and they made a right turn onto a quiet, leafy, side street. It was lined with old brick mansions converted into trendy studio apartments for the young professionals. Steve eased over to the curb.

Sprawled on the front steps of the building, in the shade from a giant hickory tree, was a lanky young man in T-shirt, shorts and sandals reading a book. With a graceful, fluid motion, he stood and grabbed his duffle bag from the steps beside him. In four paces, he was opening the rear door of the BMW, throwing in his bag, followed by himself. He squeezed his six foot eight-inch frame in doing no damage to himself.

"Sorry I'm late Liam."

"No problem, Steve, just as long as we get down to Benji Beach in time for our first game tomorrow morning."

"Despite the Friday traffic, we should be there by ten o'clock."

Sue Anne muttered under her breath, "We were supposed to have been down there by eight."

Steve ignored her, as he shouted at Liam, "How's it hanging Liam?"

"To the right."

Steve laughed and asked, "You ready to make this the third year in a row that we win this volley ball tournament?"

"You're damn right.".

Steve, half turned and put his hand up so Liam could high five it from the back seat. Sue Anne ignored them and thought to herself, boys will be boys.

Soon they had crossed over the Chesapeake and were heading East towards Delaware, the beaches and the cooling breezes off the Atlantic. Steve's cell phone rang. He hesitated and debated whether he should answer it. It rang again. Curiosity got the better of him. It was month end. Perhaps something had gone wrong. He answered it by pressing the hands-free phone button on his steering wheel.

"Hello?"

"Hi Steve, it's me, Barry. Did I get you on your ride home?"

Barry's voice boomed out over Steve's radio speakers. Steve turned the volume down, but there was nothing wrong with Sue Anne's and Liam's hearing. They eavesdropped on the conversation.

"Yeah, you did."

"I got a message to phone you as soon as I got in."

"Yeah, did Pete hand in his resignation?"

There was a long silence. Steve wondered if they had lost their connection. Finally, Barry responded. "Awww... No... Not, actually I meant to phone you about that earlier. It will be a real pain in the ass filling that slot in the summer. Maybe it would be best to keep him around for another couple of months."

"Barry, this is the third month in a row that he's missed quota. You gave him a letter on first of the month that told him that if he did not make it this month that he would be fired. The other reps need to know we mean what we say."

After a loud sigh Barry replied, "Yeah, I know, but he's been with us for ten years."

"I don't give a shit if he's been with us for a hundred years. If I lose my job because of your results, you can be assured that you are going to be losing your job, long before I lose mine. Get his ass out of here, first thing, Monday morning. If he had any brains, he would have handed in his resignation before we had to fire him."

Steve clicks off without saying goodbye. The telephone conversation with its harsh realities deflated the mood in the car. Liam and Sue Anne pretended that they had not listened to the conversation. Liam, being more introspective, wondered, if Steve's, tough guy approach, was him playing to the audience in the car. Showing them what an important, powerful person he was.

Steve half turned in his seat, to glance at Liam and Sue Anne before he turned back and said, "I hope you don't mind but I've got to make another phone call."

They both nodded but said nothing. It was his car, and they were getting a free ride. Steve pressed the voice command on his phone system and told the computer to phone Pete Kingston. The call was answered on the second ring.

"Hi Pete, it's Steve. I just wanted to phone and congratulate you on another great month. Well done."

"Jeez, Steve, thanks, I appreciate you taking the time to phone."

"Have a great weekend Pete. I'm counting on you making it three months in a row."

"I'll do my best."

"I know you will. You've got a great future with us. Bye."

"Bye."

They drove along in silence for another few minutes before Liam tries to lighten the mood.

"Steve, did I ever tell you that Sue Ann and I were at Central High together? Not that she would have remembered me. I was a pimply faced little kid, and she was the golden goddess."

Not getting a response from Steve. He tries to get a response from Sue Anne.

"Sue Anne, are you, going to be our setter for this tournament?"

"Liam, do I look like one of those vacuous volleyball babes? Weekends are for relaxing, not jumping around on a hot beach like a flea."

"Sue Anne, you'd make a great volleyball player. I remember how high you could jump when you were a cheerleader."

"That's a long time ago, Liam. I remember you as being short, chubby and bad."

"Bad? You're kidding? You remember me? I thought I was the invisible kid."

"You were until you put that plastic dog crap in Mrs. Smith's lunch bag. You became infamous."

"How'd they know it was me?"

"Every kid in the school knew it was you."

Liam and Sue Anne laughed. Even Steve laughed.

"I find it hard to believe that you graduated from high school, went to university and hold down a responsible job in one of the biggest law firm in Washington. What do you do for them? I know you never went to law school."

"Well, I kind of have a unique job, for a law firm. My title is Manager of Research."

"Research? In a law firm?"

"Yeah, for example, we had a client who died leaving many millions of dollars to a child he had fathered in Vietnam, He was a soldier there in the early seventies and he had never even seen this child. His other heirs were contesting the will. My job was to find this child and prove that this was his son. I did it in a week. My law firm earned a big fee for my work."

"I hope you paid well for your effort."

"Oh, I received a very nice bonus. They like my work. I'm able to find witnesses that no one even knew existed. I've helped us win some big cases. Other times, I've been able to dig up enough evidence to get acquittals for our clients."

"You're like a private investigator."

"Kind of but a lot of what I do involves mining databases. Most of my work involves a computer."

"It sounds interesting."

"Most would consider it boring but I enjoy it. I sit there for hours, following different leads on a computer. I get caught up on the challenge. My weird educational background let me pick up this kind of research quickly. I am not sure if any other law firms have employees like me on their staff."

Steve who had been half listening to the conversation interrupted, "The traffic is easing up. We should hit Benjy Beach before nine".

Sue Anne, displeased, responded, "We were supposed to have been there before eight." She gave Steve a hard, cold stare which he did not see. He was staring straight ahead, concentrating on his driving, but he could feel the negative vibrations that Sue Anne was broadcasting. In a quiet, condescending voice, he asked, "What's wrong?

With a voice dripping with sarcasm, she replied, "Nothing."

Steve let her reply float free. He did not reel it in. They were moving quickly, on secondary roads, through rural Delaware. He glanced in the rearview mirror and saw that Liam was now unconscious, sleeping with his mouth open. Sue Anne stared straight ahead, wondering why she had agreed to go away this weekend with Steve.

Steve's cell phone rang again and jerked everyone awake. Steve pressed the button on his steering wheel and answered it.

"Hello?"

A voice boomed over the radio's speakers, "Hi Steve. Bob here. Thought you might want the month's final results."

"You bet."

"You did it again. The fourth month in a row that your sales team has got the best sales gain of any region in the country, in both numbers and dollars. You exceeded the closest region by 10%. Congratulations. Well Done."

"Thanks Bob, that's great news, I'll let the team know, right away."

"Have you reached a decision yet on taking over the West Coast region? It's a fantastic opportunity for you. I would have killed to get it at your age. Its revenues are more than triple your region and as I told you before, your bonus, salary and stock options will reflect this increased responsibility. Opportunity knocks only once."

Steve grimaced. He wished that Bob had not brought that up. He could see out of the corner of his eye that Sue Anne had just sat straight up as if hit by a bolt of lightning. She was giving him a very hard questioning look. Steve realized he was in trouble. He tried to find a response to Bob's question that would appease two opposing forces.

"Hello, Steve, are you still there?"

"Yeah, Bob, give me the weekend to sort it all out. I'll give you my answer, first thing on Monday morning. It sure sounds like a great opportunity."

"Sorry Steve, I don't mean to put pressure on you but it's really important that we fill this slot now and you're the best man. You'll have the rest of the summer to get that West coast sales team up to speed before our big Fall push."

"Thanks Bob. I'll get back to you first thing Monday. OK?"

"OK Buddy, talk to you Monday but if you can phone me before then, just get me on my cell."

Bob hung up without waiting for Steve to say goodbye. The silence after this conversation was pregnant with unspoken emotion. Sue Anne's anger was like a fast approaching, thunder cloud, moving across a still, calm lake.

Sue Anne knew, she shouldn't confront Steve with Liam as an audience, but she could not stop herself, "Whose Bob?" She asked frostily.

Steve, sighed, before he quietly replied, "He's the Senior Vice President of Sales. You met him at the Christmas party?"

"You mean the big, fat, creepy, guy with the wig."

"Yep, that's him."

"When would you be moving?"

"I haven't said I would take the job."

"Who are you kidding?"

"I wanted to talk to you first."

"Really, when were you going to do that?"

"Over the weekend."

"And how am I included in your move?"

"I don't know. It is something we can work out."

"Were you expecting me to give up my career and follow you there?"

"No, but I do make more money than you."

"Was it to be a long-distance relationship?"

"Well, with a big increase in income, I could afford to fly back East and you could fly out to Los Angeles."

'Steve who are you kidding. Every promotion you've ever gotten, you've put more and more hours into your job. How would you find the time?"

"I'd make the time."

"When does this new job start?"

"Bob wants me to meet him in Los Angeles next week so that I can meet the team and find a place to move into. I'd be flying back and forth during the transition as I help settle in whoever takes over from me."

"What happened to the regional manager in Los Angeles?"

"He got fired."

"Why?

"His sales stank, every month, this year, he missed target." Steve paused before continuing, "He couldn't seem to turn things around."

"What was his problem?"

"I am not sure but rumors are that he was splitting with his wife."

That answer, ended the exchange. Steve mentioned nothing about marriage and Sue Anne was not about to confront him with it. They ignored the eight-hundred-pound gorilla in the car as to what her response would have been if he had said they should get married.

The exchange made her aware, that in Steve's list of priorities, his career came first and that he would sacrifice everything to achieve the wealth and power he hungered for. Once she was out of his sight, she expected to be out of his mind. Her rejection left her feeling disorientated and lost.

For those few moments they had forgot that Liam was sitting in the back seat taking it all in. It was not appropriate for him to intervene in this verbal confrontation between two people he liked. He sat there and said nothing until he thought they had missed the turn for Benji Beach, "Steve, did we just miss the turn off?

"No. It's coming up. Hungry? Who wants to eat at the roadhouse or should we wait until we reach the Beach?"

Sue Anne was the first to reply, "I'm hungry. I haven't eaten since breakfast."

Liam piped up, "Yeah, I'm starving, and I had breakfast and lunch."

"Liam," Steve said, "You're always hungry. You must have a tape worm. OK. Let's pull in. They've got great ribs."

Steve pulled into a parking spot close to the entrance of the low-slung road house. As Liam and Sue Anne got out of the car, Steve took out his cell phone and typed in an email.

Sue Anne asked, "Are you coming Steve?"

"I'll be right in. Order some ribs for me. I just want to let my sales team know that we kicked ass again this month."

Sue Anne gave Steve a long, hard look, as she remembered, where in his list of priorities, she stood. She again wondered why she had agreed to this weekend. She banged the car door behind her, harder than needed and stomped very into the roadhouse. Liam noticed. Steve didn't.

The food had already arrived by the time Steve strode into the bar. Good, old fashioned, rock-and-roll was blasting from the bar's speakers. He found Liam and Sue Anne in a booth, at the back. He was elated. His outstanding abilities had got him another promotion. Life was sweet. He smiled as he approached the booth and yelled loudly over the music, "Hey, did you guys leave anything for me?

Sue Anne was in no mood for his humor or dumb questions. She responded with, "Your food has gotten cold and the beer I ordered for you is probably warm."

Liam added, "Maybe you should get the waitress to warm up your ribs.".

"That's OK."

Steve was hungry. He attacked the barely warm ribs. They had been slow cooked for hours and the rich, fatty meat fell off the bone leaving it dry. He used the creamy mashed potatoes, that had come with the meal, as a glue to pick up the green peas and gravy. Liam and Sue Anne were finishing up their apple pie and ice cream when Steve finally finished. Noticing this, Steve skipped desert and asked for the check. Then, over the protests, from Liam and Sue Anne, that they could pay for their own meals, he put the dinner on his company credit card. Steve figured after a great month like he had had, no one would dare question this expense.

They thanked him for his generosity as they exited the roadhouse. There was little conversation on the remaining half hour drive.

☒CHAPTER 30

RELATIONSHIPS

They could see the lights of Benji Beach, reflected high in the clouds, long before they reached it. They sped along the coastal road. Out to sea, the night ocean appeared as black and foreboding as a shark's eye.

The bright lights of Benji Beach's main drag soon engulfed them. The signs hawked pizzas, hamburgers, fudge and beer. Schools of young people swam between the bars. Many of them were unusually tall and fit. They were volleyball players or fans of volleyball players. Tomorrow, many of these tall ones would be fiercely competing on beach volleyball courts. Tonight, was for fun, for renewing friendships with former teammates, for making out, for drinking lots of beer and for dancing to the loud pulsating music that escaped from the bars each time a bar door opened.

Cars crawled down the strip towards the beach. They then turned around and crawled back. The drivers and their passengers solicited the girls on the sidewalk and hurled loud, ribald insults at former volleyball competitors.

Steve's car escaped the conga line by making a left onto Beach Boulevard. A few seconds later he pulled into the wide circular driveway of The Benji Beach Grand Hotel, the most expensive hotel on the beach. It was lit up like a four-tiered wedding cake. Those guests with the more expensive, prestigious cars had their cars on display in the driveway in front of the hotel. Steve's BMW goy twenty minutes to check in before he had to hide it in the underground garage.

Steve handed his and Sue Anne's bags to the bellhop. Liam unfolded himself from the backseat and slipped, the strap of his duffle bag, over his shoulder. As he walked down the hotel driveway, towards Beach Boulevard, he yelled back at Steve, "See you at The Blind Pig, for a drink, in half an hour. We'll celebrate your promotion. You can pay." Unlike Steve, Liam had no interest in paying four hundred dollars a night for a beach front hotel room. He felt no need to impress anyone. His motel room was three streets back from the beach and was costing him less than a hundred dollars a night.

Steve smiled at Liam's invitation. He felt on top of the world. Sue Anne followed him into the lobby. She wished she were back in Washington.

The advertised suite was one large room with a living room area in one corner. A microwave, tiny refrigerator and sink graced the other corner. A divider separated the king size bed from the more active areas. After he had slipped the bellhop a five-dollar bill, Steve murmured to Sue Anne, "Nice suite."

With more than a little sarcasm in her voice, Sue Anne snapped back, "Nothing but the best for Steve Parker. Right Steve?"

"Yeah Sue Anne, nothing but the best. I've earned it."

"When were, you going to tell me?"

"Tonight."

"Bull shit."

"I wanted to."

"Really? Why didn't you?"

"You know damn well why I didn't."

"Why? Have I become excess baggage?"

"No."

"Come on Steve. Let's get real. What's the matter? Didn't want to ruin your weekend? Afraid you weren't going to get any nooky?"

"Don't be such a bitch. The reason I didn't tell you right away..."

Steve paused, as he searched for a politically correct, but logical response, that would appease Sue Anne. Finally, he replied, "I had to work out my future in my head before I could talk to you about our future together. Hey, I didn't give Bob an immediate answer, did I?"

"Crap. I know you. You were just playing hard to get so you could squeeze more money out of him.

"Am I really that greedy and devious?"

"You are damn right you are."

"Well, I have to consider what is best for my career."

"Fuck your career. A week ago, you told me you loved me. Don't you remember?"

"Yes, I remember, and I do love you.

Emotional tears welled in Sue Anne's eyes. She tried not to cry and show Steve how vulnerable and fragile she felt. She turned away from Steve and reached into her purse for a Kleenex.

Steve hesitantly moved towards her, then paused, looking embarrassed, he was not sure what her reaction would be if he touched her. Finally, he reached out and puts his hand on her shoulder and gently tried to turn her around to face him. Sue Anne shrugged off his hand and moved away from him, her head bowed. At that moment, Steve's cell phone rang. Instead of ignoring it, before the second ring, he reached for it. Instinctively he turned his back to Sue Anne. With the phone to his ear, he answered it with a very businesslike, "Hello" and then carried on a conversation about contracts that had not got into the month's results.

Incensed by his insensitivity Sue Anne walked over to her small suit case and picked it up. She looked back over her shoulder, Steve still had his back to her, lost in his conversation.

Sue Anne walked to the door, opened it and closed it gently behind her. The click of the lock snapping into place, alerted Steve. He turned and saw she had left. Her suitcase was gone. He brought the phone call to an end, "Sorry Tim. Something just came up. Sorry, but I've got to take care of this. I'll phone you later. Goodbye."

Steve rushed to the door and opened it but she was not in the hallway. Running down the hall to the elevator, he frantically punched the elevator button, knowing full well that repeatedly pressing it would have no effect in speeding it up. Why had he insisted on a suite on the top floor? Finally, the elevator arrived. He entered and waited as it crawled down to the lobby, stopping on each floor to load more passengers, intent on a night of partying.

The elevator finally arrived at the lobby. he searched the entire floor for Sue Anne. At the hotel entrance he peered down the long driveway. Not seeing her, he approached the desk clerk and asked if she had seen the girl he had come in with. She shook her head that she had not. The clerk wondered what this jerk had done to cause his girlfriend to ditch him.

Steve left the hotel and walked out to Beach Boulevard. He looked up and down the street. She was nowhere in sight. The bright lights of the main drag seemed the best place to start his search. All he found there was a street full of volleyball players and fans, intent upon having a good time. He headed towards The Blind Pig hoping that Liam could help him find her.

Steve pushed by a chunky bouncer at the bar's entrance, the pounding beat of a live band greeted him. The large room was pulsating with virile bodies set free. The band, played with little skill, on a stage that was barely big enough to hold the drum set. Steve ignored the clientele who were all intent upon reliving previous years' games. An antique, mirrored, disco ball sent random flashes of light speeding around the darkened room. From a table in a far corner, Steve heard shouting over the din, "Hey Champ, Hey Steve, over here."

Steve waved, to acknowledge them, but he continued to scan the room to see if Sue Anne had joined any of the merry makers. He finally located Liam, whose back was to him, surrounded by current and former teammates, chugging back bottles of beer. Steve headed towards him. When he reached him, he had to yell, so Liam could hear him over the din, "Liam have you seen Sue Anne?"

"Sue Anne? I haven't seen her since I left you at the hotel. She hasn't come in here. Are you guys fighting?

Steve ignored the question. "Call me on your cell phone if she comes in."

He escaped the noisy bar to phone Sue Anne from the quieter street. On his cell phone keypad, he hit the speed dial for Sue Anne's cell phone. It rang four times. He quietly mumbled, "Come on, come on Sue Anne, pick up the goddam phone". When the phone reverted to taking a message, Steve terminated the call, without leaving a message. Not knowing where to search for her, he stepped back into The Blind Pig and made his way to Liam's table. Someone found a chair and everyone squeezed closer around the small metal table to make room for him.

Steve was angry with Sue Anne and angry with himself. A perfect weekend of expected sex, partying and volleyball now blown to smithereens. He emptied the bottle of beer that had been put down in front of him, in two gulps. Liam leaned over, close enough for Steve to hear him, "Did you find her?"

Steve shook his head to show that he had not.

"You hadn't told her about Los Angeles?"

Steve glared at Liam. He did not reply.

Liam ignored Steve's desire to end the conversation, "Well, well, well that, is called the sin of omission."

"Fuck you, Liam."

"Hey, don't get mad at me. You're the one who blew it, not me. Sue Anne is a nice girl. It's bad enough to be dumped but being dumped for a job, establishes how important you are in a person's life. You know, I think she's right, you are a selfish prick."

"Hey Liam, wasn't it you, who said find'em, feel'em, fuck'em, forget'em?"

"Yeah, maybe when I was fourteen."

A waitress set down another round of beer on the table. Steve picked one up and drained half of it in one big gulp. Liam responded, "Come on Steve, don't get pissed. We've got a tournament to win tomorrow. Get up off your ass and let's look for Sue Anne. She shouldn't be wandering around by herself."

Steve looked at Liam and nodded. He rose from his chair and threw down twenty dollars for the two beer and they headed for the door. Crowds filled the sidewalks. Four eyes instead of two were now scanning the crowd for Sue Anne. They searched every bar along the strip.

CHAPTER 31

RUNNING

Sue Anne did not go to the elevator when she left Steve, talking on the phone. The entrance to the stairs was just a few feet away from the suite. She almost ran down the four flights. Her suitcase banged against the stair case's metal railing. On the ground floor, the stairs terminated next to the rear entrance of the hotel. Guests used this rear entrance to access the beach and the boardwalk.

Her anger had triggered an adrenaline rush that caused her to hurry along the boardwalk. Pulling her suitcase behind her, she walked towards the main drag and then went past it. Her cell phone rang. She checked to see who was phoning. Steve's cell phone number appeared on the screen, she turned her phone off and put it in her purse.

As Sue Anne walked along the wooden board walked, she passed from one pool of light to another cast by the street lamps. Couples strolled arm and arm. They paid her no attention.

Every time she thought about Steve, she became angry. She wondered how she could have been so blind as to not see what a selfish, egotistical prick he was. His honeyed words of love were just words to get her into bed. The commitment, that she thought was there, must have been her wishful thinking. She wondered was she that desperate for a relationship? She sat on a park bench for almost an hour reliving and questioning every experience she had ever shared with Steve.

She looked at her watch. It was getting late, and she wanted to go to bed. She turned away from the water and noticed a flashing green neon sign on the roof of a small, old-fashioned, one-story strip motel. It announced to the world that this was the Seahorse Motel. She wondered if she would be able to find a room there.

She made her way up a walkway to the front of the Motel. The "NO VACANCY" sign was lit. She was about to take the sidewalk back to the main drag when she saw someone moving in the motel's office. Sometimes, she thought, people who reserved rooms do not show up. Since she was here, it was worth a try. With the thousands of fans and players, in Benji Beach for the volleyball tournament, she recognized that her chances of finding a hotel room that night were not good.

Although she had never slept on a beach in her life, she convinced herself that she would, if that was her only option. Crawling back to Steve's suite was not an option.

The elderly man, behind the motel's counter, looked startled when she pushed open the motel's office door. This had triggered a loud buzzer. He recovered and asked, "May I help you?"

"I saw your sign outside that said NO VACANCY, but I wondered if you have had a late cancellation".

He stared at her. Noted her suitcase, and that she looked sad and tired. He had a daughter about the same age. Finally, he replied, "Well, we don't but we do have one room where the guest has not yet checked in. If you can pay cash and if they are not here by midnight, you can have it."

He recognized that he was taking a chance. It was a prepaid room. If that guest showed up, they would not only be angry that they no longer had a room but would want their money back. With the crowd in town this weekend, he figured he should be able to get double the rate that the discount booking service had already paid him months ago, for that room. The temptation to keep the prepayment and pocket the cash from the girl was just too great for him to resist.

Sue Anne looked at her watch. It was eleven-thirty. Without asking what the room charge would be, she said, "I'll wait."

The desk clerk waved her to a worn, red, vinyl, arm chair in the corner. It was only while she was sitting there that she thought about the cost and hoped she had enough cash to cover it.

CNN was playing on a television, suspended from the ceiling above the counter. In their usual excited babble, the talking heads repeating the same dire story of the latest disaster, over and over again. She watched the second hand on a large, round, ancient wall clock, crawl towards midnight. It amazed her how long a minute could be when you stared at a clock waiting for it to reach your chosen destination

No cars pulled into the Motel. Everything was quiet. At midnight, she approached the counter. The elderly man had disappeared through a door at the back. She stood waiting at the counter for him to appear. A toilet flushed. The old fellow shuffled back to counter looking surprised as if he had forgotten she was waiting.

"It's Midnight", Sue Anne said, anxious to get into her room.

"So, it is, so it is. Do you have the cash?"

"How much is it?".

"One eighty. It is our special tournament, cash, discount rate."

Sue Anne shrugged and took out her wallet. She figured she was being screwed but was too tired to protest. She took out two, one hundred-dollar bills, from her purse and laid them on the counter.

"How many nights will you be staying?"

"Probably two."

"Well, I'll need to make a credit card impression then."

Sue Anne handed him a credit card. While it was being authorized, he then asked for her name and address. He keyed it into some database whose location was not evident.

"You'll be in suite five."

He gave her an old-fashioned key with a leather disk attached that had the number five burned into it. As she turned to pick up her suitcase, he asked, "Can I have the license number of your car?"

"I don't have a car."

"Oh. Well, have a good night."

Sue Anne wished him a good night and pushed open the door and made her way past several parked cars to room five. Everything was quiet, except for the muffled rumble of the waves rolling up the beach.

She had difficulty with the lock but after a couple of tries it finally gave a click. She gave the door a push. It opened into a room that was so small that it could barely accommodate the double bed with its ugly, red bedspread. The motel's cheap, pine scented, air freshener had not removed the musty odor. An old-fashioned wooden box of a television set took up one corner of the room. In the other corner, was a hard, uncomfortable looking, wooden chair. The kind of chair, you would find in a school room for teachers to sit on. A print of a seascape, with random blotches of mildew, decorated the wall above the bed head.

A small, window, plugged by an air conditioner, sat mute. She turned on the air conditioner. Awoken out of its slumber, it rattled and roared to life. In a few minutes, a faint cool breeze escaped from it and battled the heat and humidity.

The bathroom was barely big enough to contain the small sink, the small toilet and the shower. The bathroom would be a tight squeeze for anyone who weighed over one hundred pounds.

Spent from the emotional turmoil. Sue Anne took off her clothes, threw them on the chair and fell into bed naked not having the energy to even open her suitcase.

About six thirty, the sun projected stripes from the venetian blinds onto the walls. She awoke, swimming up from a deep well of unconsciousness, aware of the waves noisily visiting the beach behind the motel. Warm memories of walking on a beach as a child, hand-in-hand with her father, beat back any thoughts of further sleep.

She reached out and groped for her cell phone on the night table and checked the time. It was just before seven o'clock. At first, she considered it was too early to get up on a Saturday morning. It was not as if she had to hustle to get to work.

Sue Anne put the cell phone back on the dresser and lay there a few moments. All of last evening's anger and disappointment came rushing back. Sleep was no longer possible. She needed to get out of the hotel room and walk off her frustration.

After she had had her shower and put on her makeup, she opened her suitcase for the first time. This was her chance to wear that new, flaming red, bikini.

It looked as good now as it did yesterday when she had tried it on at the store. A sexy, black, tassel fringed, swimsuit cover completed her outfit. Yesterday, she had been looking forward to enticing Steve with it.

With a toned, feminine body, she had no trouble in getting men to look twice at her. The bikini was unnecessary bait.

As she sat on the bed, putting on her sandals, she checked her cell phone for messages. The screen filled with urgent messages from Steve. "Screw him," she whispered to herself. As she left the room, she put the phone in her purse.

It was a glorious morning. Not a cloud in a brilliant blue sky. Frothy waves rolled up the beach only to retreat, defeated, as the next wave charged forward. Seagulls mewed as they coasted and wheeled on the morning breeze, dipping down now and then to pick some sweet morsel from the brine. Only a few early risers had made it to the boardwalk.

It felt good to be out of the city and walking beside the ocean. Sue Anne breathed the clean, salty sea air. She thought about what her dying mother used to say over and over again, "Every day is a gift. What will be, will be."

In front of her a long pier, high above the water, protruded from the beach. It beckoned her, appealing to her curiosity. She strode along the pier, listening to waves rushing through the wooden pilings below.

As she approached the end of the pier, she noticed a tanned man with a shaved head, blond beard and glasses, He was wearing an old white shirt and faded, cutoff jeans, that had seen better days. He sat on a bench, built into the pier's railing, bent over, absorbed in something. He seemed to be paying her no attention. Curious, she maneuvered closer, so she could sneak a look over his shoulder.

With oil pastels, he was creating a seascape of Benji Beach on a sketch pad. He had not looked up from his work when he startled her by saying, "Good morning."

Feeling shy, she paused then hesitantly said, "Good morning. Your seascape is beautiful."

"Thank you, but what do you like about it?"

"I don't know. I guess I like your impressionistic style and the way you've got the beach fading off into the soft colors in the background. Those colored kiosks on the boardwalk, against that blue sky, really bring it alive."

Still not looking up, he enquired, "Are you an artist?"

"No, but my father was. I grew up in house full of paintings."

He looked up and said, "Are you from around here? I am sure I would not have forgotten you if I had ever seen you before." He smiled.

"No, I'm from D.C. Is your seascape for sale?"

This elicited a laugh from the artist. The irony amused him as he realized that she thought, he was some poor starving artist. He mischievously replied with a twinkle in his eyes, "No".

Sue Anne looked disappointed and turned as if she would go. The artist quickly responded, "My pleasure is in the challenge of creating them. I give them away to people I like. I'll finish this one in a few minutes and it will be yours."

"That would be nice but the only way I could accept it would be if I gave you something."

The artist smiled again as he asked, "Have you had breakfast."

"No."

"Then you can buy me breakfast."

"Would that be fair?"

"Of course, that would be more than fair. I know a great restaurant, along the strip, that serves a wonderful breakfast. I am sure you would like it. What hotel are you staying at? I'll drive you over, so you can change."

"You have a car?"

"I sure do."

"I'm staying at the Seahorse Motel. Do you know it?"

"Of course. There are not that many hotels in Benji Beach. Here, I'm finished, it's yours."

He tore the sheet off the pad and handed it to her. She clutched it as if it were million-dollar acquisition. As John Cross closed the lid of the box that he kept his oil pastels in, he stood up and said, "By the way, my name is Raymond Powell."

"I'm Sue Anne Baker."

"Well, Sue Anne Baker, let's go get some breakfast."

Side by side, they walked down the long pier towards the beach. Sue Anne laughed as this charming man took the time to amuse her and to concentrate all his attention on just her.

⊠CHAPTER 32

TOURNAMENT

At eight in the morning, The Benji Beach Grand Hotel was running on all cylinders. An impatient line had formed at the dining room entrance. The lobby was full of excited guests who spoke loudly as they greeted friends they had not seen since last year's volleyball tournament. Cars pulled up to let people off and pick up passengers. A harassed-looking concierge, manned a lobby desk, fielding questions about destinations that would amuse the visitors from the big city, arranging car rentals and booking restaurant reservations. The front desk was busy checking in guests.

Liam, like a stork moving through a flock of pigeons, hurried in long loping strides across the lobby to the bank of elevators. He rode to the top floor and almost ran down the hallway to Steve's suite. Here, he pounded on his door.

Inside that dark room, Steve came awake. He and Liam had looked for Sue Anne, in every bar along the strip, until the wee hours in the morning. At almost every bar, they had run into players that they had played with or against. This required much drinking, accompanied by shouting and loud laughter. In between bar hops, every half hour, Steve had phoned Sue Anne or sent her a text message. It was all to no avail. She had not responded.

He and Liam had finally reached the bleary conclusion that Sue Anne did not want to be found. Steve muttered that she was a big girl who knew where she could find him, when she was ready and that it was time they got back to their rooms, to get a little sleep. Along with their teammates, they had to register and be ready to play by nine in the morning.

Still half asleep, Steve croaked, "I'm coming", as he stumbled, in his underwear, across the carpeted floor. He undid the chain and yanked open the door, just as Liam, had stopped in mid knock and shouted, "Steve, get your ass in motion, we've got to check in before nine o'clock."

Steve replied, "Yeah, yeah, I know. I'll be there. Let me get a quick shower. I'll meet you downstairs in the dining room. Order me an Eggs Benedict."

Having done this early wake-up service, more than once in the past, at other tournaments. Liam turned around and headed back to the elevator. He knew that once Steve was up and moving that he could depend on him being downstairs, in time to wolf down his breakfast.

The lineup, in front of the dining room, had shrunk to half a dozen hungry guests. Liam only had to wait a few minutes. He ordered breakfast for himself and Steve.

A half hour later, Steve made his appearance. He is looking alert and ready to play. He wolfed down his cold Eggs Benedict. This one was different. The hotel made with smoked salmon, instead of back bacon. They paid their bills and headed towards the beach.

The Benji Beach Annual Beach Volleyball Tournament was a charity fundraiser. Two thousand players took it very seriously. They were just a small percentage of the thousands attending the event.

Volleyball courts stretched for almost half a mile along the beach. Product sampling stations and kiosks, selling everything from T-shirts to hamburgers, bordered the volleyball courts. Many, well-spaced, beer gardens provided the lubricant to keep the players and the spectators happy.

In the hot morning sun, tall, lean, muscular, half naked men and women, in bathing suits and team T-shirts, were gathering. Hundreds of volunteers and officials were busy. It was their responsibility to keep, what was the largest beach volleyball tournament in the Washington-Maryland-New Jersey region, running smoothly.

An auction of donated trinkets, hot air balloon rides and live bands, that played in a temporary amphitheater, created a carnival atmosphere. The bands would blast away, nonstop, for the full two days. Millions of dollars were brought in to the local businesses and to the charities the tournament supported.

While the team check-in started at nine o'clock, Steve as team captain needed to be there before nine to attend the Team Captain's meeting. The first game would start before ten and play would end at four o'clock. On Sunday, the play offs would start at noon. This later start allowed enough time, for everyone to recover from their hangovers and Saturday night debauchery.

The teams were self-classified as beginners, recreational, intermediate and competitive. The "competitive" teams were current and former varsity players. They were the only group permitted to spike the ball, do jump serves and play in a physically intimidating manner. All the teams had to be co-ed, with a minimum of two women team members, on the court during play. While the teams registered up to ten players, during a game, only six players could be on the court.

At nine-thirty the starting horn sounded. Play began on all the courts up and down the beach. Each game ended at the sound of the horn every fourteen minutes or when a team reached twenty-five points. To win, they had to beat their opponent by at least two points.

Steve played very aggressively. Leaping high, he spiked the ball into the face of one of the attractive girls on the opposing team so hard that she staggered. Her face acquired a beet red bruise. There were tears welling in her eyes, which she struggled to control. When it was their turn to serve, the same girl leaped high and smashed the ball into Steve's face. He looked stunned, then he laughed and shook off the pain. When that game finished, he went over to see her. She was tall but appeared short standing next to him.

He nodded and said, "You're good."

"So are you. I understand that your team has won the tournament for the last two years."

Steve replied with a laugh, "Actually, it is three years in a row but I see we are going to have a tough time winning it this year. Can I get you something to drink?

"You don't have to."

"I'd like to. What would you like?"

"Whatever you're getting for yourself?"

"Whoa, that's very brave of you."

"I trust you."

"Trust no one."

"I don't, but it sounds good to say it."

"Sorry, but I don't know your name."

"Rachel."

"No last name?"

"That's right, Rachel No Last Name."

Steve laughed and said, "We must be related. My name is Steve No Last Name. I'll be right back with something cold and wet."

Rachel gave him a warm smile and said, "Thanks."

Steve didn't have to go far for drinks. Since they had more games to play, he just got Cokes. In a few minutes, he was back to where he had left Rachel. Like flies around honey, she was surrounded by several very tall admirers. Steve stood there, holding the two, red, disposable, Coke containers, feeling like a fifth wheel. He shifted his weight from on foot to the other, so Rachel would have to be blind not to see his impatience at being left to just stand there holding two Cokes.

Rachel continued to smile and laugh at her admirers' witticisms and clever repartees. She pretended she didn't see Steve. She knew how to handle arrogant gamers like Steve. Finally, losing all patience, Steve began drink his Coke. Worried that he might drink her Coke too, Rachel took this as her cue and turned towards him and said, "Oh Steve, you're back. Thanks for bringing me a Coke."

Her gang of admirers, all turned, as one, to stare daggers at this interloper. They then turned back to Rachel, who coyly reengaged them. Once again, she ignored Steve.

He stood there, excluded from the conversation. He started again to shift from one foot to another, but it was to no avail. Finally, he turned around and walked off to join his team for their next game.

They played hard all day and were one of the eight teams that qualified for the playoffs, the next morning. A little after four o'clock, Steve and Liam were packing their water bottles into Steve's gym bag. Steve congratulated Liam on playing well but what he was really doing was stroking his own ego. He knew he was the outstanding player on the team. Liam was used to Steve's ego. He recognized that if Steve did not have such a strong ego, he would not have been able to rally the team to perform at the high level that they reached in every tournament. Pausing, he turned to Steve and said, "I kept an eye out for Sue Anne but I didn't see her. Did you?"

"To be honest, I wasn't really looking for her."

"Bull shit."

Steve laughed and then responded, "Christ, Liam, you'd think she was your girlfriend."

Liam ignored the jibe and replied, "It worries me that we haven't seen her since last night."

"Liam, you worry about everything. Yeah, she's pissed off with me, but it isn't the first time and it probably will not be the last. Yeah, I'm probably an insensitive, self-centered ass hole, but she's a big girl. She can take care of herself. If she wants to see me, she knows where to find me, if she doesn't want to see me anymore, I will miss her, because I do care about her, but sometimes that is just the way things work out. We're not married. I don't own her. She doesn't own me."

"Yeah Steve, you are an arrogant asshole. You're also irresponsible. Sue Anne came with us and I think she should ride back with us. I'm going to go down the strip and see if I can find her. I hope she hasn't got into any trouble."

"OK Liam. I'll see you later."

⊠CHAPTER 33

SIGHTSEEING

John Cross parked, just outside Sue Anne's room at the Seahorse Motel, while she changed her clothes. It had been a surprise when, what she had assumed to be a poor penniless artist, had a car that turned out to be a green Porsche 911, Carrera convertible with a tan leather interior. Although it was not new, she still thought it must be worth at least $70,000. In fifteen minutes, she had changed into white shorts, that showed off her long-tanned legs, and a yellow halter top, that complimented her long blond hair.

When she stepped out of the motel room, she could see that she had impressed John. He went around to open her door. A few minutes later they had turned onto the very busy main street. A Porsche attracts attention. The younger crowd in town for the big volleyball tournament turned to admire it.

Half way up the strip, John made a quick right turn, into an alleyway next to the Lobster Haven restaurant. Sue Anne noticed a long line of hungry customers, standing on the sidewalk, waiting to get into the restaurant. At the back of the Lobster Haven, John wheeled into a parking spot guarded by a large sign that read, "Private. No Parking. Tow Away Zone". She turned to verify that he had seen the sign. He looked at her and gave her a smirk of a smile as if to reassure her that it was OK. He then got out of the car and opened her door for her. They walked past a giant disposal bin and entered a rear door into a brightly lit, hot, busy kitchen. Chefs and helpers were preparing dozens of plates. No one challenged John's sudden appearance in the kitchen. The busiest man in the Kitchen greeted John with, "Raymond, have you and your friend come for one of my world-famous lobster omelets?"

"We sure have. It looks like you've got a record sales day going."

"It sure does. We need some help back here. How about it?"

"I learned a long time ago to stick to what I do best. You want these customers to come back, don't you?"

"We sure do. Yeah, you better stick to what you're good at."

John led Sue Anne down a hallway, towards the swinging doors leading into the dining room. Half way down the hallway was an alcove with a horseshoe shaped table. It had a padded bench that could have sat six people. He motioned for her to have a seat. He sat beside her.

Waiters and waitresses were quickly moving up and down the hallway with steaming plates of food. In seconds, a silent waitress had put place mats, napkins and cutlery in front of them. She gave John a big knowing smile. A few minutes later, two large omelets arrived with toast, home fries and a steaming jug of coffee. Sue Anne looked overwhelmed by the quick service and how John had just made himself at home.

Noticing her puzzled look. He smiled and said, "I should have asked if you like lobster."

"Oh, I do love lobster and this lobster omelet is delicious." She paused before she asked, "Do you work here?"

"Kind of."

"What does 'kind of' mean?"

John paused and wondered just how much he wished to reveal to what was still a stranger. Finally, he responded, "Well, I own it."

"You own it?"

"Yes, I own it."

"So, you don't work here."

"No, I have an office a few blocks away but I drop in here a couple of times a week, just to keep an eye on my investment. I also like to eat here. I'm the one who switched it over from a typical greasy spoon to the best lobster restaurant in the state. This is my special table. I added it when we renovated the restaurant."

"Should I feel honored to be at your table?"

"Absolutely."

"So, you live in Benji Beach?"

"Yes, I do. I've got a little beach house just north of town."

"Lucky dog."

"Yeah, it's great."

"You must do something else?"

"Oh, a bit of this and that. I have other investments. I even sell my art. What about you?"

"I'm a legal manager in a commercial collection agency."

"That sounds intimidating. Should I run away?"

"Only if you're a deadbeat."

John Cross laughed and asked, feigning ignorance of collection operations, "What does a legal manager in a collection agency do?"

"Well, when our collectors can't persuade a debtor to pay the debt, they then resort to the only option that now have left, to collect the debt through the courts. This requires getting written permission from our client to sue their debtor. If the client agrees to this strategy, then they must give us, up front, enough money to cover the initial legal costs. The transfer the file to me. I determine if the debtor will have sufficient assets to cover the debt if we do get a judgment against them."

John interjected, "Litigation is not cheap."

"No, it isn't. There is no point in spending money suing a debtor if there will be no assets to seize when you win the case. If I do find enough assets, I put together the paper work the law firm needs to prepare the writ. From then on, I act as the liaison between the law firm and the client until the legal action is settled."

"How long would that take?"

"Oh, it could take years but while it is going through the courts, I try to reach an out-of-court settlement with the debtor. Only about five percent of the legal actions we start ever go to trial."

"This must mean that you are a very patient person."

"I think more persistent than patient. You are at the mercy of the courts and your customers, but you learn to live with the process. If you didn't it would drive you crazy. It requires creative thinking because although you start the legal action, you really don't want to go to court because you can never be sure the judge will rule in your favor. You always look for ways to reach a settlement without going to trial."

"You know your stuff. I once owned a collection agency."

"Really, where?"

"Oh, that was a long time ago. I used to live out West." To change the subject, John asked, "You said your father was an artist. Was he a painter?"

"Yeah, he painted. He liked doing seascapes. The reason I liked your oil pastel so much is that it reminded me of his work. Where did you get your creativity from?"

John Cross paused for a long time before answering. Boy hood memories of his poor, unfortunate mother came flooding back. None of those memories included art. "I'm not really sure. I could always draw and paint. It is something I do without thinking about it. It must be some kind of eye, hand, coordination, thing. I just do it. I'll see something that gives me a compulsion to paint it. It happens a lot here. There are some interesting sights in Delaware. Have you seen any of the light houses further up the coast?"

"No, I've never been to the Delaware coast before."

"What are your plans for today?"

"I don't really have any plans."

"Why don't you let me show you some of Delaware's sights."

"You can just take the day off? I thought this was one of Benji Beaches busiest weekends."

"Yeah, it is, but even the boss needs some time off and beside that I've got excellent managers who don't need me looking over their shoulders. They've got their objectives and their budgets. If they miss them, they will see more of me than they might wish. Are you ready to go sightseeing?"

"Oh, I would like that, but only if I can buy you lunch."

"Two free meals in one day. Sounds good to me. I know a great crab shack up the coast. Let's go."

"Shouldn't we wait for the check?"

"You'll be waiting for a very long time if you think they are going to give me a check."

"But the agreement was that I would buy you breakfast."

"You shall but not today."

"Well, thank you."

"You're welcome.

They left through the kitchen. The chef who had greeted them, smiled at her and asked if she had enjoyed the omelet. She told him, it was the best omelet she had ever had. The chef beamed from ear-to-ear. John Cross said, "Don't flatter him like that, he'll want a raise."

As they exited the alley, Sue Anne noticed that the line in front of the restaurant looked even longer than when they had come in. The main drag was bustling with people as they headed towards the coast highway. John enjoyed driving his high-performance sports car. At every opportunity, he would crank it up and pass every car in front of him.

After driving for half an hour, Sue Anne asked, "Where are we heading?"

"I want to show you the quaint town of New Castle. It is just South of Wilmington. After I show you Wilmington, we will drive to Bellfonte. It's got an interesting light house. On the way, back, we can stop at Sambo's for fresh crabs. It is just north of Dover."

"How far is Wilmington?"

"Over one hundred miles. It won't take us long."

They took almost two hours to reach New Castle. The cobbled streets and the centuries old colonial houses, left Sue Anne with the feeling that she had just stepped out of a time machine. John pointed out the many scenes that he had painted. Sue Anne took pictures with her cell phone.

It was a short drive through Wilmington to the Bellefonte light house. Sue Anne found the light house disappointing. It was not the round, stereotypical, white tube she had imagined it would be. It was a long thin concrete box in a residential area. John told her the lighthouse no longer operated.

He asked her if she were hungry. She said she was. They headed back through Wilmington and soon were pulling into Sambo's Tavern.

The restaurant was in the small town of Leipsic. John explained that it was a famous, long established tavern that specialized in selling crabs. He said it was a great example of a Delaware-Maryland crab house. Nothing fancy, but if you want the freshest and best prepared local blue crabs in Delaware, this was the place. Fishermen came up the river each morning and delivered their fresh crabs right to the restaurant.

John ordered a dozen crabs, a half pitcher of beer, a basket of fries, cups of crab bisque and a basket of fried clams. Sue Anne felt stuffed when they finished.

Sue Anne took out her credit card and signaled to the owner's wife to bring her the check. The wife shook her head and indicated that John had paid it. The bill had come to almost one hundred dollars with the tip. John was not about to stick Sue Anne with it. She complained to him that he had said, she could pay for it. He just laughed and smiled. They got back in the Porsche and headed south.

As they approached Benji Beach, John turned to Sue Anne and said, "I can't remember when I've had such a great day."

"Me too."

"Your reward for such a great day is letting me cook your dinner. Do you like steak?"

"I sure do."

"OK, I'll drop you off at the motel, so you can freshen up and I'll pick you up around 7:00 PM."

"That sounds great. Are you sure?"

"Are you kidding? The company of a beautiful, intelligent woman. A chance to show off my culinary skills, a great steak. What more could a man want?"

Once again, they drove down Benji Beach's main drag. That day's volley ball competition was over. Tomorrow was the playoffs. Tired players and thirsty tourists, who had braved the sweltering sun on the beach, were now crowded the late afternoon sidewalks. Dehydrated drinkers crowded the outdoor patios The crowd was intent on having a good time. Tomorrow they would head home to reality.

Bumper to bumper traffic crawled towards the beach. Liam was on the sidewalk, walking away from the beach. He had always lusted after an expensive sports car, just like the green Porsche that was now approaching him. He, like several heads on the sidewalk, turned to stare at it. Liam took out his cell phone to make a video of it as it went by. He was astounded to see Sue Anne as a passenger in the car. He paid no attention to the driver who he had also captured in the video. Sue Anne was concentrating on the cars in front of them, she did not notice Liam taking their picture.

Turning off the main drag, it was only a few hundred yards to the Seahorse Motel. John pulled to a stop in front of her door. Sue Anne got out and waved goodbye as he drove away. She had more than an hour to shower and get herself ready. It was only then that she considered that the whole purpose of this weekend was supposed to have been volleyball and partying. She had not seen one game or even felt that she had missed anything, especially Steve. Raymond Powell's charm and sensitivity had been welcome and appreciated.

These days, John spent little time at the beach house. Usually, he slept in an apartment, he kept on the second floor, above one of his bars on the main drag. Occasionally, he slept in the apartment at the golf course.

John drove to Beckman's meat market. They had the best steaks in town, hand cut and well marbled. He then stopped at Freshco for vegetables and wine. At the beach house, he opened windows, so the sea breezes could air it out.

After a quick shower and a change of clothes, he turned on the barbecue, to let it get hot, while he left to pick up Sue Anne. Before he left, to set the mood, he had turned on soft, mellow music. At a small, white, metal table on the deck, he had set down place mats, linen napkins, cutlery and wine glasses.

The sun was getting low on the horizon when he pulled up in front of her room at the Seahorse Motel. He got out of the car and knocked on Sue Anne's door. She yelled from inside, "I'll be ready in a minute."

"No problem, take your time."

He went back to the car, turned on the Bloomberg channel, on his Sirius radio, and waited. In ten minutes, Sue Anne made her entrance. She looked stunning. As John got out and opened her car door, he murmured, "You look great."

"Well, thank you, kind sir. You look good too."

On the drive to the beach house they said little. When John pulled into the driveway, Sue Anne gasped and said, "You live here?"

"Yes, well, to be honest, I probably spend more time in an apartment that I have on the strip, but yeah, I live here too."

"This is a small place on the beach?"

"Well, things are neither great nor small except by comparison. There are bigger places."

"I haven't seen any."

He gave her a quick tour of the first floor, made her a drink and told her to relax in one of the lounge chairs on the deck, while he prepared dinner. As she finished her drink, John went to a refrigerator, beside the giant barbeque, and took out a chilled bottle of Moet & Chandon Champagne Brut Imperial. He popped the cork, poured two glasses and proposed a toast, "To an enduring friendship."

They clinked glasses together. The dry, ice cold, nectar went down smoothly.

"You sit here and relax while I put dinner together."

John went back into the kitchen and sliced the zucchini length wise so that he could grill them with the steak. Quickly he made his very special salad and put some frozen French fries in the air fryer to crisp. Everything for the barbeque was carried out to the deck. Soon the steaks were sizzling.

After he poured Sue Anne another glass of Champagne, he turned on the small pin lights that circled the deck at floor level and lit a candle, inside a glass globe. Soon everything was ready. The salad was half an avocado, stuffed with baby shrimp, walnuts and celery, on a bed of baby spinach leaves. The steak, French fries and grilled zucchini followed with an Italian Banfi Brunello red wine.

Sue Anne whispered, between mouthfuls of the steak, "I'm very impressed. This is really delicious."

"Thank you. How was your salad?"

"Great, *merci beaucoup, Monsieur. La service et la cuisine est tres elegant.*"

"*C'est mon plasir.* Where did you learn to speak French?"

"My parents had a friend with a villa in Ville France- Sur- la -Mer, just outside of Nice. We used to spend time there, in the summers when I was a kid. What about you?"

You won't believe this, but in another life, I was a missionary in Paris."

"Really, a missionary? You mean like a monk, a priest? You have got to be kidding?"

"No, I kid you not. I was an orphan, and I was taken in, by I guess, you would call it a sect. After feeding me and educating me for ten years, I agreed to serve them two years as a missionary. They sent me to Paris."

"What was the sect called?"

"The Sanctuary."

"I've never heard of it."

"That is why they need missionaries."

"Were they the sect who don't smoke, don't drink, don't even drink coffee? You seem to enjoy your wine."

John Cross laughed, "No, that was another South West sect, the Mormons. I acquired my taste for wine in France."

It was the quiet of the evening. A gentle breeze wafted in from the ocean, lessening the humidity. Soft music was playing. John crossed over to Sue Anne and held out his hand. She looked puzzled but took it. He quietly said, "Would you give me the pleasure of this dance?"

She smiled up at him but said nothing and rose. He gently took her into his arms held her close. They danced. The soft music paused for a few moments. He looked down at her. She looked up at him. He leaned forward and kissed her. She responded. The music started again. Still holding each other tightly, they kissed again and swayed to the slow rhythm. The music paused again. John picked her up in his arms, as if she were child, and carried her through the patio door, into the house.

Taking the elevator to the second floor, he lay her down on the bed and then lay down beside her. They kissed. He unbuttoned her blouse and undid her brassiere. His shirt quickly came off. They hungrily kissed again. He explored her body with his tongue.

Headlights from a car, coming up the driveway, shone into the room through the open window. They heard the car approaching. John went to the window.

Angrily, he said, "Ah shit. Sue Anne, I'm sorry, please get dressed. We have to leave."

Sue Anne was already putting on her brassiere and blouse. John dressed and took Sue Anne's hand. He heard the car come to a stop in the garage below the house.

After leading her down the steps to the first floor, they headed towards the rear of the house. The elevator moved up from the garage. Quickly Sue Anne and John crossed the deck and took the long wooden bridge to the beach. They disappeared into the dark.

On the beach, their eyes quickly adjusted to the dark. Their feet sank into the soft sand. Sue Anne took off her sandals and held them. They walked down the beach towards the bright lights of Benji Beach. He held her hand. It helped her walk on the sand.

Sue Anne had not said a word since he told her to get dressed. She asked, "Raymond, what's going on?"

"It's my in-laws."

"Your in-laws? You're married?"

Sue Anne let go of his hand. John quickly responded, "Sorry, my ex-in-laws."

"You're divorced?"

"No, my wife died."

"Whose beach house was that?"

"It's complicated. My wife and her father owned it. So, half of it is mine."

"Well, why did we have to leave?"

"My wife didn't just die. She took out her cruiser and never returned. They found the boat abandoned at sea. She must have had an accident and fallen overboard. The courts declared that it was an accidental death. For some strange reason, that I do not understand, her parents feel that, somehow, I am responsible for her death. I can understand their pain and wanting to blame somebody. It was their only child. I didn't want you to suffer through the usual embarrassing confrontations I have with them. They're supposed to send me an email before they drive down from Baltimore, so I can I can stay out of their way, but sometimes they don't. I think they do it just to piss me off."

They walked along in silence. The lights of the strip got closer and closer, brighter and brighter. John took Sue Anne's hand. She did not take it away. They reached the boardwalk. Sue Anne put her sandals back on. They walked along it to the main drag. Crowds of players and fans celebrating their last night in Benji Beach filled the sidewalks.

Liam stepped out of bar. He almost bumped into the two of them.

Happy to find her, Liam called out, "Hey, Sue Anne?"

"Hi Liam"

"You Okay?"

"Yeah, I'm fine."

She turned to John Cross who was standing beside her and said, "Ray meet Liam. We went the same high school. Liam, this is Raymond Powell."

"It's a small world. Hi Liam, glad to meet you."

"Hi, nice meeting you too, Ray." Liam paused. He gave John a long hard look and asked, "Haven't we met before? You look familiar. Didn't I play against you in last year's tournament?

"No, I'm a golfer and a dirt biker. I've not played volley ball since high school."

"Wait a minute, now I remember. Wasn't your picture in the all newspapers and TV? Didn't they find your wife's boat was drifting off the coast? I think the press tried to turn it into a killer-husband-gains-millions story."

"You've got a good memory."

"No, it's a professional thing, collecting and storing data is what I do for a living. I'm a researcher for a law firm in Washington." Liam paused as if building up his nerve, before he asked, "I'm curious, did they ever find her body?

John was becoming uncomfortable with the question. Liam's rudeness embarrassed Sue Anne. To bring the conversation to an end, John quickly replied with a very abrupt, "No."

"Sorry, I guess you don't need me dredging up something so traumatic. I apologize for my insensitivity."

C'est la vie. It happened. I wish it hadn't happened, but life goes on, *mais non*?

"*Parlez vous Francais?*"

"*Oui, monsieur et vous?*"

"Yeah. I taught French for a year after college when I lived in California."

"My home state. My French really improved after I spent two years working in Paris."

"Great city. No wonder your accent is so good. OK. You guys have a good evening and once again, I'm sorry for my insensitivity." Liam paused as if he had something more to say. John and Sue Anne stared at him expectantly. Finally, he got it out, "Sue Ann, how are you getting home tomorrow night?"

"Don't worry about me, Liam. I'm sure I can hitch a ride back."

"OK, that's great. I'll see you around."

Sue Anne and John Cross continue down the strip, hand-in-hand. Liam stared after them. Soon they were swallowed up by the crowd in the street.

⊠CHAPTER 34

REVEALED

Liam had last seen Steve in a bar further up the street, talking to a girl and he would still be trying to hustle her. He headed back to that bar. They were still sitting at a table, with drunken team mates gathered around them. When Liam appeared at their table, Steve shouted out, "Hey, Liam. Take a load off. Pull up a chair. Have you met Rachel?"

Liam nodded at Rachel. He recognized her from when they had played her team that morning. He sat down and quickly replied, "I seem to remember, that she tried to smash a ball into my face this afternoon."

All the drunks at the table laughed at his quick wit.

Rachel smiled and said, "Hey, if you can't stand the heat, get out of the kitchen. We intend to win this tournament."

Liam couldn't pass that up, "Many have tried but we are unbeatable." In the next breath, he turned to Steve and said," I just saw Sue Anne outside with a guy."

Steve, who did not welcome a discussion about a possible ex-girlfriend while he was trying to hustle a potential new girlfriend, grunted a reply, "What guy?"

"That guy, two years ago, who the media suggested had conspired to have his rich wife murdered. They suggested he made it look like she had died in a boating accident. This guy's face appeared in all the newspapers and TV."

"Yeah, I remember that. They never found a body. What happened to him?"

"Nothing, as far as I can remember. I assume he got all her money. I tried to clue Sue Anne in on who he was, but it was awkward with him being right there."

"Why were you so sure he was the same guy?"

"I asked him."

"What? You asked him? You've got to be kidding. Christ Liam, this guy could be some kind of psychopathic killer. And then, you let Sue Anne go off with him? Did you see where they went?"

"Nope. They were just moving up the strip. Before we jump to the wrong conclusions and we get Sue Anne even more pissed off, than she already is with you, I think we better check out, what the hell happened two years ago. Did you bring your laptop?"

"Yeah, it's in my room. Here's my key. It's on the desk. I'll see you later."

Steve threw Liam his room key. Liam scooped it up and put it in his pocket. He nodded goodbye to Rachel and all the drunks at the table. The group, at the table, had become quiet listening to the exchange between Steve and Liam but they quickly reverted to loud, boisterous jock talk. Steve showed little sign, that he would follow Liam back to his hotel room anytime soon.

Liam had been working away on Steve's laptop for almost an hour when there was a knock at the room's door. He got up and let Steve in. The laptop, that he had left behind on the desk, was displaying a story from the NBC television station in Delmarva, Maryland. It read in big headlines, "WAS FOUL PLAY BEHIND BOATING ACCIDENT?"

As Steve entered the room, he quickly asked, "So, what did you find?

Liam, looking very serious and worried, replied, "Listen to this." He then clicked on the TV station's video and turned up the volume on the laptop to hear a deep, professional voice say,

"WRDE's reporter, Chris Smith, began his investigation of the mysterious disappearance of wealthy socialite, Mrs. Naomi Powell, shortly after her boat was found abandoned in Delaware Bay. The courts have now ruled that this mysterious disappearance was tragic fatal accident. Her body has never been recovered. In this special report, Smith explores the many unanswered questions that suggest foul play may be involved."

The television reporter is seen standing with a marina, full of expensive pleasure boats, serving as a backdrop. He began his report, "Captain Jim Randal, of the Coast Guard stated that they used a bull horn to rouse the people on the boat. Not getting a response, he boarded the boat and found no one on board. A stereo was playing, and glasses of beverage were sitting half full on the bridge. Captain Randal said that, in his thirty years with the Coast Guard, he had never encountered a situation where it appeared the occupants had just been there one second and gone the next. He also said that the FBI investigators, had told him that the absence of any struggle or damage to the vessel was unusual if a criminal act had occurred. They had also told him that while they found the disappearance suspicious, they could only conclude that a tragic accident had occurred. When interviewed, Mrs. Powell's father, wealthy industrialist Howard Green, a former coast guardsman, said that his daughter was a skilled and experienced mariner who took no chances and adhered to all safe boating practices. He said that he had great difficulty in believing that his daughter could have encountered a situation that she was not prepared to cope with. She was a strong swimmer and, on board, always wore a life vest that would have inflated as soon as she the water. He had concluded that some trusted third party must have boarded the boat and disabled her. When asked if his daughter kept a weapon on the boat. He replied that he had trained her in using the weapon found in a locked cabinet on the boat. Now back to the studio."

Steve listened to the television report. At its conclusion, he said, "Well Liam, is this guy, that Sue Anne is with, a murderer or not?"

Lien threw up his hands, as a sign of inconclusiveness, and responded, "No, despite all the innuendos, trying to tie her husband into her disappearance, there is nothing to show that he was on that boat. People saw her leave the marina, with a man who was not her husband. That man also disappeared. The press raised all kinds of wild theories from pirates, to a mafia hit, but there is no evidence to support them."

"What else did you find of interest?"

"Well, just over a year ago, her husband brought the case to court to have her declared legally dead. Apparently, her parents were not happy about that. In most states five years must past before a missing person can be presumed dead. However, her husband petitioned the court, to end the speculation that his wife was still alive and to put to rest the rumors that he was involved in her death. The only subpoenaed witness, was an investigator who said that after a thorough investigation in his opinion she was deceased. Her will stipulated that all of her estate went to her husband."

"How big an estate?"

"No figures published, but the press reported that she had inherited a big chunk of her grandfather's shares in a several major corporations. They speculated that she was worth hundreds of millions. That could certainly give an unhappy spouse motivation to do more than just ask for a divorce. What do we do now?

"Well, I've got no credibility with Sue Anne, so I guess you're the one who has got to find her and warn her that she may have put herself in danger. If she thinks I'm a shit, then this guy may make me look like a choir boy. Were you able to find anything that indicated he had a history of violence?"

"That is the strange thing. Raymond Powell just seemed to show up, out of the blue, in Benji Beach, several years ago. He bought a local golf course and his business interests grew from there."

"Liam, if he is a murderer then you would think there should be some kind of history of violence. For example, did you check the FBI Most Wanted website? A small, coastal, resort town would be a good place, for someone on the run to hide out in."

"No, I didn't check the FBI list. It seems a little farfetched and paranoid to think that this guy could be a murderer. He doesn't look like one."

"What do you mean he doesn't look like one?"

"You know, wild eyed, jerky, hard looking. He looks like a successful, hip businessman, the kind who drives a Porsche, which is what I saw him driving."

"You can't trust guys who drive Porches."

"You're kidding, aren't you?"

"Yeah, I'm kidding but you never know. Why not check the FBI Most Wanted List, anyway?"

"Okay, let's see who the FBI are looking for. I've seen him, so I should be able to go through this list quickly."

Liam saw that the FBI had organized their website into sections, "Ten Most Wanted, Fugitives, Terrorism, Kidnappings/Missing Persons, Seeking Information, Bank Robbers, ECAP"

He started with bank robbers and worked backwards. It didn't take him long to skim through the pages. He was looking for a blond haired, white guy and there were not many matching that criteria. When he finally got to the "Ten Most Wanted" he finally found someone who resembled Raymond Powell.

Liam called out to Steve, "Holy shit, I think we've got a hit. See this guy. I think if you shaved his hair, gave him a blond beard and put glasses on him, that it could be him. The eyes, height and weight would be about right. You've got a PhotoShop program in your PC. Give me a couple of minutes with this picture and let me show you."

Liam copied the picture from the FBI website and transferred it into PhotoShop. He added a beard to the face and removed the hair from his head. Finally, he drew in glasses. Liam compared the picture on the computer screen to the photograph he had taken with his cell phone of John Cross in the Porsche with Sue Anne. Holding the cell phone, next to the computer screen he said to Steve, "What do you think?"

Steve looked at one picture and then the other before he quietly said, "They sure look like the same person to me." Liam brought up the entire wanted notice. Steve leaned over Liam's shoulder and read it.

JOHN DAVID CROSS
DESCRIPTION:

- Aliases: Jay Cross, Dan Cross
- Date(s) of Birth Used: December 25, 1978
- Place of Birth: California
- Hair: Blond, Eyes: blue, Height: 6'1", Weight: 185 pounds, Sex: Male, Race: White,

☒ Nationality: American. Scars and marks: Cross has scars on his chest and left forearm.

☒ Occupation: businessman, financial services

REWARD: The FBI is offering a reward of up to $100,000 for information leading directly to the arrest of John David Cross.

REMARKS

Cross spent two years in France as a missionary for an organization identified as The Sanctuary. He speaks French fluently. A university graduate with a Master of Business Administration degree, for several years he owned a collection agency in Las Vegas, Nevada. A sportsman, he is an avid golfer, snowboarder, boater and motorcycle enthusiast.

CAUTION

John David Cross is wanted for his alleged involvement in the robbery of a casino. A male suspect in helmet, sunglasses and bicycle racing gear, later identified as Cross, intercepted an armored truck guard outside the Cheers Casino in Laughlin, Nevada. The guard resisted Cross' attempt to seize a bag containing $3,500,000 of the casino's cash. Cross fatally shot the guard and escaped on a bicycle with the deposit. His automobile was found abandoned two days later in the Mexican border town of Nogales, Arizona.

A federal arrest warrant was issued for Cross in the United States District Court, District of Nevada, Las Vegas, Nevada, after he was charged with first degree murder and aggravated robbery.

SHOULD BE CONSIDERED ARMED AND DANGEROUS If you have any information concerning this person, please contact your local FBI office or the nearest American Embassy or Consulate. Field Office: Las Vegas.

Steve and Liam looked at each other. Liam let out a low whistle and said, "Wow."

"Liam, you're sure it's him?

"Absolutely."

"Just do a search under his name alone and see what else you can find out about him."

Liam did another search and got pages of hits. The first one was a newspaper article, He read it silently and then read it out loud for Steve, "Cross didn't fit the image of a hardened criminal. He looked more like a surfer dude from California, which is where he grew up. He boasted about a privileged lifestyle filled with beautiful women, expensive cars and vacations at luxury resorts."

Glancing up from the computer, Liam said, "This sure sounds like a guy who would want to latch on to a rich heiress and then knock her off. Get this, it says he is a former missionary of The Sanctuary, whatever that is, and speaks French fluently. When I was talking to him and Sue Anne, he said that he had grown up in

California and had worked in Paris. Too many coincidences. He's grown a beard, shaved his hair and wears glasses. It's a disguise. Even his own mother wouldn't recognize him if he walked by her on the street."

Steve sighed and said, "What do we do?

"We should contact the local police or even the FBI," Liam suggested.

"It would probably take too long for the FBI to react. The most important thing is to get Sue Anne away from him as quickly as we can. Let me try to reach her again."

Steve took out his cell phone and speed dialed her cell phone number again. He listened and then handed the phone to Liam and said, "She still has her phone turned off. I've got her voice mail, here. you leave her a message. You will have more credibility with her than me right now."

Liam took Steve's cell phone and left the following message, "Hi Sue Anne, this is Liam. Please phone us back. I'm on Steve's phone. The guy you are with is not who he says he is. Your life could be in danger. Leave him, as quickly as you can, and meet us at the hotel."

Steve had wanted to leave a message for her that said he loved her but with Liam there he felt too inhibited. Liam said, "Now What?"

"Let's see, if we can track down where she is staying. She may be there. It can't be that far away. She was lugging a suitcase when she left here."

Liam went back to the laptop and did a Google search of Benji Beach hotels. A map came up. He could see all the hotels within an easy walking distance. He copied the names and phone numbers and then transferred them into the laptop's notebook. The next step was to phone each of the hotels and asking for Sue Anne. Steve sat slumped, in an upholstered arm chair, listening to him. On the third call, he turned to Steve and said, "Hey, I've got a live one. She is at the Seahorse Motel. They are putting me through to her room."

The telephone rang and rang. Finally, the desk clerk came back on the line and said, "I'm sorry but she is not answering."

"Could you leave a message for her to contact Liam and that it's urgent and that it's regarding Raymond."

"Leon?"

"No, not Leon. It's Liam. That is L- I -A-M"

"Does she have your phone number, Mister Leon"?

"The phone number is 721-322-4999"

"That is 721-233-4999?"

"No, 721-322-4999"

Feeling frustrated, Liam hangs up the phone and turns to Steve and says, "Now, what do we do."

"Check and see if there is a phone listing for a Raymond Powell."

189

Liam did a telephone number search for a Raymond Powell in Benji Beach, Delaware. The Google search found nothing. He tried several variations of Powell's name but all he got were newspaper articles, commenting on Powell's numerous business enterprises. No home address or phone number was found. He turned to Steve and said, "He must have an unlisted phone number and stays away from Facebook and LinkedIn. Now What?"

Steve pondered their dead end for several seconds before replying, "We could go out on the strip and look for her, which would probably be like looking for a needle in a hay stack or we could contact the FBI and see if they are interested. It could be embarrassing, if we are wrong about finding this, John David Cross. We could also contact the local police which could might be embarrassing but at least they probably know where to find Powell. This is a small town and Powell is a big wheel. I don't think this isn't something we could explain over the phone. Can you find out where the police station is?"

In a few seconds, Liam had done another search and located the Benji Beach police station. The Google map indicated it was just a short walk from the hotel.

Ten minutes later they were standing outside the unimpressive, one and a half story police station. It was on a quiet, residential side street lined with vacation rental apartment buildings and modest houses. A police cruiser parked close to the entrance, confirmed they had the right building.

They entered and stood at a counter. No one jumped up to see why they were there. They could see a female employee, a dispatcher, working in a glassed-in area at the back of the room. Through an open door, they could see a fat balding, policeman absorbed in typing with two fingers on an old desk top computer with an ancient cathode ray monitor. It was Wally, the police chief. They waited for several minutes. Finally, Steve called out, "Hello?".

Wally looked up and stared vacantly at them, then waved his hand to show that he would be right there. He resumed typing and did not seem happy about being interrupted by the two out-of-towners.

Wally was sorry that he had put all the police officers out patrolling the main drag. "Thank God," he whispered to himself, "this volleyball tournament is over tomorrow." With most of the help, out of the station, he had taken over the responsibility of manning the front counter. With thousands of visitors in town he wanted as many feet on the street as possible.

Ten minutes later, Wally rose from behind his desk and strolled unenthusiastically over to the counter. He greeted them with, "What can I do for you boys?"

"It's a long story," Steve responded.

The police chief stared at Steve expectantly, wondering how much of his time this story would waste. He hoped, his nice quiet shift, was not about to get busy.

With no way to avoid hearing this long story, he nodded at Steve, pretending that he was interested in hearing their story.

Steve recognized he was being cued and started his story, "Do you remember, two years ago, when a wealthy woman from Benji Beach fell off her boat and disappeared. They found her abandoned boat in the bay but no body."

"Yeah, Mrs. Powell. I remember it well. Do you have some new information about it?"

"Maybe. Did her husband inherit her estate?"

"Yes, that's right. There was a special trial to declare that she was deceased by an accident at sea."

"This is my friend Liam." Steve, turned towards Liam before he continued, "He is a researcher for one of the big law firms in Washington. He just did some research, and that shows that Mrs. Powell's former husband, Raymond Powell, is a murderer wanted by the FBI. His real name is John David Cross."

Not impressed by Liam's credentials and with a bit of a condescending tone, Wally responded, "Now. What proof do you have to back that up?"

Steve and the policeman now both turned to stare at Liam. He quickly responded, "Raymond Powell was introduced to me this evening. He was with a friend of ours. I remembered him, from the pictures in the papers and on TV. I couldn't remember all the details or what happened to his wife, so I researched it on the internet. There were a lot of innuendos that the husband had arranged her disappearance to get his hands on her money."

The police chief thought to himself, here we go with those same old bull shit conspiracy theories. Why did these two idiots have to interrupt my quiet Saturday night?

He finally sighed and said, "That was all idle chatter by a bunch of busybodies. The trial put a stop to that nonsense. Her loss was just an unfortunate accident. I was part of the team that investigated her disappearance. Raymond Powell was miles away when she took her boat out. I confirmed it. He had nothing to do with her death."

Liam ignored the Chief of Police's response, and continued, "I also checked the FBI's Most Wanted list because we felt that if he were a murderer, then he could well have done something like this before. I went through it and I found a wanted posting for a John David Cross. He killed an armored truck guard in a Nevada robbery. If you shaved John Cross' head, put a beard and glasses on him, he looks like Raymond Powell. When I was talking to him, he said that he was from California, just like where the wanted poster said Cross was from. Powell also speaks French fluently. John Cross lived in France for two years and speaks French fluently. That was also in the poster."

Wally felt like he was getting a headache. With one of those voices, that indicated that he wished that they would just leave, he responded, "Listen, this is a closed case. I will not waste any more of my time on it, especially if it means irritating someone, I trust, and I have nothing but respect for. I've known Raymond Powell for years. He is a pillar of this community. For Christ sakes, he employs a big percentage of the damn people in Benji Beach. He's a Rotarian and has done more for this community than anyone else has ever done. The very success of this volley ball tournament is his doing. He's a good guy. Your friend is in good hands if he's with Ray."

Steve piped up, "Our friend is a she".

"Well then, she's in good hands. He's a real gentleman. Now, why don't you guys go home to bed and let me get back to my work."

Steve, disappointed, with an incredulous voice asked "So you will do nothing?"

"No, I am not going to anything. I sure as hell am not going to bother Ray Powell and neither are you. He's had to put up with enough of this kind of crap. Now go home."

As Liam and Steve left. The policeman went back to his desk and resumed typing his report. Just as he finished, a police officer came in with a young drunk who had thrown a beer can through a store window. Billy helped process the booking.

When things quieted down, and he picked up the phone and dialed the number of his good friend, Raymond Powell. The following was the one-way phone call, "Hi Ray, it's Wally. Did I wake you?... Oh, good. I thought you could do with a laugh. Two city boys came in here asking about you. They said their friend was with you. They thought you were a murderer by the name of Cross, who is on some FBI most wanted list ... Yeah that's a good one.... If they should bother you, just let me know.... No problem. Take it easy... Well thank you Ray, you don't have to do that... No, no we love eating at Matteo's.... Bye."

He smiled as he put the phone down, thinking what a great guy Raymond Powell was. Peering at his watch, he realized it was almost time for him to go home and get some sleep. He was so glad that the tournament would be over tomorrow.

CHAPTER 35

REWARD

Dejected, Steve and Liam left the police station and headed back to Steve's suite. On the short walk, Liam mumbled, "Well that was a big waste of time. That cop made me feel like a real asshole."

Steve responded, "Are you really sure that Raymond Powell is John David Cross?"

"Yeah, but not as sure as I was before. It's like we just hit a brick wall. That cop wouldn't even consider the possibility."

"Well, I think he's wrong. The wanted poster said there was a hundred-thousand-dollar reward for information leading to his apprehension. What do we have to lose? The only option is to phone the FBI. If we get nowhere with them, then I guess, we have hit a brick wall. Get the FBI phone number off the wanted poster. Let's see what happens."

Back in Steve's room, Liam again pulled up the wanted notice with the FBI's Las Vegas office phone number. He wrote the phone number down on the hotel notepaper and handed it to Steve. Steve took out his cell phone and dialed the number. Steve figured his company could absorb the long-distance charge.

The phone was answered by a soft, melodious, feminine voice, "FBI Las Vegas, how may I direct your call?"

"I have sighted a fugitive that appears on your most wanted list."

"One moment, Please."

The phone was answered on the first ring, "Agent Michael Smith here, to who am I talking?"

"My name is Steve Kennedy."

"Thank you, Mister Kennedy. Just in case our phone call is interrupted, and I must phone you back, can you please give me a phone number where I can reach you?"

"989-800-3298"

"Is that a cell phone number?"

"Yes, it is."

"Thank you. Now, how can I assist you?"

"I would like to report sighting a fugitive on your most wanted list."

"Who would that be?"

"John David Cross."

"Where was, he sighted?"

""In Benji Beach, Delaware."

"Where was he?"

"On the main street"

"What was he doing?"

"Walking down the street with my girlfriend."

"Your girlfriend?"

"Yes, my girlfriend."

"Why do you think this was John Cross?"

"He was introduced to my friend Liam, who is here with me now, as Raymond Powell. Mister Powell is a rich and powerful man in Benji Beach. Two years ago, his wealthy wife disappeared, in a boating mishap, under mysterious circumstances. Her will left him with over one hundred million dollars. He pushed the courts to declare that she was dead. Rumors have circulated that he murdered her for her money"

"Sorry, where is Benji Beach?"

"In Delaware. It is a small beach town, just south of Dover, Delaware. There is a big air force base in Dover."

"Is Powell spelled the way it sounds, P-O-W-E-L-L?"

"Yes, that's right."

"Why do you think this Mister Powell is John Cross?"

"He is a blond, about the right height, weight and age. He's shaved off all his hair, has grown a beard and wears glasses, which is an attempt at a disguise. When Liam talked to him, he mentioned that he was from California and had worked in Paris, France. They conversed in French."

"What made you check him on our most wanted List?"

"When my friend came back to my room and told me who my girlfriend was with, I became worried that she was with someone who might harm her. Liam is an expert researcher. As soon as he told me she was with this guy, who may have murdered his wife, I told him to check for a prior murder. He might have done it before. Benji Beach is off the beaten path, a great place to hide. When Liam checked your wanted website, he found, the only blond in it, was John Cross and that he sure looked like he could be Powell. Liam Photo Shopped the picture of Powell that he had taken of him in the street. After he erased the hair and the glasses, and then added the beard, it looked just like your wanted poster. It was too strong a match to ignore. During his conversation with Powell, Liam said Powell mentioned his French fluency and his roots in California. There are just too many coincidences.

"Where is Powell now?"

"I don't know but he has extensive property holdings in Benji Beach."

"Is there anything else you can tell me about him?"

"No but I am worried that my girlfriend may be in great danger."

"Mister Kennedy. Can you make a note of the following case number?"

"Yes, I've got a pen and paper."

"The case number is JC494678. Use this case number, if you remember anything else, or if you wish to contact us, to learn what is going on."

"I'm worried about her. Are you going to do something tonight?"

"I will be immediately forwarding everything you have given me to the agent in charge of this investigation. My advice, would be for you to approach the local police."

"We already did that. It was a waste of time. He told us Mister Powell was a very important person in Benji Beach and that he would not do anything."

"Okay, I will make sure the agent in charge knows that. Thanks for contacting us."

Steve hung up, turned to Liam and said, "What do you think, Liam?"

"I don't know. He didn't seem to want to commit them to anything. I guess, it all comes down to this agent in charge of the investigation. We've given them enough to get moving on it.

"We can't do anymore tonight. We might as well get some sleep. Why don't you pull out the fold away bed in that couch and sleep here, just in case something comes up."

"OK, good idea."

⌧CHAPTER 36

DANGER

After parting company with Liam, Sue Anne and John Cross had continued walking up the crowded main drag. John held her hand. Sue Anne felt very safe and at peace. He had treated her with the respect and tenderness which is something every woman appreciates. As they passed one of the noisier bars, John released her hand, stopped, took out a set of keys and inserted a key into a nondescript door, between the two bars. As he pushed the door open, Sue Anne asked, "What is this?"

"This is home for me. I own these two bars and many others along the strip. I live and work upstairs. Come on up. I'll make you a drink."

They climbed the steps and ended up in a luxurious foyer of white marble floors and brilliant white walls. Large paintings in vibrant colors leaped from the foyer's walls. The air conditioning was a welcome relief from the hot, humid street below. John led her into an immense living room decorated in white and black. The white suede furniture surrounded a black marble cube table. Some of the paintings in this room looked like the oil pastel that John had given her on the pier, except they were oils and much larger. She went over to one and confirmed that the oil painting was one of Raymond Powell's. She turned to him and said, "What a beautiful painting."

"I'm glad you like it. Take a seat. Let me get you a drink. What would you like?"

"This is a great time for a vodka martini. Do you have any olives?

"No problem."

John crossed the room to a well-stocked bar hidden behind the doors of a cabinet. Sue Anne could hear the ice cubes tinkling in the glass as he stirred the martini. She saw him lean forward and touch dimmer switches that softened the room. He hit another switch, and she heard the distinctive tones of Oscar Peterson's jazz trio. He also made a drink for himself and carried them back to her on a silver tray. When he sat down next to her on the couch, she nestled up to him. His arm circled around her and he pulled her towards him. She tilted her head back, and he kissed her. She passionately responded.

Standing, he picked her up in his arms, crossed the living room and pushed open a door with his knee. A king size bed dominated the dark room. John lay her on the bed and kissed her. Holding her with one hand, he unbuttoned her blouse with his other hand. She shrugged herself out of it as he undid her brassiere. She helped to undress him. His hard, muscled body pulsed with desire.

Much later, as they lay sated holding each other, spent and at peace with the world, the ringing of a telephone on the night table brought them back to reality. John whispered to Sue Anne, "Sorry, it's an unlisted phone. Few people know the number. It might be an emergency."

In the dim light coming from the open door to the living room, Sue Anne saw him reach out and pick up the phone. She then heard a one-way conversation.

"Hi Wally.... No. What can I do for you ... Really, that's a strange one... Would I be in any danger?... Thanks, Wally I appreciate that.... Why don't you and the wife drop around to Matteo's for dinner tomorrow night, on me?.. What's the matter, you don't like Matteo's?... That's great. Thanks for phoning Wally. Bye..."

John placed the phone back into its holder on the night table. He lay there, staring at the ceiling, The phone call had destroyed the warm, cocoon of intimacy they had shared. Sue Anne rolled on to her side towards him and reached out to touch his arm.

"Is there a problem?", she asked.

John turned to her and stared into her eyes. His eyes had a cold hardness that she had not seen before. His voice had lost its softness and tenderness. When he spoke, it was as if they had just met her, "I never asked how you got down here?"

"I came with two friends. They're playing in the volley ball tournament. They've won it for the last three years. You met one of them, on the strip, when we were on our way here."

"Liam? Was that his name?"

"That's right."

"Who is the other one?"

"Steve Kennedy."

"Where are they staying?"

"'Steve has a suite at the Benji Beach Grand Hotel. I'm not sure where Liam is staying. Why are you asking? Has this got to do with that phone call?"

John didn't answer her. He got out of bed, naked, and padded across the room to a high dresser. He pulled open a drawer. With his back was to her, he took out a Glock 17 9X19 pistol and screwed a GMT-300BLK silencer on to it. He turned around and pointed the pistol at Sue Anne.

She thought, "I must be dreaming. This cannot be happening." She stared wide eyed at him

"Sue Anne, I'm sorry, but I'm afraid that you've become my safe ticket out of here. Your friends, Liam and Steve, seem to have stumbled on a little secret of mine. If you cooperate with me, then everything will be OK. I do not want to kill you, but I will, if I have to. I'm going to tie you up so I can get some things together. Lie down with your hands behind your back."

Sue Anne, shaking with fear, got out of the bed and lay face down on the carpet. Her beautiful naked body contrasted with black carpet.

"Don't move. Keep your head down."

John went into the adjoining bath room and returned with a pair of scissors and cut the draw cord of a curtain. Putting his weapon on the carpet beside him, a he knelt beside her and tied her feet together with the cord. He pulled her arms behind her back and tied them together. He then ran a cord, from her tied arms to her tied feet and pulled it tight. Her legs were bent and pulled back at the knees. She could not move. When she had tried to move an arm, the ropes cut into her wrist and it made the knots tighter.

John dressed, as if he were going to a meeting, a dark suit, white shirt and tie. From a closet in the bedroom, he picked up a suitcase and quickly strode through the apartment to his office. In front of a small painting on the office wall, he grasped the frame and pulled on it. It swung on hinges to reveal a hidden wall safe. With a few spins of the dial, the safe opened. He reached in and extracted bundles of one hundred-dollar bills. These were stuffed into the suitcase. When the suitcase was full, he returned to the bedroom.

Sue Anne twisted her head, so she could see him. She pleaded, "Raymond. please let me go. I promise I won't tell anybody."

"Tell anybody, what?"

Sue Anne began to cry. Her sobs shook her body. She feared this madman might take her life.

"Sue Anne, I'm not worried about you telling anyone anything. Unless, I can shut up your two friends, I'm finished in this town. You and I are going on a little trip and you will be my shield." He reached down and undid her feet before he continued, "I have to gag you, to make sure you don't call out. You co-operate and do what I tell you, then I promise I'll set you free as soon as I am in the clear."

He ripped a pillow case into strips and stuffed the strips into her mouth. One long strip was tied around her head to hold the gag in place. In his closet, he found a black hoody. He pulled it over Sue Anne's head. With her arms tied behind her back, the sweatshirt's long, empty sleeves dangled down by her side. The extra-large sweat shirt hung down to her knees. It hid her naked body like a dress. He helped her to stand.

With one hand on her shoulders, he guided her through the apartment to a rear staircase. In the other hand, he held the suitcase full of money. As they descended the stairs, he held her bound arms firmly, to steady her. To stop herself from falling, Sue Anne slid her right shoulder against the wall of the staircase for support. She carefully descended, placing one bare foot on the next step before she moved the other foot to the same step. At the bottom, they entered a dark room with a cold, hard, gritty concrete floor. She could smell the car before she saw it. A motion detector had switched on bright overhead lights. In the garage, was an SUV, a BMW X6 M.

John opened the back door of the car and helped Sue Ann in. He made her curl up in a fetal position on the back seat. Once again, he had her bend her legs, so he could tie her feet and hands together. He buckled the rear seat belts to hold her in place. She lay there mute and immobile.

The cars, dark tinted windows, made it impossible for anyone to see her inside. John threw the suit case full of money on the floor of the front seat, on the passenger side. As he was getting into the car, he noticed at the bottom of the stairs, a red plastic container that he kept gasoline in for emergencies. He picked the container up and put it in the back of the SUV.

Sue Anne could smell the gasoline. She wondered why Raymond would have put a container of gasoline in the car. The heavy cotton hoody that John had pulled over her was hot. She was sweating. The hoody was getting damp. The thought terrified her that a sweatshirt soaked in gasoline would serve as excellent wick.

John climbed in, started the car and then pushed the garage door button. He backed out into the alleyway, behind his building, and drove to the Benji Beach Grand Hotel and parked by its rear entrance.

He had shoved the Glock into the waist band of his pants and got out of the car. Despite the late hour the hotel's lobby was still full of loud partyers. John recognized the night desk clerk as an avid golfer, even though he did not know his name. The clerk greeted him enthusiastically, "Good evening, Mister Powell. How can I help you?"

"You have a guest, Steve Kennedy. I am supposed to be meeting with him. He gave me his suite number, but I've lost it. What would the number be?"

The clerk went to his computer and quickly found it. He cheerily said," He's in suite Five Zero One."

"Well thank you. Let me buy you a drink next time you're at the club."

"That would be great Mister Powell."

John walked, across the lobby, to the bank of elevators and waited. The elevators were notoriously slow. With the crowd in the hotel, they were slower than ever.

The desk clerk was always looking for opportunities to ingratiate himself to those who might advance his career. It occurred to him if Steve Kennedy was important enough to know Mister Powell then it would be a good idea to make sure Mister Kennedy realized that the Benji Beach Grand Hotel appreciated his choosing to stay with them. The clerk phoned room 501.

He woke Steve out of a deep sleep. Groggily, Steve answered the phone and heard the desk clerk say, "Good Evening, Mister Kennedy. Mister Powell has arrived for your meeting and is on his way up to your suite. Is there anything we can get you for your meeting?

Steve was so stunned by this announcement that he took several seconds to reply. Finally, he responded, "No thank you. We are just fine."

Yelling at Liam, who the phone call also woke, he said, "Holy shit, John Cross is on his way up here. That isn't good. Let's get the hell out of here."

They quickly pulled on pants and shirts but left their shoes behind, Steve headed towards the hallway door. Liam stopped him, "Don't go out in the hall. He may be out there. We can get out through the balcony."

They went out on the balcony. There was a gap of about three feet between their balcony and the next balcony. Being tall, Steve could lean out and grasp the railing of the neighboring balcony. He ignored the fifty-foot drop as he pulled himself over to it. Liam was right behind him.

They tried their neighbor's balcony door. It was locked. They crossed over to the next balcony it was also locked. The next one was not locked. They entered the dark room and waited.

By the faint light coming in through the window, Liam stumbled across to the hallway door and put his ear to the closed door and listened. He heard the ding of an elevator door opening. A few seconds late he eased the door open a crack. Liam could see a bald man with a blonde beard. He watched him knocking with one hand the door to Steve's suite while holding a pistol in the other hand. Liam quietly eased the door shut and whispered to Steve what he had seen.

A loud thump echoed down the hall. They assumed John Cross must have kicked in the door. They speculated quietly on what Cross would do next. Would he sit in the suite and wait for them to return or would he leave the room and start looking for them? Since they had, left their suite's balcony door open, he might conclude that they had escaped that way and were now hiding in one of the other suites on this floor. Would he then start kicking in every door on the floor looking for them? If they ventured out into the hall, he might decide, at that very moment, to leave Steve's suite and come into the hall and would then shoot them. If they went out on the balcony to escape, he might be on the other balcony. As soon as he saw them, he might shoot them.

Liam whispered to Steve, "How the hell did he find us? Why is he here?"

Steve whispered back, "Sue Anne knew I was here. That cop we saw, must have told Powell that we thought he was a John Cross. I sure hope Sue Anne is OK."

"What do we do now?"

"I don't know. Maybe that guy at the FBI that we just talked to can help us."

Steve took out his cell phone and speed dialed the FBI number. This time, when it was answered, he asked for agent Michael Smith. Smith came on the phone. Steve told him of the danger they were in. He told them to barricade their door until help arrived.

After he had hung up on their first call, agent Smith had phoned agent Connor who their records identified as being the agent in charge of the John Cross file. He reached Connor, at home, just as he was getting ready for bed. Agent Smith related what Steve had told him about John Cross. When he got to the name of Raymond Powell, agent Connor stopped him and said, "Did you say Raymond Powell?"

"Yes, he said he was introduced to him, as Raymond Powell, and that he was a blond-haired Californian who speaks fluent French and had worked in Paris."

"Son-of-a-bitch, it's him. We've got him. During our investigation, we learned that Raymond Powell was working and living with John Cross in Paris. We tried to find Powell, so he could lead us to Cross. Powell never returned to the States. Our agents, at the embassy looked for him in Paris. They said the sect, that sent Powell and Cross to France, were very evasive, when they visited The Sanctuary's office in Paris. They got the impression, that the sect knew what happened to Raymond Powell, but gave no explanation for his disappearance. Of course, Cross has assumed his identity. We need to get a jet to fly us to Delaware."

"When?"

"Now, tonight.

Tonight?

Yes, tonight. I'll be at the airport in half an hour. Arrange it with whoever is in charge tonight."

"Are you sure about this?"

"You're damn right, I'm sure about this. Tell the agent in charge that there is a couple of US senators and a casino owner, by the name of Mike Asino, very anxious to bring this murderer back to Las Vegas. If they find out, Cross got away because someone didn't approve a flight, there will be hell to pay. Phone me back on my cell phone. I'm heading to the airport and I'm going to pick up Tully on the way."

Connor was in the Astra/Gulfstream 1125, travelling at six hundred miles an hour, when Agent Smith phoned him and told him that John Cross had shown up, with a gun at the hotel, looking for Steve and Liam. Connor interpreted this to mean that Cross would now expect the FBI to be on their way.

The reason Cross was at the hotel, Connor believed was to silence Liam and Steve. Connor agreed they should stay in the room they were hiding in and barricade the door.

The pilot had told Connor that the Sussex County Airport in Georgetown, Delaware was the only airport, near Benji Beach, that had a runway long enough to handle their small corporate jet. Agent Connor calculated that they would land in an hour and that it would then take half an hour to drive to Benji Beach. A lot could happen in an hour and a half. If they were to capture Cross before he disappeared again Connor decided they needed help and they needed it now.

The call for help was to the Delaware State Police in Georgetown. While the Benji Beach police department would be the most logical ones to rescue the two volley ball players, Connor believed that instead of helping, they might tell John Cross where Liam and Steve were hiding. Agent Smith had warned him that the Benji Beach police department appeared to be in John Cross' hip pocket.

The Delaware State Police trooper who answered the phone directed Connor to Lieutenant Rob Ford, the Assistant Troop Commander. After Connor explained the violent fugitive situation to him, the Lieutenant said that he would immediately dispatch all free units to the Benji Beach Grand Hotel. He was sure one could be there in ten minutes.

The lieutenant also said that the state police's helicopter would be waiting for agents Connor and Tully when their jet arrived at the airport. Ford told Connor to tell his pilot to taxi the corporate jet over to the state police hangar, in the North-West corner of the airport. They would see the helicopter's flashing lights. From the airport, it should take them only fifteen minutes, for the helicopter, to reach the hotel. The helicopter would land on the beach beside the hotel.

Aware of Connor's distrust of the Benji Beach police force, the lieutenant said he would drive to Benji Beach and meet with the chief to make sure that there would be no interference from the local police or leaks to John Cross. Ford said the situation would then become a joint federal/state/local police initiative.

Agent Smith had supplied Agent Connor with Steve's cell phone number. Connor phoned Steve and told him that, within a few minutes, state police would be there to take them to safety. Steve then raised the further problem of Sue Anne being in danger and not knowing where she was. Connor phoned the state police lieutenant back and relayed this added complication. The State Police said that they would need the additional manpower of the local police, to raid all the possible places that John Cross had in Benji Beach. All Connor could do was sit as the plane traveled to Delaware.

⊠CHAPTER 37

REVENGE

Within ten minutes of Agent Connor receiving the first phone call from Agent Smith, a telephone rang in Michael Asino's study. He suffered from insomnia and often worked through the night. His enemies would have said it was because of his guilty conscience.

Several phones were on his desk. The phone that rang was the one, that only his most senior executives and a few of his most trusted informants, had the number for. He picked up the phone and growled, "Yeah."

"Mister Asino?"

"Yeah."

"You know who this is?"

"Yeah."

"You still interested in John Cross?"

"Yeah."

"He's turned up in Benji Beach. It's a small resort town in Delaware, on the coast, just north of Ocean City, Maryland. He's using the name Raymond Powell. Apparently, he's a multi-millionaire, who owns several businesses there. FBI agents from Las Vegas are on their way there, by corporate jet. It will take them a couple of hours. They intend to arrest him tonight. That's all I got."

"That's all I need. See Tony, in the morning. He'll take care of you."

Michael Asino slowly hung up the phone and leaned back in his soft, red, Italian leather executive chair. It was more a throne than a chair. Slowly, he let a sigh

escape and then said out loud, "I'm finally going to get you, you son-of-a-bitch."
He picked up a phone and speed dialed a number.

The phone was answered with a, "Yeah, boss?"

"Louie, who we got handling Benji Beach?"

"Where the fuck is Benji Beach?"

"In Delaware, on the coast, its north of Ocean City, Maryland."

"Give me a minute let me check."

Within three minutes, Louie was back, "Yeah, there's a guy, out of D.C."

"Have they got someone right in the town?"

"I don't know but it would surprise me if they didn't. Those beach towns are hopping in the summer. It keeps the weed and coke people real busy. I'll find out."

"OK, presuming they do have someone there, I need someone to take out a target. I'll guarantee them one hundred thousand dollars and half of any money they can recover. This piece of shit stole three and a half million dollars from me. I want to see John Cross, dead tonight."

"OK, boss, let me get hold of this guy and see if he can put me in touch with someone who can handle this for you. I'll phone you right back."

Michael Asino sat back in his throne and rolled a pen back and forth on his desk. Finally, after what seemed like hours, but were only minutes, the phone suddenly rang loudly in the quiet room. Even though he had been expecting it, he still jumped. Quickly, he picked up the phone and said, "Yeah Louie?

"Mister Asino, I have a Mister Vincent Lupo on the phone with us."

"Good Evening, Mister Lupo. Can you assist us?"

"I'll do my best."

"Do you know of a Raymond Powell in Benji Beach?"

"I sure do. He's a very important man here. He owns several bars along the main drag, a golf course and several other businesses."

"Well, Mister Powell is actually a Mister John Cross. That piece of shit stole three and a half million dollars from me and killed one of my employees. I want you to take care of him before the cops can get to him. Apparently, they are on their way, so you are going to have to get moving. You've probably got at least an hour before the police show. He's a smart guy and probably knows they are coming for him. I'm guaranteeing you a hundred thousand dollars for the job, but you get to keep half of anything he's carrying with him. These guys on the run, always have a big bundle of emergency cash stashed away, to set up in a new life. Do you know where he lives?"

"Yeah, he's got a couple of places. From what I understand, he spends most of his time at an apartment above one of his bars on the main drag."

"You should get someone over there right away and some people on the main roads going out of town. Is there an airport?

"Yeah, about eighteen miles away."

"Someone should get over there just in case he tries to fly out. You're on the coast. Does he have a boat?"

"Yeah, a big cruiser."

"Do you know where he keeps it."

"The closest yacht club is down the coastal highway. It would be there. I'll get someone over there too."

"Mister Lupo, I'm a betting man. The John Cross, I knew, would take that the safest route out and that would be by water. He would be right in thinking that the police will concentrate all their efforts on the roads. Once he is at sea, they will never find him.

"OK Mister Asino. We're on our way. I'll cover off the yacht club myself."

"Good. Make sure I never have a problem with that fucker again"

"Don't worry Mister Asino we'll take care of him for you."

✕

CHAPTER 38

ESCAPE

After smashing open the door into Steve's suite, John Cross was surprised to find the lights on and the sliding glass door to the balcony open. Being diligent, he checked closets and behind the shower curtain in the bathroom. No one was there.

On the balcony he looked for them on the neighboring balconies. While the gap, to the neighboring balcony was not much over three feet, John discarded the thought of leaping it and searching the neighboring hotel rooms. Heights made him nervous. It was a long way down to the ground. He looked down; it seemed impossible to him that anyone could escape by dropping from balcony to balcony

Puzzled, as to where they could be, he went back inside the room. It looked like; they had cleared out so fast that they had left their shoes behind. He felt the bed. It was still warm. How could they have known that he was on his way?

John concluded that it was doubtful they would come back to the room. Since they must have been warned about him coming to their room, then they would now seek help from the FBI. They had told Wally that they had seen his FBI wanted poster.

With only minutes before the FBI might show up. There was no time to waste. If he had only arrived at the suite earlier, he might have eliminated this threat, but now it was too late.

It was time to flee. He would still need the Sue Anne as a bargaining chip, so she would have to go with him. Since the police would now have blocked off all the roads leading out of town, the only opportunity for escape seemed to be by water, just as

Gabriel had anticipated. He took out the cell phone that Gabriel had given him and pressed the red button. It would alert Gabriel that he was in trouble and allow Gabriel to come to his aid.

He left the suite and took the stairs, two at a time, down to the ground floor. He did not want to risk getting trapped in the elevator. The stair well ended at a side door, opening into a hallway, that ran from the lobby to the rear entrance of the hotel. He took the rear entrance and returned to the BMW.

He checked to make sure his hostage was still in the back seat. Sue Anne made strange animal noises that John could not understand, and he was not about to take out her gag to find out what she was saying.

John drove down the coast road. It took only a few minutes to reach the yacht club's entrance. He used his pass card to open the gate. He entered the quiet parking lot. There were no lights on in the club house.

John bent over and untied Sue Anne's feet, leaving only her hands tied. She could not immediately stand. John held her upright and waited for her circulation to return to her legs. As soon as she could stand on her own, he reached into the car and took out his suit case full of money. With his one free arm, he pushed her along the path, down the hill to the floating docks. The hundreds of boats, tied up, to what seemed to be miles of floating docks, showed no lights. Even those drunken boaters, who partied late into the night, were now in their berths.

As they tread along the floating docks, they could hear the water lapping against the boats. The smell of salt, seaweed and gasoline hung on the humid night air.

When they reached the cruiser, he had to carry her on board because with her arms tied, she could not manage the big step from the dock to boat's stern. Once on board, he sat her in one of the bridge's captain's chair. It was the same captain's chair, that Naomi Green had been sitting in, when he had shot her with the tranquilizer dart. With the cord from his apartment drapes, he tied Sue Anne's feet to the captain's chair.

Once he was certain she was immobile, he took his pistol out of his belt and placed it in the open map pocket in the boat's instrument panel. It was about the same height as the chair's arms. He returned to the dock and undid the lines. Before the boat could drift away, he leaped aboard and made his way to the bridge to start the diesel engine. It soon settled down to a throaty rumble. In the silence of the night it sounded very loud. This made him anxious to get under way. The engine may have woken a dozen boaters in the surrounding boats. He did not want them coming to investigate this late-night activity.

With the boat, free from its tethers, he sat down in the other captain's chair, switched on the bow flood lights and prepared to shift out of neutral. Focused, on how he would maneuver the fifty-foot cruiser, between the dock on one side and the large, expensive boat on the other side, he was unaware that the hatch, to the unlit main cabin, had opened behind him. A figure silently emerged with a gun in his hand. Just as John's arm muscles tensed, ready to push the throttle forward, he felt something cold and hard press against the back of his neck. As if annoyed by a mosquito, he brought up his right hand, as if to slap it away but stopped when he realized that it was the muzzle of a gun. Swiftly, he reached into the map pocket and extracted his Glock. He aimed it at Sue Anne who was sitting beside him. In a calm voice, which hid his fear very well, he said, "Lower your gun or I'll kill her".

Vincent Lupo laughed and responded, "Go ahead asshole. I'm not the police. She's nothing to me."

John kept his gun aimed at Sue Anne head. Her pleading eyes were wide in horror. Her gag turned her scream into an inaudible gurgle. John let the pistol slide from his fingers onto the bridge's deck. Vincent quickly reached down and picked it up. He shoved it into his belt. John turned around. In a surprised voice, he said, "Vincent?"

"Good Evening Mr. Powell or should I say Mr. Cross. Michael Asino asked me to give you his warmest regards. Untie her."

John undid the cord that he had tied around her feet. He pulled up the sweatshirt, so he could untie her hands. Sue Anne quickly pulled the sweatshirt back down, over her naked body and then snaked her arms into the sleeves. She rolled the sleeves up to expose her hands and rubbed her numb wrists. Her eyes were wide with terror as she reached up to rip the gag out of her mouth and threw it on the deck, unsure as to whether Vincent would kill her or spare her.

Vincent turned to John and asked, "Where are your car keys?"

John reached into his pant pocket and moved to hand the keys to Vincent.

Vincent said, "No, give them to her."

When Sue Anne took the keys, Vincent told her, "OK, get off the boat. Go, before I change my mind."

Sue Anne stared at him, not moving. Louder, Vincent said, "Go, get out of here. Take his car, he won't be needing it anymore. Just remember two things. One, my people are a vengeful people and two, that it was so dark that you could not identify who freed you."

Sue Anne ran to the stern, hesitated, and then jumped the three feet from the boat onto the floating dock. The engine was still rumbling away and bubbles from the exhaust were making popping sounds on the surface. The starboard side of the boat gently banged against the dock's bumpers. She ran, as fast as she could, through the network of connecting docks to the shore.

Vincent watched Sue Anne leave, then he turned to John and said, "OK, since you want to get out of here. Let's go. The police are on their way and will soon be here."

John carefully moved the boat out of the slip. He slid between the cabin cruiser on the port side and the dock on the starboard. Once the boat reached the narrow channel, he made a turn and headed towards the opening in the breakwater. Passing through it, they entered Delaware Bay. Still hopeful, that somehow, he could get out of this situation, he turned towards Vincent and said, "Which way do you want to go?"

"Head East, into the Bay."

John pushed the accelerator. The boat sped into the darkness. Ten minutes later, Vincent told him, "Cut the engine."

John cut the engine. The boat rocked in the ocean swells.

Pleading for his life, John tried to bargain, "There's a million dollars in that suitcase at my feet. It yours and another million if you let me go."

"Mister Asino says you took him for three and a half. You can do better than a lousy two million. I figure, after you knocked off Naomi Green that you are now worth at least a hundred million."

There was a pause, before John quietly replied, "How much do you want?"

They were now several miles into Delaware Bay. Before he responded, Vincent laughed, pleased at his chance to gain sudden wealth. Waving his pistol at John, he said "I tell you what Mister Powell. Move to the back of the boat. I want to check and see just how much money there really is in your suitcase."

A million stars shone in the heaven above. The distant lights on the Delaware shore seemed very far away. John moved to the unlit stern and sat down. Vincent pushed the suitcase with his foot into a position where he could watch it and also John in the stern. Holding his pistol in his right hand, he reached down with his left hand and snapped the catches. He opened the suitcase. It was full. It was too dark to see the denomination of the bills. He stood, reached up and switched on an overhead light. The light blinded him and made John Cross, disappear. Vincent heard a loud splash. Vincent turned off the overhead light. It took his eyes a few seconds to adjust to the dark.

John Cross was no longer in the stern. Vincent rushed to the back of the boat. There was splashing in the water, but he could not see John. He fired shots in the direction where he thought he had heard splashing. They seemed to have worked. There was no more splashing, Vincent ran back and retrieved a large flash light. Back in the stern he shone it on the ocean and fired at any shadow or ripple that might be John Cross.

With continued dead silence, Vincent returned to the bridge and started the boat's engine with a roar. Turning on a searchlight, he directed it onto the water in front of the boat. He guided the boat in small tight circles as he searched the water for John. After ten minutes of futile circling, his wishful thinking led him to conclude that he must have killed John, and the body had sunk into the deep.

With the suitcase, full of money, now being his primary concern, Vincent wanted to get back to the yacht club, before any early rising boaters were around, to ask him where Raymond Powell was. As he turned the boat towards Benji Beach, he noticed another boat, without running lights, half mile away, just sitting there. He speculated that it might be fishermen, just getting an early start. He ignored it as he sped back to the yacht club.

The dawn was drawing a faint pink smudge on the horizon when Vincent got back to the marina. Soon he was back in his bar, much richer than he had been when he had left. The first thing he did was dump the money on the table and count it. John Cross had not exaggerated. The one hundred-dollar bills were in packages of one hundred. There were one hundred packages in the suitcase.

He lay down on a couch in a back room and slept. At ten o'clock, staff coming in for the first shift, woke him. Vincent closed his office door and phoned Michael Asino.

Asino answered the phone with his usual, "Yeah?"

"Mister Asino, it's Vincent, in Benji Beach. I took care of your problem. One of my men will fly to Las Vegas this afternoon with your $500,000. Forget about the $100,000. I appreciate the opportunity you gave me. I hope, that, I can be of help to you again."

"You are sure that Cross is dead."

"Yes, he is now food for the fish."

"Good. Now, I will have my lawyers go after his estate to recover the $3,500,000 he stole from me. Would his estate be big enough to cover that amount plus accumulative interest?"

"Local rumors say he was worth well over a hundred million."

"Thanks for your help."

⊠CHAPTER 39

TOGETHER

The two FBI agents made the short commute by helicopter from the Georgetown airport to Benji Beach in less than fifteen minutes. About the same time as John Cross arrived at the yacht club, the State Police Helicopter was landing on the beach, a hundred feet from the Benji Beach Grand Hotel. The helicopter's floodlights and the roar of its engine immediately drew the few revelers still on the street down to the beach.

The FBI agents made their way into the hotel. The State Police troopers had arrived a half hour earlier to await the imminent arrival of their Acting Commander, the two FBI agents and the Benji Beach police chief. The hotel provided free coffee. Some joker asked for doughnuts, but no one thought it was funny.

When they first arrived, in full assault gear, the State Police had rushed to the hotel's top floor and through the broken door, into Steve's suite. No one was in the room.

As they returned to the lobby, one of the policemen banged on the hotel room door where Steve and Liam were hiding. He told them that it was now safe for them to return to their suite.

In a few hours they had to be ready to play volleyball. Sleep eluded them.

The State Police's acting commander, the two FBI agents and police chief Wally met in the lobby. They agreed to send armed teams to Raymond Powell's beach house, his golf club and his apartment, above the bar on the main street. The arrest teams were warned that John Cross was armed and dangerous.

The arrest teams returned empty-handed within half an hour. When pressed for other locations where John might be, Chief Wally recalled, that after finishing their forensic examination of Naomi Green's boat, the FBI had returned it to the Benji Beach Yacht Club. Since the yacht was part of Naomi's estate, it would now be

Raymond Powell's. As far as Wally knew it never been sold. He presumed it must still be at the yacht club. Since roadblocks, on all the roads out of town had reported no sightings of Powell, this left escape by boat as the most logical option. A dozen of more of them climbed into their vehicles and with sirens wailing headed towards the yacht club.

A red ball of a sun was just peeking over the flat line of the ocean's horizon when the contingent of policemen descended on the yacht club. The boat's mooring location was obtained from the staff in the club house.

Down, the floating docks the herd thundered. Much to their surprise, they found the boat moored in its berth.

Agent Connor was both disappointed and surprised that John Cross had not used this obvious escape option. He couldn't believe it. he opened the hatch to the engine room and stuck his head into it and immediately felt the heat coming off the hot engine.

With no other search options, open to them, the teams dispersed. The state police kept the road blocks up. It snarled traffic for the next two days. The two FBI agents returned to the Benji Beach Grand Hotel. As they were arranging for the rental of two rooms, Agent Connor's cell phone rang. It was Chief Wally who told him that Sue Anne had walked into the police station with Steve and Liam. Connor said they would be right over.

The group assembled in Wally's cramped conference room at the police station. Sue Anne told, the group how a pleasant day with Raymond Powell had turned into a nightmare They perked up when she said that, someone who was hiding on the boat, freed her. This intruder had appeared as they were getting underway. He had held a gun to John Cross' head and had helped her escape.

When asked to describe the intruder, Sue Anne said it was too dark to provide a useful description. She could only describe him as being of average height and weight with no noticeable accent. As she ran from the boat, she said she had heard the boat leaving the marina.

Connor was more puzzled than ever. The boat went out. The boat came back. Where was John Cross? Was he dead? Was his body buried at sea? Perhaps John Cross had overcame his assailant and returning to the marina but that would make no sense. An escape by sea would have made sense.

While they were discussing where John Cross could be, an excited police officer burst into the room to tell them that John Cross' SUV was in front of the Benji Beach Grand Hotel. Sue Anne explained that she was the one who had parked it there. After she had parked it, she explained that she had gone to Steve's suite in the hotel. Steve had been the one who insisted that they walk over to the police station.

After reviewing her story, of the last few hours, agent Connor felt depressed. Their flight to Delaware had been a waste of time. Someone had got to John Cross before them. He suspected, he knew who it was, and that no one would object if they now closed their file on John Cross.

⊠CHAPTER 40

ASCENSION

Gabriel LaChance checked his cell phone again. On the cell's bright screen, he could see that John Cross's cell phone, still appeared to be on John's cruiser, a half mile away. John's boat had come to a halt for no apparent reason. Gabriel had shifted his engine into neutral and let his boat gently rock on the Atlantic swells. The late-night sky was full of a million stars. He had turned off the boat's running lights, when he had started this pursuit, and hoped, that under the cloak of darkness, his boat was invisible to John's boat.

Gabriel watched as John's cruiser raking the surface of the ocean with its spotlight while making slow circles. Someone or something had fallen overboard. The searcher finally stopped circling and with a mighty roar, at full throttle, headed back towards Benji Beach.

After, John's boat left, Gabriel's cell phone map still showed that John's cell phone remained a half mile away. Gabriel shifted the engine into forward and moved towards where the blip on his screen showed the cell phone's position. In front of his bow, the ocean was black and empty. The blip would disappear from the cell screen map for several seconds but would reappear.

A half hour ago, when Gabriel's cell phone had gone off in the middle of the night and woken him, it had taken him a few seconds before he accepted that John Cross had pushed the emergency button, on his cell phone, and was seeking help. The sturdy, water proof, Runbo Q5, cell phone, invented for the Israeli military, was the best money could buy. Gabriel had purchased the two cell phones as a precaution. He had never expected to use them. John's contact number appeared on the cell phone's screen. He touched the screen. The phone rang and then immediately went to message mode

The red emergency light on his phone was still lit. John had not cancelled the emergency call. Gabriel went to the cell's map screen. It would pinpoint where John was. The blip on the map screen was moving. It showed John travelling south. Gabriel guessed that John was on his way to the yacht club, just as they had planned. If discovered, John was to immediately get on his boat and head out to sea. Gabriel would then find him and assist in his escape.

Dressing as fast as he could, Gabriel left his apartment and got into his car. He headed towards the yacht club. As he drove through the quiet streets, he continued to glance at the map on his cell phone. He saw that John was now at the yacht club.

Reaching the yacht club, he parked a hundred feet away from John's BMW. He walked over to it and confirmed that John was not in it. Next, he headed for the docks.

Keeping as low a profile as possible, he made his way along the floating docks towards John's boat. As he drew close to it, he heard the engine in John's boat start up. A few minutes later, a young woman, in obvious distress, wearing just a sweatshirt, leaped from the boat and came running towards him. He ducked down behind a boat on an adjoining dock and waited for her to run by. John's boat was reversing out of its slip. Gabriel checked his cell phone to see if John still needed his help. The red light was still lit.

Gabriel ran to his own boat. He cast off the lines and started the engine. Moving quickly through the yacht club channels, his boat's wake violently rocked the moored boats Passing the breakwater, he could see John's boat ahead. He sped up and then throttled back when he got too close. When John's boat stopped, Gabriel shifted the boat into neutral and waited to see what would happen. He watched the boat with its searchlight on circling and then head back to Benji Beach at full throttle.

Gabriel now moved, across the dark ocean towards where the other boat had been circling. When the map on his cell phone screen, showed him that he had reached the blip's coordinates, he hit the walkie-talkie mode on his Runbo cell phone. Shouting into it, he called out, "John, where are you. Turn on the flashlight, on your phone. I can't see you." He wondered if he would get a response, maybe John was dead, and the phone was just floating on the ocean's surface. Within seconds, a bright light appeared fifty feet away.

After he had rolled off the back of his cruiser into the ocean, John had transferred the cell phone to his jockey shorts, as he stripped off his suit. The suit had felt as constricting and heavy as concrete. He swam away from the boat. When Vincent shot into the ocean, John dived as deep as he could, and would then surface for a quick breath, before diving again. He did the same thing whenever the spot light came close to him.

When he heard the boat, move away, he surfaced, floated and considered what to do next. He appeared to be several miles off the coast and wasn't at all sure if he could swim that distance.

When Gabriel had insisted that he always carry the Runbo, John had thought that Gabriel was being overly cautious. Now, as he floated, he remembered that he had shoved the phone into his undershorts. He pulled it out and held it in the air above him. The screen was lit. He wasn't sure why it surprised him to find that it really was waterproof. As he held it up, he noticed a cruiser, without running lights, moving towards him. One of the most wonderful sounds he had ever heard was Gabriel shouting for him to turn on the cell phone's flash light, so he could find him. It took John a couple of seconds to find the flashlight app. It lit up the night.

Gabriel maneuvered the stern of the boat close to John. He put down the swimming ladder and helped John into the boat.

As John, lay recovering on the boat's deck, he thought how ironic it was that he had saved this boy from the wretched streets of Paris. Now Gabriel was saving him. The Sanctuary had anticipated, the day would come when Raymond Powell would be revealed to be the fugitive, John Cross.

John changed into dry clothes. Gabriel restarted the engine and charted a due East course.

Soon, John joined Gabriel on the bridge. As they sped towards the Eastern horizon, it was now a pink-grey line as a new day began. "Where are, we are heading?" John asked.

"Bermuda."

"How far is it?"

"About eight hundred miles, east of here. It will take a couple of days. We'll relieve each other every four hours."

"What happens when we get there."

"You will catch the first plane to London and then take the Chunnel to Paris. I will charter a corporate jet and fly back to Benji Beach. It is important that I get back, as quickly as possible, to protect The Sanctuary's assets. The government and Michael Asino are going to try to seize everything you built up in Benji Beach. Now, you understand why it was so important to set up those offshore companies and transfer all your assets to The Sanctuary. I'll want to get the courts, to declare you lost at sea, as quickly as I can., that should end the manhunt for John Cross."

"How do I travel without a passport?"

"Oh, but you do have a passport."

"I do?"

Gabriel opened a drawer and took out a brown manila envelope and handed it to John. John emptied the contents onto a small table that he had pulled out. The first thing he noticed was a worn, brown, leather wallet. He opened it. It contained credit cards, a pinkish-blue French driver's license, a green French health card and Euros. The next thing he noticed, was a French passport with its Bordeaux-red cover. He opened it, and was astounded to see, that the name in it was Gabriel LaChance but the picture was John Cross."

"Gabriel, I'm assuming your identity?"

"Yes, an identity that was abandoned when The Sanctuary spirited me from France to America. With my French birth certificate and the help of The Sanctuary in Paris, we obtained the passport."

"What will I do in Paris?"

Gabriel smiled as he said, "Exactly what you have been doing all these years. Saving murderous little bastards like us."

The End

If you enjoyed **BEWARE THE ABANDONED**, you will also enjoy DUEL. It is Ian Duncan MacDonald's first book in the Roy Lyons series.

It is an entertaining, action packed, suspense novel that is hard to put down. It explores the transfer of world domination from the United States to The People's Republic of China.

Rob Lyons a State Department analyst is sent from Washington to the Caribbean Island of Saint Matts to determine why China is suddenly so bold as to lease an old, abandoned British naval base on the island. The

Caribbean has been America's private lake for centuries. He encounters assignation, evacuation, corruption, greed and romance as the world teeters on the edge of annellation.

For more information go to **informus.ca/WKLY_MAGAZINE_1html.**

****

The second action packed, suspense novel in the Rob Lyons series, **USING DROUGHT USA** will also be another page turner.

With no time for negotiations, Rob Lyons is sent to Canada to convince separatists in Quebec and Alberta; as well as the aboriginal people in the area, to step aside and not interfere in the American invasion of Ontario.

It is an election year. California, Arizona, Nevada and New Mexico face economic ruin. They are running out of water. The President feels if he presents a solution to the water shortage, he will win votes from the 80,000,000 citizens in those states. His secret plan is to reroute the water that flows through the barren lands of

Canada's sub-Arctic to the headwaters of the Colorado River that irrigates the South West..

A lobbyist sells the secret plan to the Canadian government. The treasonous Rob Lyons immediately becomes a fugitive with a price on his head. Will Rob be able to get back across the border? Will the native people's plan to assassinate the President stop the American invasion?

For more information on this novel go to informus.ca/DROUGHT_USA.html